ₑ

The Affacombe Affair

Elizabeth Lemarchand

Hart-Davis, MacGibbon   London

Granada Publishing Limited
First published in Great Britain 1968 by
Rupert Hart-Davis Limited.
Second impression 1975 by
Hart-Davis, MacGibbon Ltd
Frogmore, St Albans, Hertfordshire AL2 2NF and
3 Upper James Street, London W1R 4BP

ISBN 0 246 97455 9

Printed in Great Britain by
Fletcher & Son Ltd, Norwich

To B.V.
my oldest friend

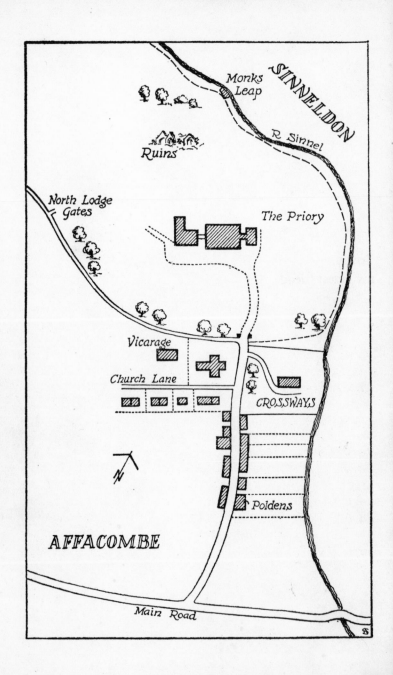

Chapter One

The Crownmoor village of Affacombe lay in an enormous silence under the midnight stars. A solitary lighted rectangle indicated the sitting-room window of Poldens where Olivia Strode sat absorbed at a workmanlike desk. Presently she turned a page with a rasp. The church clock gave three metallic hiccoughs which vanished without trace, like stones dropped into deep water. Surfacing, Olivia swept off a large pair of horn-rimmed spectacles, blinked and realized that her son David could arrive at any moment. She leant back and listened, but the intensity of the silence seemed to sound in her ears. Then an expression of certainty came over her face, and she got up and went to her kitchen to heat a saucepan of soup. Leaving it on the cooker, she flung open the front door, letting a shaft of light fall across the street. As a powerful car streaked along the main road below the village she was disappointed, but almost at once noticed the lights of a stationary vehicle which had already taken the Affacombe turning. Surely it must be David – what on earth was he doing? But as the question framed in her mind the car began to move forward, and in less than a minute a mini braked outside Poldens. Her son grinned through the driver's window.

' Sorry I'm so appallingly late, Mamma,' he said, extracting his six feet of length and giving her a hug. ' Just on twelve, isn't it?'

9

'It doesn't matter a scrap,' she told him, 'especially as you were so thoughtful about ringing up to say you'd feed on the way down. I've got soup and sandwiches laid on, and the garage is open.'

'Jolly good. I'll run her in and be with you.'

Affacombe was nine hundred feet up, and there was a nip in the September night. The Strodes drew armchairs up to the electric fire in the sitting-room and settled themselves for an exchange of news.

'Thank heaven it wasn't raining,' David remarked as he wolfed ham sandwiches. 'Perfect night for the run, really, except for the odd patch of mist in the valleys. I'd hoped to get off much earlier, but there's been a rush of work this week, and in the end I got caught up in the Friday evening traffic snarl. Better not to make difficulties when you're a new boy, though.'

Olivia nodded, thankful for his horse sense. Things might have been so different. Her husband's sudden death when David was ten had left her with the responsibility for the boy's education and launching, but she'd been incredibly fortunate. He'd gone straight through school and his articles, and now was a partner – even if a very junior one – in a well-established firm of London solicitors at thirty. There remained the marriage that she wanted for him so badly...

'You see,' he was saying with apparent inconsequence, 'I particularly wanted to get down this week-end.'

She felt a tremor of excitement as she recognized the indirect statement which he'd employed from childhood to tell her something important which he didn't want to discuss for the moment. This must mean that he'd known Julian Wrey was coming home too. Could he be going to propose to her at last? Had he got himself over the hurdle of her money?

'Well, you've hit on some marvellous weather,' she replied, taking her cue. 'The Ainsworths have got up a bathing-cum-tea party at the school swimming pool tomorrow afternoon. I said

10

you were coming down, but didn't commit you, of course. It's a kind of open invitation.'

As she expected, David refrained from giving any undertaking.

' Aren't the boys back yet?' he asked.

' No. Term begins next week. Boys' prep schools always seem to have fantastically long holidays.'

He put down his cup and saucer, stretched, and smothered a huge yawn.

' Time we turned in, isn't it? I feel I could sleep for a week. It's so marvellously quiet after London, especially the hellish planes.'

Her mind went back to his arrival.

' Why did you draw up just beyond the turning tonight?'

David looked at her with amusement.

' Little escapes the notice of Mrs Olivia Strode, the well-known local historian,' he enunciated with the inflections of a broadcast talk. ' It's all this scouring the countryside for hut circles and what-not, I suppose...I was intrigued by a car which was determined not to pass me, and thought I might get a glimpse of it in the mirror, but it went past the turning at such a lick once I was out of the way that I wasn't much the wiser.'

' Was it a van? There's been some sheep-stealing from moor farms lately.'

' Definitely not a van. A big dark saloon of the high-powered sort. Someone fairly local out with somebody else's wife is my guess.'

White mist blanketed the combe at dawn on Saturday, September 20th, but by ten-thirty when Olivia Strode came out of Poldens the sun was unchallenged in a cloudless sky. She carried a trug of gladioli from her garden, and set off briskly up the village street in the direction of the church, her comfortably plump, rather short figure sensibly dressed in a navy-blue tub frock. Her progress was marked by exchanges of greetings with passers-by and figures in doorways, for she was no longer

11

considered an incomer. It was on her honeymoon, thirty years ago, that she and John Strode had chanced on Affacombe, found Poldens up for sale, and decided to buy it for a holiday cottage. She still found the village and its setting enchanting, and on this perfect September morning gazed with pleasure at the granite and cob cottages curving up the hill, their gardens blazing with rich autumn colour. On the far side of the combe the massive ridge of Sinneldon was already touched here and there with dull gold, crimson and purple, promise of splendour to come.

Turning down Church Lane she went through the lych-gate and up the path to the south porch. The door stood open, and she was greeted by a buzz of conversation, and a strong smell of flowers, greengrocery and metal polish. An angular figure emerged from the space under the tower at the west end, wearing a straw hat and an overall and carrying a dustpan and brush.

' Oh, there you are, Olivia. I was beginning to wonder, but you've got your boy, of course. Your vases are all ready for you, over by the font. I've kept a sharp look-out after what happened at Easter – Yes, Mrs Allcut, I'm just coming. One thing about Patronal and Harvest, it gets the green frontal off, and we can give the altar a good brush down.'

Before Olivia could reply, Hilda Rainbird, an energetic spinster who functioned as sacristan, had darted up the aisle to superintend operations in the chancel. The church was dedicated to St Matthew, and sensibly combined its patronal festival on September 21st with its harvest festival, although a minority of the parishioners strongly resented the arrangement. After a little tactful admiration of other people's efforts Olivia went over to the font and set to work herself. Crudely fashioned and roughly ornamented the font never failed to stir her imagination. It was far older than the existing church, and almost certainly older than the replaced Norman church. Its millenium of association with human faith and religious emotion gave it great serenity and dignity, she thought, as she began grouping her flowers. She noticed that Barbara Winship's window had already

12

been decorated, and wondered if Julian had taken her mother into Leeford for shopping. David would almost certainly have gone round to Crossways as soon as he'd finished his very late breakfast.

A voice broke in on her thoughts.

' Mornin', Mrs Strode. Real beautiful, your flowers.'

Olivia looked up from her knees to see Mrs Earwaker, a buxom young Affacombe matron, vigorously polishing the brass ewer.

' Good morning, Ethel,' she said. ' Yes, they've done well this year. The church is going to be a mass of colour, isn't it?'

Ethel Earwaker, who belonged to the dissident minority, refused to be placated.

' Maybe 'twill,' she replied, ' but I still says 'tis a shame Patronal's bin put atop o' Harvest. Does us out of a festival, like. Festival should be Revel Day, shouldn't'n?'

' Us doan't want Patronal ten days afore Christmas,' protested another voice. ' You'm daft, Ethel Earwaker.'

' Patronal oughter be Revel Day b'rights,' Ethel persisted. ' Allus wur, till some ole bishop altered'n.'

Olivia listened fascinated to this evidence of the incredible length of village memories. The original dedication had been to a St Lucca, undoubtedly a Saxon goddess of light taken over by Christian missionaries, and associated with the Roman St Lucy, whose feast-day falls on December 15th, significantly near the winter solstice. Affacombe's St Lucca had retained a ' revel ', far removed from Christian piety, and the church had been allowed to fall into a ruinous state. It had been rebuilt in the thirteenth century during the reign of the indefatigable Bishop Whitcombe, who had no doubt insisted on a fresh dedication, well separated in the calendar from the dubious St Lucca and the junketings. But resentment at this interference by a foreigner still lingered on into the late twentieth century.

Her flowers arranged to her satisfaction, Olivia began reluctantly to heap the inevitable fruit and vegetables between the vases.

'It's the thought of distributing it all on Monday that makes me feel weak,' remarked Jane Fairhall, the Vicar's wife, as she passed.

'I'll be along with the car as usual,' Olivia told her. 'David has to go back tomorrow.'

'Careful!' trumpeted Hilda Rainbird from the altar steps.

Jane Fairhall winked at Olivia. A small procession advanced awkwardly up the aisle, supporting the best golden frontal slung on a pole. It gleamed in the sunlight which streamed through the south windows. Olivia thought with amusement that St Lucca might still be said to have a stake in the land.

Chapter Two

Finishing his breakfast in the kitchen at Poldens, David Strode was suddenly possessed by panic. Suppose Julian turned him down? A tacit understanding was all very well, but what an arrogant fool he'd been to imagine that she was going to hang about for him until he brought himself to make a move. All because his idiotic pride had jibbed at her money. All those doctors at the Highcastle Hospital where she'd been working because she wanted to do something useful – a vision of TV medicos invaded his agitated mind. He set down his cup with a clatter and got up from the table. He'd go round to Crossways at once, and only hope they'd be able to shake off her mother and old Winship.

A little surprised to find himself in the role of a frantic lover he set off up the village street. Admittedly he'd been a bloody fool about the money, but if you hadn't had a father since you were a kid, and had seen your mother carrying the can for years, you felt you wanted to do absolutely everything for the woman you married. Illogical, perhaps, but that was how he felt. All at once he knew for a certainty that Julian would understand.

Crossways, the home of the retired Colonel Hugh Winship, Julian's step-father, was a small Queen Anne house opposite the Church Lane turning. David went up the drive and round to the front. The Colonel was in his shirtsleeves, bedding out wallflowers, and raised a trowel in greeting.

'Morning, m'boy,' he said. 'Glad to see you. M'wife and Julian have gone into Leeford. Should be back any minute. We'll have a cup of coffee. Julian said she thought you might be turning up this week-end.'

An odd little trait of Julian's, this reluctance to count chickens, David thought. He'd written to tell her he was coming.

'Morning, sir,' he said. 'Nice healthy lot of plants you've got there.'

'Raised 'em from seed. Should have got 'em out before. Touch of frost last night. How's the law?'

David sat down on the grass, clasping his hands round his knees, and obliged with anecdotes from his recent professional activities. Colonel Winship worked with dexterity and speed, inching along on his knees, and uttering a guffaw from time to time. At last, after what seemed an eternity, there was a toot from the direction of the gate, and a car came round the side of the house. As David scrambled to his feet to open the door for Barbara Winship he intercepted a look and a smile from Julian which set his heart racing.

'My dear David, how delightful,' Barbara said, making herself heard with difficulty above the frenzy of two Jack Russell terriers struggling to get out of the car. She handed him a shopping basket. 'Thanks so much. Your mother's still in church, I suppose? Noble woman! I'm afraid I did my window early and gave the Rainbird the slip. Otherwise I'd be there now. Ju, darling, some coffee would be quite marvellous, don't you think?'

It was generally conceded that Barbara Winship was an attractive woman. Her fair prettiness had lasted on into the forties, and she was invariably soignée and becomingly dressed. David found her rather languid charm irritating. He thought her self-centred, and unobtrusively skilled in engineering her own comfort. It came home to him once again how uncongenial he would find her as a mother-in-law.

16

' I'll take the basket in. There are some things for the fridge.'

Julian had come round the front of the car, and he wondered how even the Rockefeller millions could have mattered to
him for a single moment. She was small and lightly-built, with
shining dark hair and bright dark eyes, and when she smiled
the corners of her rather wide mouth curved up puckishly, dis-
solving the gravity of her face in repose.

' Can't I help?'

Their fingers touched as he handed over the basket.

' No, thanks. There's really nothing to do. I left the coffee
perking. Stay and talk to Mummy while I collect it.'

She was quite right, of course. This wasn't the context for the
most important decision of their lives. He stared after her until
Barbara's voice broke in.

' Could you move this chair just a tiny bit, so that my head's
in the shade, David? Thanks so much. That's perfect. Come
and sit down and talk to me.'

He took the seat she indicated, aware of a keen, if veiled
scrutiny. He suspected that Julian's marriage might well affect
her financially.

' I gather from Mamma that we've all been asked up to the
Priory this afternoon,' he said by way of conversation.

' I simply adore that heavenly house,' Barbara remarked, her
eyes half-closed as though visualising it. ' I could sit and look
at it indefinitely. It makes me yearn for the days of gracious
living.'

' Must have been damn cold to live in before central heating,'
said her husband, coming up to join them and winking at
David.

' Darling, you're laughing at me as usual, but just imagine
walking down that glorious staircase in the manner born, taking
it all for granted. Rather wonderful, don't you think?' She
turned interrogatively to David.

' Personally I should have disliked quite a lot of things in
the Country House Age,' he replied, deliberately judicial. ' The
place crawling with servants, for one thing. Popping up when

you weren't expecting them. No real privacy.'

The Colonel agreed, ramming tobacco into a pipe with an earthy thumb.

'Menace,' he commented briefly.

There was a chinking of china in the background. David rose thankfully to take the coffee tray from Julian.

It emerged that they were all four going to the Ainsworths party, and that Julian and David intended to swim.

'It's a super bath,' Julian remarked. 'Those boys are jolly lucky.'

'Garnish must have spent a fortune on modernizing the place,' said David. 'Unless Ainsworth pays him a whacking rent for the school part he can't be seeing much of a return on his money.'

'It seems to me a pretty good arrangement from the Garnishes' side, all the same. The West Wing makes them a lovely little country house. It's quite private, but near enough for the Ainsworths to keep an eye on it when it's empty. And a well-run school's about the least objectionable thing to have in the rest of the place. It only functions for about eight months of the year.'

'Anyway, I don't suppose money enters into it,' said Barbara. 'They're absolutely rolling. There was a lot about Countrywide Properties in the paper the other day, wasn't there, Hugh, and then there's his Mayfair estate agency.'

'Can't think why the chap doesn't pull out and come down here, away from the stink and racket of London,' said Colonel Winship, puffing contentedly. 'Just can't stop making a bit more, I suppose. Becomes a habit.'

Presently David caught Julian's eye and looked at his watch.

'I'd better be pushing off,' he said. 'Many thanks for the coffee. We'll be foregathering this afternoon, then?'

Julian got up too. They strolled towards the drive.

'Will you come out to dinner with me afterwards?' he asked her, when they had rounded the corner of the house. 'I rang up the Foxtor and booked a table on chance.'

'I'd like to,' she replied.

Silence descended. David stared at the long crest of Sinneldon, crowned with its three Bronze Age barrows, imprint of a time infinitely remote. All at once the evening seemed equally far removed. He stopped dead.

'Julian,' he said jerkily, 'you will marry me, won't you?'

In his arms, her face pressed against him, he felt her give a little choking sigh of relief.

'I was so afraid you were never going to ask me. It—it has only been grandfather's money, hasn't it?'

'Of course. I've been an utter clot. I know you understand, though, don't you? Darling, you won't ever hold it against me, will you?'

'Why should I? I've been just as miserable about having the wretched money.'

He realized that in his intolerable self-centredness he'd hardly thought about her feelings in the matter. Bereft of speech he held her closer.

'The capital's tied up like grim death,' she told him when they surfaced. 'On—our children. Doesn't that sound marvellous? You do want children, don't you?'

'By God I do!' He was surprised at his own vehemence. 'Growing up with both their parents, which neither of us did.'

'And with brothers and sisters, too, which we never had. A real family. It's quite frightening to feel so happy, isn't it? Almost tempting Providence.'

There it was again, that reluctance to believe that things would turn out all right. He'd have to supply a good bit of unobtrusive reassurance.

'If I were Providence, I'd feel wounded to the core by that remark,' he said, kissing her again. 'Look, what are we going to do about breaking it to our respective parents? I feel as though I want to proclaim it from the housetops.'

Julian considered.

'Let's go and find your Mamma first, and bring her up here.

Daddy will insist on opening a bottle. I'm so fond of her, David.'

'I am, too,' he said, gratified. 'It's great that you feel like that about her.'

The news of the engagement spread rapidly and had an exhilarating effect on the Ainsworths' party, which became a kind of informal celebration. The general setting was idyllic. The swimming bath was near the South Lodge of Affacombe Priory, on the right of the drive. It had been refilled for the occasion, and the crystal-clear water sparkled in the sun. Gay garden chairs and umbrellas had been brought down and dotted about, and a buffet tea set out in the shade of a cedar tree. The guests were local people, and the fact that the engagement was within the circle gave keen satisfaction. Congratulations rained upon David and Julian, as well as on Olivia and the Winships.

'Olivia darling!' Faith Ainsworth came hurrying forward, both hands outstretched. 'I didn't see you arrive.' She embraced Olivia affectionately and stood gazing at her with large, cowlike eyes. 'I'm so terribly happy for you. I mean, it's such agonizing anxiety for a mum these days, isn't it? I simply dread our two getting to that stage. But really, if you'd searched the world over you couldn't have found David a nicer girl, could you? I think she's simply sweet.'

Olivia liked Faith, as well as being amused by her.

'I've been secretly hoping for it for some time,' she said. 'People are being incredibly nice about it. I'm afraid we're dominating your party quite outrageously.'

Faith Ainsworth's large flat face flushed with pleasure.

'Why, it's *making* the party!' she exclaimed. 'It's the happiest thing that could have happened. Oh, dear, there are the Matlocks arriving—I must fly. See you presently, of course.'

Olivia passed slowly from one group of friends to another.

Soon, she thought, she must link up with the Winships. It was quite odd to feel that an official relationship had suddenly sprung into being. She'd had to make an effort to find out what Barbara was really like behind her affectation. Hugh was easy enough, if a bit inarticulate . . .

A good deal of hilarity was coming from the swimming bath, where John Ainsworth was organising a relay race between two teams captained by David and Julian respectively. Forty-five, fair and fattish, he radiated bonhomie and enjoyment as the prospective competitors milled noisily around him. By dint of blasts on a referee's whistle he finally managed to get the two teams to the opposite ends of the bath.

'Thank God I could plead my cloth,' the Reverend Simon Fairhall remarked to Olivia as they watched. 'I see Dr Coppin's been press-ganged.'

'The teams are disgracefully weighted in Julian's favour,' said Jane Fairhall. 'Do look. She's got young Hyde who's won endless cups at school, and the games master, too.'

'ON YOUR MARKS!' roared John Ainsworth, brandishing a starting gun. He fired it, and a chorus of squeals arose from the drenched spectators who had ventured too near.

After the race had been handsomely won by Julian's team, and the competitors had emerged to sunbathe and recover, Olivia spotted the Winships, Barbara elegant in an expensively simple pale blue suit and what was unmistakably a model hat. She made her way towards them, and was greeted by a welcoming gesture.

'My dear, how too terribly hearty,' Barbara said. 'For heaven's sake let's find some chairs and sink into them. I'm quite exhausted by all this excitement, aren't you?'

It certainly was very pleasant, Olivia thought, when they were settled. From where they sat the park sloped gently upwards to the gracious late eighteenth-century house, the central block of which was linked by short colonnades to two charming wings.

Her mind reverted to her Parish History, and she wondered where the inspiration and money had come from for so lavish a reconstruction. The Georgian house replaced an earlier one built from the stone of the despoiled Augustinian priory, the ruins of which could still be seen a little higher up the slope. Finding out all about it was going to be so exciting. As she speculated, the surface layer of her consciousness attended to Barbara Winship, who was once again lamenting the disappearance of the age of gracious living.

'All the same,' Olivia said, curbing her natural forthrightness. 'I'd rather have a school here than one of those National Trust museums. So much more alive, and I'm sure the boys gain from surroundings like these, even if they don't realize it at the time.'

They turned their heads at the sound of a powerful car which shot up the drive and vanished in the direction of the West Wing.

'That's the Garnishes' Mercedes, that was,' remarked John Ainsworth, who had come up behind them, and stood with a hand on the back of Olivia's chair. 'I always hope they won't mow down a boy when they come during term. They're here just for the week-end.'

'Long way to come for a week-end,' grunted Hugh Winship.

'Not in that car, Colonel.'

'John,' broke in Olivia, 'I know it's an understood thing that they don't want to get involved socially down here, but I really do want to contact Mr Garnish. I think it's quite likely he took over papers dealing with the selling up of the estate in the eighteen-fifties, and if he did it would be an enormous help to me to have a look at them. Should I just get a flea in my ear?'

'It's worth having a go, I think. He gets a terrific kick out of being the owner of a place like this. I'd ring up rather than call, though – Hallo, David. Drowned your bride-to-be in the bath?'

'She's been stung quite badly by a wasp,' said David briefly.

22

'On her hand. Your Sister's taken her off to the San to put something on it.'

There were dismayed exclamations.

'What about rounding up some grub?' suggested Hugh Winship. 'She'll be glad of her tea. Nasty thing, a wasp sting.'

Two more chairs were collected, and David manoeuvered over a garden table surmounted by a striped umbrella.

'Now this is really delightful,' pronounced Barbara, as her husband returned with plates of sandwiches and cakes. 'Oh, and here's Ju. Better, darling?'

'Mummy, I don't think you and Sister Roach have met,' said Julian, ushering forward her companion. 'She's been so kind and given me first aid.'

Barbara rose to shake hands with a neat, unobtrusive little woman with a sallow complexion and black eyes, and proceeded to thank her charmingly. Sister Roach stood listening attentively, just as though a patient were describing symptoms, Olivia thought with amusement.

'Lucky I was on hand, wasn't it?' she said pleasantly.

'Won't you join us, Sister?' Barbara suggested.

'That's very kind of you, Mrs Winship. But I know Mrs Ainsworth would be glad of extra help with the tea, thank you all the same.'

'Thank heaven for that,' said Barbara a moment later, subsiding into her chair. 'I felt I simply had to ask her.'

'She certainly produced something pretty effective for the sting. It hardly hurts at all now.' Julian glanced round. 'Here come Daddy and David with cups of tea. Gorgeous!'

The circle of chairs was drawn a little closer, the two families slightly self-conscious in their new relationship.

At Poldens that evening, after David had taken Julian off to dine at the Foxtor Inn, Olivia relaxed over a glass of sherry. What a wonderful day it had been. David home and dry—almost. Emotion was a bit wearing, though. After all, she thought, I'm nearly an Old Age Pensioner. She glanced happily round her sitting-room. Books, familiar pictures, flowers, desk and filing cabinet all adding up to a comfortable sense of security and fulfilment.

Next week looked like being fairly peaceful, once the Harvest Festival stuff had been disposed of, and she ought to be able to get a good long stretch at the Parish History. Presently she'd ring up the Garnishes, about nine, perhaps.

She began thinking about David again. She simply must do him credit at the wedding. Barbara would go to town over her outfit. If it really was to be early in January she'd better go up to Town herself before the fogs started, and get something. Nice to work in a call on dear old M.B., too, and get his opinion on her book up-to-date.

To help out financially during David's education Olivia had taken a post as secretary to Professor Moreton-Blake, a distinguished authority on Saxon and Norman England. Her interest in the past had soon developed into an enthusiasm for local history. Now, home for good at Affacombe and free of family responsibilities, she had been able to embark on a piece of research of her own.

Soon after nine she consulted the telephone directory and dialled the West Wing of the Priory. A woman's voice answered promptly, giving the number.

'Mrs Garnish?'

'Speaking.' The voice sounded guarded.

'I hope you'll forgive my disturbing you, Mrs Garnish. My name's Strode, Mrs Olivia Strode. I live in the village, and I'm writing a history of Affacombe parish. Naturally the Priory has played an important part, and I wondered if your husband has any papers dealing with the selling up of the estate about a hundred years ago, and if so, if he'd allow me to see them? I should be most grateful.'

'Oh – I see.' Mrs Garnish was clearly out of her depth. 'I'm afraid my husband's in his bath at the moment. We don't go by the clock when we're down here for a break – '

24

'How very sensible of you. Shall I ring up at a more convenient time, then? Tomorrow, perhaps?'

'Oh, no. It's quite all right. I'll just go and ask him. Hold on a sec, will you?'

Olivia could hear steps dying away, and a door shutting. She sat idly fingering a paperweight, and wondering what it was like to be married to a tycoon. After two or three minutes she heard Mrs Garnish returning.

'Hallo?' The intonation was more friendly.

'Yes, Mrs Garnish?'

'My husband's sorry he isn't available. He can't be sure about the papers you want, but he'll have a look and bring down anything there is next time we come. That'll be in about a fortnight, as far as we know. All right?'

Olivia thanked her appreciatively and rang off.

Chapter Three

Faithful to her promise Olivia Strode drove up to the church on Monday morning. She found the Harvest Festival decorations disintegrating under the attack of the Fairhalls and a small band of helpers. Large cardboard containers occupied the back pews, bearing labels such as HOSPITAL, EVENTIDE, and SISTERS OF CHARITY, and were filling up fast.

'Angel!' Jane Fairhall glanced up from the list in her hand. 'Eggs for Eventide over here, please, Mrs Yeo.'

What a relief to clear away everything but the flowers from the font, Olivia thought, scooping up the last of the apples. All the same, there was none of Saturday morning's zip in the air. Curious how depressing it always was to dismantle things. She fetched a can of water and carefully topped up her vases before clearing a crowded window ledge. A high-pitched whine started up in the chancel, where Hilda Rainbird had gone into action with a vacuum cleaner.

'Shall I do the Sisters as usual?' she asked Simon Fairhall.

'Splendid,' he replied automatically. 'It's awfully good of you, Olivia, if you really can manage it.'

'Help you load up?' Hugh Winship came through the south door.

His estate car was outside, stacked to the roof with produce. There was no sign of Barbara. He darted a glance at Olivia.

'Heavy job for women. Make 'em help you at the other end,' he added illogically.

After lunch Olivia drove the twenty miles into Highcastle and discharged her cargo at the convent, assisted by beaming nuns and orphans. Afterwards she managed to find a parking space, and did some shopping before having tea at her favourite café. As she headed for home again she was surprised to find how fast the weather was deteriorating. Dirty-looking low cloud was streaming up from the south-west, and before long raindrops appeared on the windscreen. Back at Affacombe she had difficulty in shutting the garage doors in the rising wind. By dusk a gale was screaming over the village, lashing it with rain.

Poldens was solidly built with walls over a foot thick, but Olivia could feel the whole cottage vibrating as she lay in bed that night. The noise made sleep impossible, and she read into the small hours, worrying intermittently about the thatch and TV aerial. From time to time her bedside lamp gave a flicker, ominously suggestive of a power failure. It was nearly three before she began to nod.

She awoke to broad daylight and was relieved to find that the electricity supply was still functioning. The gale was dying down a little, and fleeting chinks of blue appeared in the tumbling mass of clouds. She decided to postpone going to the shop until later, and spent the first part of the morning at her desk. Venturing out later she found the thatch intact, but a trellis fence in the garden was listing badly. As she arrived at the village shop, breathless from struggling against the wind, a figure in thigh boots and macintosh came scorching down the hill and jumped off a bicycle.

'Mornin', Mis' Strode. Turrible wild night, an' a lot o' damage done. All right down to your place?'

Fred Earwaker, a lusty young giant in his late twenties, worked as groundsman and gardener at the Priory School. He was a favourite of Olivia's, who was interested by the unusual

27

persistence of his family in the parish records, and by her discovery that the original meaning of his surname was almost certainly ' wild boar watcher '. He did odd jobs in her garden in his spare time.

' Good morning, Fred. Yes, it was pretty rough, wasn't it? That bit of trellis is heeling over, but nothing worse seems to have happened, thank goodness.'

' I'll come along an' fix'n for you, soon as the wind drops a bit. One of they beeches is down up to the ruins, an' where the roots 'as 'eaved up there's more o' the old walls showin'. 'Twill interest Mis' Strode, I said to meself, soon as I'd seed 'n.'

' Whereabouts is the tree, Fred?'

' Way beyond the stickin'-up bits, over to what wur North Lodge side.'

Olivia was keenly interested. The Augustinian priory had been an entirely undistinguished foundation, and little was known of its ground plan. This new discovery suggested a gatehouse, or possibly a guest house. Perhaps the Highcastle Archaeological Society could be persuaded to sponsor an excavation if the Garnishes agreed. A pity the ruins weren't scheduled as an Ancient Monument.

After lunch she could not resist going to have a look for herself. The expedition took her up the village street and past Crossways to a small kissing gate just to the right of the drive entrance of the Priory. The gate was the beginning of a right-of-way known as the Monk's Path, which ran along the boundary of the park close to the little River Sinnel. It rose to the edge of a small gorge immediately behind the ruins. From here there was a fine view of Sinneldon and the combe, and a garden seat had been installed, protected by a railing. The spot was known locally as the Monk's Leap, and alleged to be where one of the Priory brethren had leapt over the edge, hotly pursued by the Devil in the guise of a beautiful woman, landing miraculously safe on a rock in midstream. Olivia paused to look down at the Sinnel, roaring in full spate after the heavy rain, and sweeping

28

along a surprising quantity of debris.

The ruins were partly overgrown by brambles and bushes, and interspersed with trees planted as a windbreak for the house. She picked her way through the soaking greenery, getting damp and scratched in the process. On arriving at the fallen tree she experienced a thrill of excitement. The roots, now a tangled mass in mid-air, had been interlaced with blocks of the same grey granite which formed the exposed remains of the buildings. She climbed down into the cavity for a closer look, regardless of the mud, and was interested to find that the corner of a former building had been uncovered.

After emerging and spending some time in estimating distances she made her way back to the Monk's Path, preoccupied with the possibilities of an excavation. Two small white bodies suddenly hurtled towards her, making her start. They barked furiously, scrabbling at her burberry with muddy paws. The next moment she came face to face with Barbara Winship, dog leads in hand, her hunter's green quilted raincoat and Liberty headscarf straight from the pages of a fashion glossy. They exchanged surprised greetings and Barbara quelled her Jack Russells.

'Don't apologise – they could hardly make me any muddier,' Olivia said, feeling grubby and dishevelled. 'I just simply had to go and look at some bits of wall which have come to light under a tree which has blown down.'

She expected blankness or politely concealed amusement, and was astonished at the unmistakably wistful look which flashed across Barbara Winship's face.

'I think you're so lucky, Olivia. I mean, all the things you're interested in, and know so much about. You've got such a solid kind of life…'

Olivia searched hastily for an answer. Behind her friendliness and ease she was chary of becoming intimately involved with people, but here there was something very like an appeal.

'I married late, you know,' she said, rather to her own surprise. 'Not until I was nearly thirty. So I had quite a long spell of earning my living and making a life for myself. Then, after John died I had David to see through and get started, so I took a job again to make things easier financially. I only had eleven years of married life.'

'I married far too young,' Barbara said abruptly. 'I think it's a great mistake. I don't mean Julian and David, of course,' she added hastily. 'They're both so sensible, aren't they? Really, Ju sometimes makes me feel she's older than I am. Anyway, David's thirty. I suppose we shall have to start planning the wedding soon,' she went on in her usual conversational tone. 'Ju won't hear of Highcastle Cathedral: she's determined to have quite a simple affair here. Are you going back? I think I'll turn too, then.'

They walked back to the village talking easily, and parted outside Crossways, Olivia refusing an invitation to tea on the plea of dampness and muddiness. She went on alone, intrigued by her first glance of the real Barbara Winship behind the elegant and languid façade.

Impatient though she was to get to know her prospective daughter-in-law better, Olivia wisely decided that Julian must make the going. She was, therefore, delighted by a visit from her on the following Saturday evening.

The season of log fires had begun, and they sat companionably on either side of the hearth, Julian looking most attractive in a plain dark red frock. She had suggested that they made a start on 'filling in the picture', and Olivia found herself talking freely about David's boyhood and the problems of bringing up a fatherless boy. A good listener, she thought with satisfaction.

'I don't think anything can quite make up for losing your father early on,' Julian said thoughtfully.

Olivia turned the conversation to the girl's own history. She quickly sensed that a defence of Barbara was implicit in Julian's narrative, and that she obviously realized that people found her mother irritating. Olivia began to feel rather conscience-stricken: Barbara had certainly been through a great deal. Her first husband, an R.A.F. bomber pilot, had been killed in action over Germany only six months after their marriage. A few hours after Julian's posthumous birth the nursing home was hit in a tip and run raid.

'It must have been absolutely grim for Mummy. She herself wasn't hurt at all apart from shock, and I was perfectly all right. But her cousin who was in the part of the building which collapsed was dead when they got her out, and her baby which had been born the day before died afterwards. I don't think Mummy has ever quite got over it all, you know.'

Julian looked squarely at Olivia, who nodded without speaking.

The wealthy paternal grandfather emerged as a dominating and possessive figure. He had clearly been disappointed in his son's choice of a wife, but after the former's death had concentrated all his affection and pride on Julian, insisting that she should be named after her father, and tolerating Barbara for the child's sake. He was a widower, and for the first ten years they lived with him in his Cotswold home, where an established housekeeper made Barbara's position difficult.

'He was awfully generous over Mummy's allowance and that sort of thing, and when she said she was going to marry Daddy he was simply furious. He thought she'd have more children and that I should suffer, and when he saw he couldn't stop her marrying, well – he bribed her. He said he'd go on with the allowance if she'd agree to him legally adopting me, so that I had a home in my own right. He had made me his heiress already. He was perfectly reasonable about my spending half my holidays with her and so on, and in the end she agreed. I'm afraid I've always felt a bit resentful – at being a sort of bargaining counter. David was absolutely horrified about it when I told him last week-end. He said he couldn't imagine anything in the world inducing you to have let him be adopted.'

'I don't think I can either,' said Olivia. 'But it's awfully difficult to think oneself into someone else's skin, isn't it? The adoption gave you complete material security, of course.'

'Oh, yes. Too much, really. You probably know that it nearly put David off altogether. But that side of things is going to be all right. There are trusts for children, for instance. We've talked it all over in a completely uninhibited way. And David absolutely agrees with me that Mummy's allowance must go on. Legally it stops when I marry, or in eighteen months' time when I'm twenty-five.'

'I'm so glad about that. I – '

The telephone on Olivia's desk rang. She went across the room and took up the receiver.

'A trunk call from London,' she told Julian. 'It could be David.'

Their eyes met hopefully. Then an unfamiliar masculine voice came through.

'Mrs Olivia Strode speaking – Oh, good evening, Mr Garnish.' Olivia made an astonished grimace at Julian as she listened. 'Why, I should be delighted to go through the papers you took over with the property – No, I don't mind how bad a muddle they're in. I shall almost certainly find some useful material for my book – No, I shouldn't think of accepting a fee. Local history's my hobby, you know – Next Saturday evening, about half-past six? Thank you, I shall look forward to coming and meeting you both. Good-bye.

'My dear, can you believe it?' she said to Julian, returning to the fireside. ' They've asked me up for a drink!'

'It's epoch-making! As far as I know they've never had anyone inside the door barring the Ainsworths. What do you think has done it?'

'John Ainsworth says Mr Garnish – whose antecedents are pretty humble, I imagine – gets a tremendous kick out of owning a place like the Priory, and I dare say he's thrilled at the prospect of its being written up. He's no idea what a modest affair the P.H. is going to be, of course.'

'That remains to be seen. I'm afraid I really ought to go

home now – I've loved coming. By the way I've fixed with David to go up for next week-end. We're seeing my trustees, and getting down to plans generally. Where we want to live, and so on. The vicar says January 3rd is perfectly all right for the wedding. I think Mummy would have liked the Cathedral and a big reception, but I should simply loathe it, and David feels just the same. You'll give her moral support over everything, won't you?'

' Of course I will,' Olivia promised.

Chapter Four

'Murdered the room, haven't we?' asked Roy Garnish. 'I know what you're thinking, Mrs Strode. Modern furniture instead of the right period stuff.'

He stood with his hands in the pockets of an admirable tweed suit and legs apart, stocky and ginger-haired with a grin on his reddish face as he watched for her reaction to this mild baiting.

Olivia smiled. 'You can't spoil a room with proportions and windows like these,' she said decisively. 'Besides, the furniture may be modern but it's good in its own right.'

Pleased, he turned to his wife.

'What about that?' he demanded.

'What about a drink for the visitor?' Pamela Garnish countered, bringing forward a trolley of appetising snacks. 'Try this chair, Mrs Strode. I think you'll find it's comfortable, whatever it looks like.'

'What's your pet poison?' Roy asked her, going across to a cabinet which opened at the flick of a finger to disclose an impressive array of bottles.

'A dry sherry, please,' Olivia said.

'On the rocks?'

'Please. My son introduced me to that idea.'

'Jolly good one.' Ice rattled and clinked as he busied himself.

'Isn't it your son who's just got engaged to a local girl?' Pamela Garnish enquired politely. She moved the trolley nearer. 'Do help yourself, won't you?'

Olivia was visited by a mathematical fantasy. Roy Garnish was a cube, Pamela a line. She was slightly the taller, and of a curiously elongated appearance. She had incredibly long fingers, spindly legs, and her facial features reproduced the linear pattern. Unobtrusively eyeing her suit and jewellery, Olivia wondered what it would feel like to dress oneself on that level. She was aware that she, too, was being scrutinized, but in a puzzled way. Pamela was seeing a late-middle-aged woman dressed off a middle-grade peg, and wearing cultured pearls.

'Yes,' she said, in reply to the first question. 'He's engaged to Julian Wrey, the step-daughter of Colonel Winship, who lives at Crossways.'

'I'm afraid we keep clear of the village,' Roy Garnish said, coming over with the drinks on a tray. 'I'm a very busy man, Mrs Strode, and when we manage to snatch a short break down here I just feel like sleeping most of the time. Well, cheers, everybody.'

He downed the best part of a whisky and soda.

'Are you pleased about the engagement?' Pamela pursued.

'Yes, very pleased indeed. There's nothing hasty about it: they've known each other for five years.'

'So you're writing a book about Affacombe?' Roy Garnish asked, leaning back in his chair and crossing his legs.

'I'm writing the history of Affacombe parish, actually. It's quite a big one, running right up into the moor, although nearly all the people live down here in the village.'

'Who are you publishing with?'

Olivia explained that her book was only at a very early stage.

'I don't get you,' he said. 'If you want material about this place of mine dealing with the 1855 sell-up, you can't be far short of the end, surely?'

Sources of information became progressively fewer as you went back into the past, she told him. It was easier to proceed from the known to the less known as you collected your data.

'The last hundred years are a relatively simple matter,' she elaborated. 'What I'm doing at the moment is trying to get the fullest possible idea of what the parish was like just before the railway arrived in this part of the world. That was in 1849, when the pre-machine age came to an end.'

'Ah, now I'm with you all right. Damned interesting.'

Olivia was impressed by his intelligent and unfeigned interest in a topic which had never come his way before. He's able, she thought. Naturally able. With a different background he'd have gone to a university, and been able to tackle most things.

Roy Garnish pounced on the information she could give him about the Benisson family who had owned Affacombe Priory for three centuries before the estate was sold up.

'It tickles me pink to think of a chap like me lording it in a stately home, you know,' he said with satisfaction.

Pamela pressed more refreshment on Olivia with an assiduity which suggested that this trend in the conversation was not to her taste.

'Really, it's all quite fascinating,' she said unconvincingly. 'Why, I often wonder if the house is haunted.'

'Now you're talking,' said her husband, in high good humour. 'A ghost's a status symbol, if you like. Ever heard any tales of a Priory spook, Mrs Strode?'

'Not in the house itself, I'm afraid, but there's the legend of the Monk's Leap, of course.'

She narrated it amusingly, and it went down well with both the Garnishes. Roy gave a bellow of laughter.

As he refilled the glasses it seemed a propitious moment for introducing the subject of the excavation.

'Talking about the ruins,' Olivia said, 'there's another matter of historical interest I'd rather like to put to you, Mr Garnish.'

'Fire away,' he replied.

He listened attentively as she outlined the possibilities, but reacted with decision.

'Don't think we'd care for a whole lot of strangers digging up the place, do you, Pam?'

His wife agreed.

'There are the Ainsworths, too,' she added. 'It might be inconvenient for them. We've got to think of our tenants.'

'It was just an idea I had after that tree came down in the gale,' Olivia said equably, concealing her keen disappointment. 'Apparently' – she made a split-second decision not to mention her own visit to the spot – 'the original Priory extended a good deal farther than the exposed ruins. It must have been bigger and more important than historians have thought up to now. I'm afraid we get carried away at the chance of fresh information coming to light. I quite understand how you feel.'

'Here, hold on a minute.' The good-humoured grin had returned to Roy Garnish's face. 'I'm a bit out of my depth when it comes to culture, y'know. Haven't had much time for it. But if there's something worth digging up on the property I don't want to be obstructive. Far from it. It'd be quite a thing to have a whatsit – Ancient Monument outside the back door. It's just come back to me that I ran across one of these digging johnnies last summer. He'd been down at that prehistoric place in Midshire with a lot of the high-ups, he said. Can't think of his name at the moment, but I'll soon run him to earth. He might get some real top-notchers to come along.'

Olivia tried to convey tactfully that eminent archaeologists were most unlikely to be interested in the ruins of Affacombe Priory, but her views were brushed aside almost impatiently. I can just imagine him in a board-room, she thought, as the topic was abruptly dismissed and the conversation turned to the estate papers which had been brought down from London.

Half an hour later she was driving home, mulling over her visit. Some useful ground had certainly been covered. In time it would become clear to Roy Garnish that his ruins were very small beer, and if she were tactful it should then be possible to bring in the Highcastle Archaeological Society after all, and she would be able to take part in the field work herself. The big box of papers in the boot held out fascinating possibilities. She'd made a potentially valuable contact, although one which she'd no wish to extend into the social sphere. It would be best to be 'rather non-committal when describing the evening to her friends. And she'd make quite sure that the Garnishes were not in residence before going up to the ruins again.

On the following Friday evening David rang up Poldens from London, and there was also a call from Julian when the latter had returned to her flat in Highcastle. They were both ecstatically happy, full of their plans and eager to bring Olivia into the picture. She found this heartwarming, and as the days went by did all she could to show friendliness to the Winships, dropping in on them casually and encouraging them to do the same at Poldens.

Affacombe was by now settling down to its winter seclusion. Summer visitors had departed, and even cruising motorists had become a rarity. With few interruptions Olivia spent blissful hours sorting the box of papers. As Roy Garnish had warned her, they were in hopeless confusion. Only the spare room floor offered adequate space, and she retreated upstairs with them. The musty smell of long-stored documents seeped through the cottage as the little heaps multiplied, each carefully labelled. From time to time she came on a prize. One such was the auctioneers' plan of the estate drawn up for the sale in 1855. The village was smaller then, but on the other hand some houses seemed to have disappeared. She spread the plan on the kitchen table and compared it with the six-inch map of the Ordnance Survey. It was exactly what she had hoped to find. Later she found a copy of the Benissons' rent roll for 1839. Under the heading INCROACHMENT there was an additional charge of a penny to Samuel Wollacott 'for a porch to the cottage called Poledens adjoining the road leading to the turn-pike '.

Quite a lot of these ought to be in the County Archives, she thought, surveying the floor. How would Roy Garnish react to this suggestion? She really ought to put it to him. The best thing would be to play on his vanity as a landowner. She suddenly sneezed convulsively, and decided that the air was full of dust and that she needed a freshener. Why not go up to the ruins before lunch? She had learnt from the Ainsworths that a tractor and circular saw were dealing with the tree, and that the Garnishes had left. Pulling on a coat she went out to the garage, pausing for an affectionate glance at Samuel Wollacott's porch.

This time, having forewarned the Ainsworths, Olivia drove up to the front of the Priory, parked outside the West Wing and approached the ruins from the south side. It was past twelve and the men had knocked off for the dinner hour. But the clearing-up operation was already far advanced. The trunk had been lopped of its small branches and dragged away to an open space for easier handling.

After making a careful inspection Olivia came to the conclusion that the walls were part of a small building more likely to be the gatehouse than a guesthouse. She stood with her back to it and tried to picture the general layout more clearly. Then she walked in an easterly direction and poked about in what appeared to be the cloister garth. A dense thicket of shrubs had established itself on the probable site of the chapter house. It would be a tough job to clear, she thought, idly parting the branches and peering in. To her surprise there was a kind of tunnel leading to an open space in the middle. Twigs freshly snapped off showed that its existence was known to others – young devils, she at once concluded, knowing that the ruins were out of bounds for the boys. It was irresistible to her, too. Tying a scarf over her head she bent nearly double and wormed her way through.

Her first reaction was triumph as she discovered a piece of paving and the base of a pillar. There were also signs of much more recent occupation: a ground sheet, some sacks rolled up in a polythene bag, and a squalid litter of cigarette ends, some stained with lipstick, dead matches and sweet papers. A patch of bare earth bore the imprint of stiletto heels and heavy masculine footwear.

Temperamentally averse to getting herself involved in other people's business, Olivia stared at the floor of the little clearing with dismay. Ought she to say something to the Ainsworths? Their foreign maids were the subject of endless gossip in Affacombe, but personally she believed that most of this stemmed from the local girls incensed by what they considered unfair competition. Anyway, it was surely up to the Ainsworths to keep an eye on their staff. On the other hand she didn't believe for a moment that the ban on the ruins kept the boys out of them altogether ... This wasn't the sort of situation you'd care for them to stumble on.

Undecided, and irritated by the tiresomeness of it all she extricated herself and returned to her car. It was just on one o'clock: later than she had realized. When she was halfway down the drive Fred Earwaker swung in at the gate on his bicycle, returning from his dinner, and she slowed up for a friendly word. To her utter amazement he rode past without acknowledging her, his normally open face a wooden mask. She had stalled her engine, and sat for a moment watching him in the driving mirror, pedalling on without a glance over his shoulder. What on earth could be the matter, she wondered, starting up again? An accident to Ethel or Tommy? Perhaps he was hurrying to report to John Ainsworth and ask for time off? But as the thought came into her mind she saw Fred turn left as if making for the fallen tree.

After a late lunch she tried to settle down once more to the papers in the spare room, but her attention kept wandering. I'd better face it, she thought at last, thoroughly exasperated, and went downstairs to ring up the Priory School. John Ainsworth answered.

'I want to talk to you and Faith about something,' she told him. 'Not over the line, I think. Could you be free? I can come up any time.'

'Why, of course,' he said. 'Come about half-past eight, when most of the jobs are over. Here's Faith.'

'My dear, I can't think of anybody I'd be more glad to see!' Faith sounded tired and fussed. 'We're in a good old tiz. I'll lay on coffee.'

'You must have spotted the girl down in the village,' John Ainsworth said. 'An exotic blonde with a waggling bottom, and false eyelashes like the prongs of a rake. She came after Easter, and to our flat amazement turned out to be quite a good worker. So when she said she'd like to come back after the holidays, we were only too thankful. Well, she suddenly walked out early this morning, leaving a note to say she'd been offered a good job in London if she'd go at once, and would we please forward her luggage to the address given – some club for foreign girls, it was. She's gone to some man, if I know anything about it.'

'Of course the other girls were in such a state of excitement that we could hardly get any breakfast,' said Faith. She looked harassed and shiny, and pushed back some straying wisps of hair. 'We've talked to them, and they obviously knew she was up to something, but of course, they stick together like glue. All the same, I'm quite sure they weren't expecting her to go off like that. Then on top of it all there's the Earwaker disaster.'

Olivia looked up sharply.

'Earwaker? What's happened?'

'Ethel's gone off to nurse her mother, she says. She's taken Tommy with her. They went this afternoon, apparently. She does the early shift, and goes home at half-past eleven. She got Mrs Mullings to bring up a note.'

'Mrs Mullings?' exclaimed Olivia. 'But surely Fred knew she was going?'

'A bull's eye,' said John Ainsworth. 'Blake came up from the South Lodge just now, and said he thought he'd better tell me that it was all round the Priory Arms that Ethel's left Fred.

41

She found out today that he's been having an affair with one o' they vurrin gurls up to the skule. The Paleys who live next door heard the mother and father of a row going on in the dinner hour. I suppose Luisa knew someone had found out and decided to vamoose while the going was good.'

'Oh, Lord,' said Olivia, 'I'm afraid this is where I come in.'

'Of course, there's no proof that Fred and the girl have been meeting there,' she concluded. 'The Monk's Path is a right-of-way. Anybody can step over the wall into the ruins. Do you get people trespassing much?'

'Very seldom. Village kids now and again, or a nosey hiker. No, it seems pretty conclusive: a nice handy spot for them. I'd better have some of the shrubs down in case it's a recognised love-nest. I hope to God Fred doesn't take it into his head to go off after Luisa, the silly fool. Staffing a place like this is damn-all.'

'I don't think he will,' Olivia said, remembering the expression on Fred Earwaker's face. 'And I'm pretty sure Ethel will come back when she's cooled down, and they'll weather it somehow. There's Tommy to consider.'

'Ethel's like a mule when she gets an idea into her head,' lamented Faith.

'Listen, Faith. I'm off to London tomorrow, as you know, to get something to wear at the wedding. But if you're still two down on the domestic side when I get back on Wednesday, I'll gladly help you out. It's a firm offer.'

'How simply wonderful of you, Olivia darling! You're a friend in a million. But I shouldn't dream of sending you an S.O.S. unless we're really up against it.'

Chapter Five

Olivia's visit to London was a great success. Remarking that it was the last time they'd be boy and girl on their own, David insisted on taking her out twice to dinner and a theatre. At the week-end they went down to Wimbledon and inspected the house which Julian's trustee was buying for her. A helpful assistant at Margrove's made the buying of the wedding outfit positively enjoyable. There was even time to meet some old friends.

At intervals she hoped that the Affacombe problems were sorting themselves out. On an impulse she told David about the Earwakers.

'The balloon went up jolly suddenly,' he commented. 'Was Ethel quite normal when she was up at the Priory that morning?'

'She must have been. Faith Ainsworth had no idea that she was thinking of going off to her mother until the note arrived in the afternoon.'

'How early does Ethel go up to work?'

'Half-past eight. A good half-hour before the post arrives. Are you thinking of an anonymous letter, or something of that sort?' Olivia asked with interest, having had the same idea herself.

'It looks a bit like it, doesn't it? I mean, Ethel could hardly get home before a quarter to twelve or thereabouts, and Fred was due to turn up for his dinner soon after twelve. Anyone from the village with a juicy scandal about him would surely have waited until he'd gone back to his job, and Ethel was alone for the afternoon? Does anyone occur to you as a potential writer?'

'No one at all,' replied Olivia. 'I've thought and thought about it. I'm quite sure the other foreign girls must have known about the affair, but it doesn't sound like one of them, somehow. I wish it did: it's hateful to think of someone from the village doing anything so beastly.'

'I agree. Naughty of old Fred to let himself be seduced by a glamorous blonde, but clean fun compared with the other form of amusement. I hope Ethel manages to get over it. He's an awfully decent chap.'

Olivia's last engagement was a call on her former employer, Professor Moreton-Blake, who was most encouraging and helpful about her Parish History. She came away feeling that she could hardly wait to get back to Affacombe and start work again. On the following day she returned home and rather reluctantly contacted Faith Ainsworth. She learnt that Ethel Earwaker had not returned, but that some temporary help was available, and that there was hope of a replacement for Luisa. Asked about Fred, Faith reported that attempts by Simon Fairhall and John to act as mediators had got nowhere: he was flatly refusing to discuss the situation. Olivia finally rang off with a feeling of relief at not being wanted in a domestic capacity.

By teatime on Saturday she had completely finished sorting and classifying Roy Garnish's papers, and wondered when he was coming down again. Obviously she must see him and try to persuade him to deposit the more valuable records with the County Archivist. With the comfortable feeling of a good job behind her, she presently bathed and changed and set off to supper at Crossways, wishing that she were going to spend the evening with Julian rather than *en famille*.

It turned out a more congenial party than she had expected. There was the latest report of David to give Julian, and her own activities to describe. A good visual memory enabled her to draw a detailed plan of the Wimbledon house for Barbara and Hugh, and this led to an animated discussion of colour schemes and furniture. Later, they worked on a list of those to be invited to the wedding, a matter complicated by the smallness of the church. Glancing at the clock on the mantelpiece Olivia was astonished to find that it was past eleven, and said that she really must be going home.

'Mind taking your notice of the Revel meeting?' asked Hugh Winship, returning to the room with a duplicated sheet. 'Thought it was time I got a move on with all this wedding business ahead.'

There were cries of dismay from the three women.

'Heavens! I'd completely forgotten the Revel,' exclaimed Julian. 'Must you be Hon. Sec. again this year, Daddy?'

'Can't very well rat now, m'dear. The meeting's on Monday week.'

'Personally, I think Revel's the utter end,' said Barbara. 'I feel bound to go to the wretched meeting though, to support Hugh. Come with us, Olivia?'

'Thanks very much. I'd like to. Shall whichever of us gets there first keep a place? Then we can mutter flippant remarks while Hugh looks important.'

As she walked home escorted by Hugh, Olivia reflected that she was making quite good headway over establishing friendly relations with Barbara.

Affacombe's community life revolved round the Priory Arms, the church and the parish hall. Volunteers had recently redecorated the interior of the latter with sky-blue colour wash and yellow paint, and fluorescent strip lighting had been installed. Coming in out of the dark to the Revel meeting Olivia blinked at the glare, and noticed that the characteristic smell of steamy tea urns and perspiration was as strong as ever.

The hall was already well filled. At the far end Simon Fairhall was standing at a small table, talking to George Forbes, owner of the Village Stores and honorary treasurer of the Revel. The usual voluntary segregation was in force. In the back rows youths and their girls engaged in self-conscious badinage. The older members of families who considered themselves real Affacombe filled the middle rows, forcing the incomers, who were mainly gentry, to the front, and surveying them with critical interest as they took their places. Large coloured prints of the Queen and the Duke of Edinburgh looked down on the assembly, and the hands of a wall clock stood at one minute to seven-thirty. Olivia hurried forward to find Barbara Winship, but to her surprise neither she nor Hugh had yet arrived. She slipped into a chair next to a Commander and Mrs Forsythe, and put her handbag on the empty seat on her other side. After a brief conversation she glanced round at the door, but there was still no sign of the Winships.

'Where on earth are they?' demanded Charles Forsythe. 'Old Hugh's never late. I want to get this over and be home in time for the News.'

By five and twenty to eight conversation in the hall had risen to a roar, and the Vicar and George Forbes were conferring with baffled expressions. Soon there were signs of restiveness, and Simon Fairhall hammered on the table.

'We seem to have mislaid our secretary,' he said. 'Does anyone know if he and Mrs Winship have been away for the day?'

'Maybe the clocks is wrong over to Crossways,' suggested someone, raising a laugh connected with a recent incident involving the Vicarage clocks.

There was a chorus of offers to run over to Crossways. Finally George Forbes hurried off under a good-humoured volley of enquiries as to whether he was clearing out with the balance from last year. The noise in the hall quickly rose to deafening proportions once more.

'Hope they haven't had a car smash!' screeched Celia Forsythe.

The tumult died down as George Forbes reappeared and made his way up to the front, panting heavily. Simon Fairhall listened, and turned to the rows of expectant faces.

'I'm sorry to tell you that Mrs Winship was taken ill just as she and the Colonel were starting for the meeting, but we hope it's nothing serious. He naturally didn't feel he could leave her alone in the house, and was just ringing round trying to get a message up here. Now, we must find someone to act as our temporary Revel secretary.'

'Not this fella,' Charles Forsythe murmured anxiously, trying to look inconspicuous. 'She's gone down with 'flu, I expect. Coppin was saying he's got some cases in Leeford.'

Tiresome, thought Olivia. Barbara always made such heavy weather of her ailments, and there was a lot to be done in the near future. Perhaps she'd better call in on her way home ... She tried to concentrate on the meeting, wondering what would happen if Fred Earwaker hadn't turned up. From all accounts he was still living like a hermit outside working hours.

St Lucca's Revel included some customs of interest to antiquarians. At sunset on December 15th a barrel of blazing tar was sent hurtling down the precipitous side of Sinneldon into the river. It was maintained that the longer it went on burning, the better were the prospects for the crops and for animal and human fertility in the twelve months ahead. At the moment of its final extinction the Revel Queen of the year emerged from concealment carrying a blazing torch with which she set alight a huge bonfire on the river bank. Then, attended by her retinue, all carrying lanterns, she led the way to the parish hall. The questionable festivities which had affronted Bishop Whitcombe had in the course of time been sublimated into a Parish Supper, followed by some mildly rowdy dancing in the village street. Bad weather sometimes reduced the earlier part of the proceedings to chaos, but from time immemorial nothing short of the two World Wars had ever induced the villagers to abandon it.

Getting the tar barrel to the top of Sinneldon and sending it off on its meteoritic descent called for brawn, and was the prerogative of the younger men. For some years Fred Earwaker had been regarded as the leader of the operation. As the business of the meeting slowly progressed, Olivia listened anxiously.

' Now, strong men forward, please,' Simon Fairhall said. ' Which of you hefty lads are doing the barrel this year?'

There was an awkward silence. At last one of the older men rose to his feet.

' Seein' as Fred Earwaker b'ain't yur, Vicar, I takes leave to propose Jim Brent leads barrel party.'

In default of other suggestions Jim Brent was duly seconded, and elected by a forest of raised hands. Olivia gave a sigh of relief. It had been done very tactfully, really. If only some way could be found to break the impasse, though.

Hugh Winship looked slightly lost, in the manner of men whose domestic routine has broken down.

' She was perfectly all right when I went off to the County Council this morning,' he told Olivia. ' Began to feel off colour when she got in from walking the dogs this afternoon, she says. She didn't fancy any supper, and just as we were starting off for the meeting she had a funny sort of collapse. Scared me stiff. I got on to Coppin, and he's been along and says she's got a virus infection. Means 'flu, I suppose. Left some pills, and told her to stay in bed. She's got a bit of temperature.'

' Shall I go up and see her?' she asked.

' Think not, if you don't mind. Her light's out: she said she just wanted to sleep. Nice of you to look in, though. How did the meeting go?'

Olivia gave him a brief account, and undertook to come round again after breakfast the next morning. An early telephone call, however, put her off. Barbara was feeling better, but would not hear of her risking infection. With the comforting feeling of having at least tried to do her duty she settled down to a good day's work on the Parish History.

It was a wet and dismal afternoon, and going over to draw the curtains at an early hour she saw the Garnishes' Mercedes pass, going in the direction of the Priory. She decided to ring them later, and offer to bring the box of papers up to the West Wing on the following day. They could hardly avoid asking her in, and she could then raise the matter of the County Archives.

This plan, however, was not to materialize. Roy had started off with a bit of a cold that morning, Pamela said, and he was now absolutely streaming with it. He would be sorry not to see her, but it really wouldn't be sensible. He was just here, and would like a word...

Hoarse and catarrhal, Roy thanked her for all her work and asked her to hang on to the box till he was down again. Yes, he'd got a flipping awful cold.

Olivia commiserated and rang off, wondering who it was at the front door.

Chapter Six

Julian stood with her back to the fire looking tired and strained.

'Daddy seemed bothered about Mummy,' she explained, 'so I thought I'd better come home for the night.' She hesitated. 'As a matter of fact I wondered if I might ring up David from here, just on the chance that he's in this evening?'

'My dear, of course you can,' Olivia told her. 'Any time. The Crossways telephone's rather public, isn't it? See if you can get him while I make some coffee.'

Julian took a step in the direction of the telephone and then stood irresolutely.

'I'm a bit bothered myself, come to that.'

'Why not sit down for a minute and tell me about it, if you'd care to?' Olivia suggested, pulling up another chair and throwing a log on the fire.

Julian took off her coat and sat down. For a few moments there was silence as she watched the leaping flames.

'Mummy's looking simply dreadful,' she said unequivocally. 'So white and drawn, and she's gone to pieces in the most extraordinary way. When we were alone she broke down completely, and said she couldn't possibly face the wedding and that it must be put off for the present. When I said there was no need to have a reception or any fuss at all she got quite hysterical, and said it wouldn't make any difference, and the whole thing had got to be postponed. Then Daddy came in, but neither of us could do anything with her at all. At last we persuaded her to take a sedative Dr Coppin had prescribed, and in the end she quietened down and got sleepy. It just doesn't make sense. I mean, she was perfectly happy about the wedding on Saturday evening, wasn't she? It's so sudden.'

'I expect Dr Coppin gave her an antibiotic,' Olivia said reassuringly. 'Hugh said he'd left something for her to take on Monday night. They have the most frightfully depressing effect on some people. And after all, parting with your only daughter *is* a wrench, and I think she's probably got everything out of focus at the moment.'

A look of relief came into Julian's face.

'What a clot I am,' she said. 'I never thought of that. People are always talking about antibiotic depression at the hospital.'

'Why not see if you can get David now? You'll feel much happier after a chat with him.'

Going into the kitchen Olivia listened anxiously until it became clear that David was at the other end of the line. As she went automatically through the process of coffee-making she began to feel increasingly indignant towards Barbara Winship. Of course, when people were ill their real selves were apt to come out, and Barbara was a spoilt, self-centred woman. Naturally she didn't want Julian to go off for good, nor the wear and tear of organizing the wedding, and wasn't making any attempt to disguise the fact.

The sitting-room door opened, and Julian came across to the kitchen looking relaxed and much happier.

'David sends you his love,' she reported. 'He says he thinks your diagnosis of Mummy's upset is probably correct in the light of the information available to him: the legal mind in action! We've decided to take a soothing line with her, and say we'll be talking it over when I go up to Town the week-end after next. Of course, we've no intention of putting off the wedding, but she'll have got over her 'flu by then.'

51

'You're finishing up at the hospital on Friday week, aren't you?'

'Yes. I'm coming straight back here from London on the Sunday night. My being at home all the time ought to make it easier for Mummy. Silly of me to get into such a tiz just now, but when I want a thing really desperately I'm always terrified it won't come off. David teases me about it. Do let me carry that tray for you.'

Half an hour later when Julian had gone back to Crossways Olivia settled down once more to read. After a time she found her attention wandering, and putting her book aside stared into the fire. Everything had been going so well until Barbara started this disruption. At least, almost everything. The unfortunate Earwaker business was a marginal worry, and that had come absolutely out of the blue, too. What was it David said about it? 'The balloon seems to have gone up very suddenly', wasn't it? Ethel had been her normal self on the morning of her abrupt departure, and Hugh had said that Barbara was perfectly all right when he went off to his County Council meeting. Quite an odd coincidence.

Feeling rather tired and depressed she decided to go up to bed. Tomorrow she would make another attempt to see Barbara.

On the following morning Olivia duly carried out her resolution and went to Crossways. She found Barbara installed in the drawing-room, surrounded with invalid comforts and being cosseted by Hugh. The spectacle was irritating until she caught sight of her face. Discomfited, she had to admit that Julian had not exaggerated, and that her mother did look dreadful. About ten years older, and her eyes were frightened.

'...few days in a decent hotel at Polharbour,' Hugh was saying. 'Keeps on that she doesn't feel up to going away, but I'm digging m'heels in for once.'

Barbara smiled wanly.

'I really can't face packing and shutting up the house until after the week-end. I must get on to my legs and go out once or twice first.'

'Down here today. Turn in the garden tomorrow, what?'

'Polharbour sounds a splendid idea,' Olivia said bracingly. 'I'll gladly come round and pack for you, Barbara, if it would help. You could just sit and tell me what to put in.'

'Oh, no, really. It's too sweet of you, but I'm sure I'll be able to cope by then. I wouldn't dream of letting you.'

After some rather desultory conversation Olivia rose to go, remarking that visitors were tiring when you were under the weather. Barbara made no effort to detain her, and she left feeling that she had been warned off. Various casual encounters later in the week confirmed this impression. They met in the village and once in Leeford, and on each occasion there was an unmistakable sense of a barrier having sprung up between them. We're far more out of touch than before the engagement she thought. Really, Barbara was being most peculiar and tiresome.

A further irritation to an orderly person like herself was the non-appearance of Fred Earwaker to mend the trellis fence damaged by the storm. He was avoiding her, and according to the village had been living more or less like a hermit since the departure of Ethel and Tommy. Olivia finally wrote an urgent note and took it up to his cottage. As she put it through the letter box she found herself wondering again if Ethel had learnt of his affair with Luisa through an anonymous letter, and almost simultaneously a startling idea flashed into her mind. Was it conceivably possible that Barbara's attack of nerves was the result of an anonymous letter?

Really, she thought as she walked slowly home, I'm getting anonymous letters on the brain. To begin with there's no proof that Ethel ever had one. Still, from what one reads in detective novels once people start writing them they're apt to go on, so if she did there's nothing improbable in Barbara getting one as well. But what on earth could have been in it to shatter her so completely? I can't believe that she'd take it seriously if it accused Hugh of infidelity, or Julian of doing something frightful.

Deciding that she was allowing her imagination to run away with her Olivia made a determined effort to dismiss the whole subject from her mind. But in spite of some hard work on the Parish History she found herself unable to do so, and after deliberating wrote a long letter to David at the week-end. His reply came at mid-week. It was neither teasing nor irritated, a fact which she found rather disturbing. He was very glad to have been briefed on the situation at Crossways before Julian came up to London. He still thought that a medical explanation of Barbara's behaviour was tenable, but agreed that there was an apparent odd parallel with the Earwaker explosion. However, although it seemed quite possible that Ethel had received an anonymous letter, perhaps it was going a bit far to attribute Barbara's vapours to one? All the same, it was a dangerously intriguing idea if it could be taken a stage further to imply a skeleton in his prospective mother-in-law's cupboard.

On the following Saturday afternoon a team from St Hector's, Polharbour, came over to play the Priory School. It was the chief match of the term, and John Ainsworth anxiously watched the foxy brilliance of the early morning clouding over. The weather was still holding up after lunch, however, and from half-past two onwards faint yelling and cheering came floating down to the village.

Olivia Strode had been invited to tea at the Vicarage. Shortly before four o'clock she went upstairs to get ready, and noticed that the noise had stopped. She hoped that the home team had won: John Ainsworth cared so much about such things. At any rate everybody would now be enjoying one of Faith's celebrated match teas. Judging that the rain was likely to come soon, she took an umbrella and started off on foot.

The village seemed deserted. A bus left for Polharbour at one on Saturdays, taking people in for shopping and the cinema, and would not return until six. As she reached the Church Lane turning she saw the Winships' Jack Russells dart out of the gate leading from the Monk's Path. A moment later Barbara followed them, and returned her wave as the church clock jerkily announced the first quarter. Olivia hurried on, relieved at not having to stop and engage in constrained conversation about the visit to Polharbour. But sooner or later, she thought, frowning, I'll have to tackle this situation and try to get through to her.

The Priory School had deservedly won the match, and after seeing off the St Hector's coach with the decorum demanded by the Ainsworths' presence, the boys showed every sign of getting above themselves. Mrs Claythorpe, the matron on duty, had her hands full, and when one Stephen Biggs reported that he felt sick she bundled him along the colonnade to the school sanatorium in the East Wing.

'If you're going to be sick you can do it over with Sister,' she said in an exasperated voice. 'You've overeaten at the match tea, that's what it is. You're a thoroughly greedy little boy, Stephen. I haven't forgotten what happened when your Granny took you out last term, if you have...Sister!' she called, sweeping him through the door and into the surgery. 'Here, hold this.' She thrust a white enamel bowl at him. 'Sister! You're wanted!' she called more loudly.

There was no answer. Hurrying to Sister Roach's sitting-room, Mrs Claythorpe found it empty, and a few moments were enough to establish that she was nowhere in the sanatorium. Clicking her tongue in annoyance Mrs Claythorpe returned to the surgery and ran a practised eye over the hapless Stephen, by now looking decidedly green.

'Sister must have gone over to school,' she said more mildly. 'You'd better come and lie down until she comes back. Bring that bowl, for goodness sake.'

After putting him on a bed with the bowl strategically placed, she hurried back to the main block in search of Sister Roach, but an appalling uproar in the senior boys' common room diverted her. She found Sheila Wills, an assistant matron, vainly trying to quell a free-for-all in which a chair had already been smashed. Having restored order, and made it clear that anyone who gave further trouble would be sent straight to the headmaster, she reverted to her original purpose.

'Just run across to the San, dear,' she said to Sheila Wills, 'and explain to Sister about that little wretch Stephen Biggs. She's sure to have got back by now. It's better for me to be about here with the boys being so over-excited.'

Within a few minutes Sheila returned to report that Sister Roach was still absent, and that Stephen had been frightfully sick and looked awful.

'I'm afraid you'll just have to do the best you can for the moment, then. Give him a hot-water bottle, and a few sips of water if he can keep it down. I'll run and see if she's in the kitchen.'

No one on duty in the kitchen had seen Sister Roach since she collected her tea tray at about four o'clock, or knew anything of her whereabouts. After looking for her in various other places, Mrs. Claythorpe stood hesitating. Could it be that as there were no in-patients, Sister had asked Mrs Ainsworth if she could go down to the village, and had forgotten to tell the matron on duty? It wouldn't be a bit like her to forget a thing as important as that. Reluctant to disturb the Ainsworths, and still more to risk giving away a colleague who might have slipped up, Mrs. Claythorpe was still undecided when pandemonium broke out in the little boys' playroom and tipped the balance. Stephen Biggs couldn't be left alone over there, so they simply must have a third pair of hands . . .

Chapter Seven

It was a tribute to Sister Roach's reputation for reliability that the Ainsworths assumed at once that her absence was due to some misunderstanding about off-duty time. Faith hurried across to the East Wing and relieved Sheila Wills, leaving John to ring George Forbes at the Village Stores and find out if Sister Roach was visiting his wife, her main social contact in Affacombe. On hearing that they had not seen her since the previous day, he went over to the East Wing himself, to ask Faith if she could suggest any other likely household.

Faith came out of Sister Roach's sitting-room looking puzzled and slightly bothered.

'Her everyday coat's gone,' she told him. 'It always hangs on that hook, just inside the door. But she hasn't taken her handbag – it's here on the table. I can't make it out.'

'What about her bike?' he asked.

The bicycle was in its usual shed. In the clinically clean and orderly pantry they found a teatray with an unused teapot and an apparently untouched plate of food from the match tea. A strainer had been used to brew a single cup of tea.

'John, I don't like it a bit.' There was a slight tremor in Faith's voice as she stared at him with large, anxious eyes. 'Suppose she went out into the grounds for a breather, meaning to have her tea later? She could have slipped and fallen, and be lying somewhere with a broken leg.'

He frowned.

'Could be,' he admitted reluctantly. 'Not very likely, though. She wouldn't have gone far as she was on duty. Somebody would be sure to have heard her calling for help. Still, perhaps I'd better get a torch and have a quick look round.'

'Yes, do,' she said. 'I'd feel much happier. I think I'd better put a blanket round Stephen Biggs and take him over to the spare room. It'll be easier to look after him there.'

Twenty minutes later John Ainsworth re-entered the main front door of the house. Faith came running down the staircase.

'Not a sign of her,' he said in a low voice, peeling off a wet macintosh and leading the way to their sitting-room. 'I've been all round the back and into the ruins, and along the Monk's Path a bit, and yelled and listened. It's drizzling, which doesn't help.'

As he spoke there was the sound of a car coming up the drive. They turned their heads, but it went past the window towards the West Wing.

'Garnishes,' John said. 'I saw them going off somewhere before lunch. Look here, can't you think of anywhere else in the village where she could be? I can easily run down in the car.'

'I suppose it's just possible that she might be at Hilda Rainbird's,' Faith said doubtfully. 'Or with Mrs Cummings. I've seen them talking to each other once or twice after church.'

After two more abortive telephone calls they looked at each other, torn between anxiety and the dread of involving the school in undesirable publicity.

'We'd better face it,' John said. 'It's beginning to point to a proper search. Blast and damn the woman! It would be a Saturday night with the teaching staff away. I'm going to risk getting a flea in my ear, and ring through to Garnish. If he'd lend a hand, it'd be a lot better than digging Blake out of the Priory Arms, and having the whole village buzzing.'

'What's up?' enquired Roy Garnish. 'Evening, Mrs Ainsworth.' He dominated the hearthrug, and eyed them enquiringly.

'We need a spot of help on the quiet,' John Ainsworth said. 'It's like this.'

Roy Garnish listened to his account without comment.

'Didn't you have a match on this afternoon?' he asked.

'Yes. Why?'

'Look at it this way. There were visitors and strange cars about, I take it? Suppose an old flame of the woman's turned up to see her, and suggested going off to make an evening of it somewhere? Mightn't she have risked it, seeing there weren't any kids in the sick bay?'

'She'd have known perfectly well that she'd only got to come and ask for special leave. My wife would have stood in for her. We're pretty elastic: have to be, or we couldn't keep a staff at all.'

'She wouldn't have gone out for the evening in her old coat, and without a handbag,' ventured Faith.

Roy Garnish stared at her.

'You've got a point there,' he agreed. 'Well, it's a bloody nuisance, but somebody's got to make sure she isn't lying out in the rain. I'll lend a hand, of course. I'm with you about trying to keep the village out of it. The less talk the better from the school's point of view, and ten to one it's a mare's nest, anyway. I'll cut home and get into some boots and a raincoat. Be seeing you, Mrs Ainsworth.'

Olivia Strode cautiously negotiated the turn into the drive of Affacombe Priory, the curtain of the rain glittering in her headlights. The need for concentration interrupted her speculation about what had happened at the school. Faith had sounded desperately worried over the telephone, giving no details beyond the fact that a major crisis had developed. As she drew up at the front door Olivia saw that no other car was parked in the gravel sweep, and realized that she had been subconsciously expecting to find Dr Coppin's there. Perhaps it was a domestic crisis? The foreign girls walking out en bloc, for instance.

She tied a scarf over her head and dived for the shelter of the porch. The next moment she had opened the door and was confronted by the spectacle of John Ainsworth and Roy Garnish dragging off muddy Wellington boots, while Faith carried dripping macintoshes in the direction of the cloakroom. Sounds of a large number of small boys going to bed were floating down from the upper floors: running water, feet thudding along passages in bedroom slippers, doors slamming, young voices and adult exhortation. A composite smell of baked beans on toast, Dettol and wet clothes assailed her nostrils. Roy Garnish looked up, acknowledging her arrival with a nod.

'Good of you to come up, Olivia.' John Ainsworth sounded abstracted.

In the sitting-room he dispensed drinks while giving her the facts of Sister Roach's disappearance.

'We're now absolutely certain that she isn't anywhere in the buildings. Garnish and I have been going over the grounds with torches for the past hour and have drawn a complete blank. She hadn't many contacts in the village, and none of them have seen her. Where do we go from here—if anywhere? We can call at every house, I suppose, or bring in the police. Either will get the school into the papers and set off the parents. What's your reaction, Olivia?'

Olivia glanced at the clock on the mantelpiece which registered twenty minutes past eight, and considered for a few moments.

'Let me recap,' she said. 'Sister's absence was first noticed roughly three hours ago, but as far as we know she hasn't been seen on the premises since she collected her tray about four o'clock. It certainly seems a bit soon to raise the alarm. On the other hand, the old coat, the handbag, the hurried cup of tea and the bicycle taken together suggest that she didn't intend to go far. Also, from what you say about her, she doesn't sound the sort of person to be A.W.O.L.'

The two Ainsworths made emphatic sounds of assent.

'Of course, sensational newspaper reports and so on are frightfully bad for a school, but if by any chance she really has come to harm, and it transpires that you did nothing much about it tonight, wouldn't the long-term publicity be even worse?'

'Fifty times worse!' burst out Faith. 'Anyway, there's another side to it. If you employ people, you've got to accept some responsibility for them. I'm certain she'd never have gone off like this of her own free will.'

There was an uneasy silence.

'Your last points make sense to me,' Roy Garnish remarked to Olivia. 'Not that the police or anybody else can do much round here tonight. It's raining like hell and pitch dark. But see here, Ainsworth. If you've reported it to the police you can't be caught on the wrong foot if there's trouble.'

John Ainsworth reluctantly picked up the telephone directory and began turning over the pages.

'I'd better ring the station at Leeford,' he said. 'It's hardly a 999 call – The headmaster of Affacombe Priory School speaking. Is that Sergeant Murch? –'

A couple of minutes later he replaced the receiver.

'Murch is coming over. He sounded pretty browned off, and made it quite clear that he thinks it's a fuss about nothing, and that she'll walk in later with some perfectly good explanation.'

'Well, let's hope she does,' said Olivia cheerfully. 'We can but look silly.'

'I'll be pushing off, then.' Roy Garnish got to his feet. 'There's nothing I can do at the moment. Let me know if the copper wants to hear where we searched, Ainsworth, and if the damned woman turns up, of course. Sorry you're having all this bother,' he added, with a comprehensive jerk of his head in the direction of Faith and Olivia.

As the two men went out of the room Faith thrust back her straying hair with an agitated gesture.

'I simply must run up and see how Stephen Biggs is. He's in

61

the spare room with a bilious attack. I brought him across from the San.'

' I,' said Olivia firmly, ' am dealing with Stephen Biggs, and any other casualties. Otherwise there's no point in my being here. I'm perfectly ready to stand in for Sister Roach until further notice. I've had supper, and you and John obviously haven't. For heaven's sake be sensible, and go and see about some food.'

Reinforced by John, Olivia persuaded Faith to agree to this programme, and left them eating a hasty and belated meal. Going upstairs she encountered a startled Mrs Claythorpe, and decided to bring her up to date with developments. She invented a tactful message from Faith to the effect that she was relying entirely on Mrs Claythorpe to keep the rest of the domestic and house staff on an even keel. Stephen Biggs was recovering, and showing signs of curiosity about his transfer to the Ainsworths' private quarters and Olivia's presence. As she sponged his face and hands and settled him for the night she parried his questions as best she could. She heard a car draw up, and an unfamiliar masculine voice in the hall, followed by the shutting of a door. As Stephen became drowsy she slipped out quietly and went downstairs, anxious to avoid further conversation with Mrs Claythorpe. She could hear voices in the sitting-room, but John's study would be empty. She went in and sank into an arm-chair, staring unseeingly at the impersonal office furniture and the rows of school photographs on the walls. It was impossible to smother the feeling that something sinister and unpleasant was going on below the surface in Affacombe.

After a few minutes she heard a door open and footsteps in the hall. Was Sergeant Murch going, then?

' Well, sir, we'll leave it like that then,' she heard. ' Unless you contact us meantime to say the lady's returned, we'll be over as soon as it's light.'

Ought I to have advised it, Olivia thought in sudden panic? It's landed us in quite a different context. Official, and outside our control altogether.

The rain died out during the night, but low cloud and drifting hill fog delayed the coming of daylight on Sunday morning. It was half-past eight before a police car arrived at the Priory, bringing Sergeant Murch and a couple of constables. At the former's request the Ainsworths conducted all three to the East Wing, where they briefly inspected Sister Roach's quarters and the various sheds in the rear of the building. Finally, reinforced by Blake, the head gardener, they moved off in the direction of the ruins. Olivia, preparing to receive two boys with bad colds, watched the solid uncompromising backs of the policemen from a window in one of the wards. The fact that all four men carried stout sticks horridly suggested a search of the undergrowth.

The arrival of the boys distracted her attention, and she was disconcerted to find a long jostling queue of out-patients at the surgery door. They looked extremely healthy, and it did not take her long to realize that the news of Sister Roach's disappearance had leaked out. With most of them she was crisp, and overheard some far from complimentary remarks which amused her. One or two, however, were genuinely in need of her ministrations. She was so busy that she did not notice the hurried return of Sergeant Murch to the main building shortly after ten o'clock.

John Ainsworth sat swivelled round from his desk, an incredulous expression on his face.

'In the *river*, did you say? At the bottom of the Monk's Leap?'

'A bit farther downstream, actually, sir. The body's wedged under an overhanging bit of the bank, where the current's swept it. It's going to be a job getting at it with the water running high as it is after the rain. We'll have to work along from the village end.'

'But what in God's name can have happened? There's a perfectly good railing at the Leap.'

'That'll be up to the coroner to find out, sir,' Sergeant Murch replied impassively. 'There'll be an inquest, of course. Meantime there's the next-of-kin to think of. You've got the name and address, I expect?'

'It's a sister in London as far as I remember.' John Ainsworth flicked through a card-index. 'Yes, here it is. A Mrs Grant, 167 Winterton Road, Lewisham, S.E.13. No telephone.'

'Then it'll be best to get on to the local station right away. We'll see to that.' Sergeant Murch made a note of the address. 'You'll keep the boys away from the river for the next hour or so, I take it?'

'I certainly will,' replied John Ainsworth grimly, already mentally composing an urgent circular to parents.

After the initial shock of the news a general sense of relief was perceptible. As Faith Ainsworth remarked to Olivia, it was something to feel you knew the worst and what you'd got to cope with. On their return from church the boys were assembled and sensibly addressed by John. Their reaction was what he had expected: goggle-eyed excitement, and eagerness to start their home letters. The foreign girls showed a tendency to get into huddles and mutter, but in general the normal routine was maintained. Lunch for Olivia and her patients was brought over to the East Wing, and at half-past one she was relieved by Sheila Wills and went home for a couple of hours to catch up on her own affairs.

When she returned two unfamiliar police cars were standing in the drive. She deduced that the enquiry had been passed to a higher level, and was unprepared to find a shaken and ashen-faced Sheila.

'Oh, Mrs Strode, I'm so glad you've come back,' the girl gasped, almost in tears. 'The police are saying Sister's been – been murdered! An Inspector from Highcastle's been in here,

64

asking me all sorts of questions. He said he'd be coming again to see you.'

Olivia had the sensation of having stepped out of normality into a nightmare. For a moment she stood frozen.

' How absolutely terrible,' she said slowly. Then the sight of the frightened girl restored her powers of action. ' I'd better give the boys their tea at once, I think, if the Inspector's coming back. Would you like a cup too?'

Busy in the pantry she fought an icy little fear which had taken root in her mind from the first moment. It was absurd, she told herself. Sister was in the school kitchen fetching her teatray ' about four ' – John had said so. Barbara had come through the gate on to the road as the quarter had struck, all the way down from the Monk's Leap. It wasn't as though she was a quick walker. Anyway, even to imagine for a single moment – but the police would find out, and in her present nervy state Barbara'd go to pieces. Suppose the Inspector asked where she herself was yesterday afternoon?

It's no good, she thought, steadying herself, and taking trays in to the boys. Not the slightest good pretending I didn't see her. It's bound to come out in the end, and would only make things worse. Perhaps he wouldn't ask.

The cups of tea were barely finished when there was a knock on the door from the colonnade. Olivia went to answer it. A very tall man was standing outside, and she felt a flicker of interest in his combination of dark colouring and a Scandinavian cast of features.

' Detective-Inspector Dart of the Highcastle C.I.D., madam,' he said, producing his official card. ' I'm in charge of the enquiry into the death of Sister Joan Roach, and I'd like a few minutes with you, if you're free just now.'

In the unoccupied ward where she had installed herself, Olivia explained that she was not a member of the staff, but a friend of Mr and Mrs Ainsworth, who was helping them out in the emergency. Inspector Dart, who gave the impression of finding the situation unorthodox, made a note of her full name, widowed status and address. He was polite, if tediously slow, and took her through the events of the previous evening, step by step.

'May I ask you something, Inspector?' she asked in a pause. 'The young assistant matron you interviewed here just now told me that the police think Sister Roach was murdered? Is this really true? It seems absolutely incredible.'

Dart gave her a disapproving look, and appeared to be weighing up the advisability of snubbing her.

'At present we are treating her death as a case of murder,' he said. 'Her injuries are not altogether compatible with accident or suicide.'

As he reverted to a study of his notebook, Olivia realized that the idea of suicide had not even occurred to her, and she felt a momentary relief, but Dart's next words confirmed her earlier apprehensions. In such a case, he told her, a full routine enquiry was, of course, essential. It was only by checking and counterchecking statements that the police could arrive at the movements of people over the crucial period. Would she tell him where she herself was yesterday afternoon, purely as a matter of routine?

'Certainly, Inspector,' she replied. It was important to be relaxed, matter-of-fact, unemphatic. 'I was in my cottage until about five minutes past four, when I left to go to tea at the Vicarage in Church Lane. I returned home just before six, and didn't go out again until Mrs Ainsworth telephoned asking me to come up here. That was at eight o'clock, as I told you.'

There was another pause.

'Did you go to the Vicarage by car, Mrs Strode?'

'No. I walked.'

'Did you notice anyone about?'

'Very few people. The village is always rather empty on Saturday afternoons. There's a shopping bus into Polharbour.'

'I should like the names of the people you did see, if you can remember them. Take your time.'

Olivia closed her eyes and wrinkled her brow.

' I saw George Forbes behind the counter of the shop. It was a dark afternoon and the lights were on. Several people were inside, but I only saw their backs. I think one of them was old Andy Pethybridge...Mrs Moon was going up the street ahead of me, carrying a basket. She went into her cottage – Pear Tree Cottage, it's called. That's all, I think...Oh, Mrs Winship. I just caught sight of her coming back from exercising her dogs as I turned into Church Lane. We waved to each other.'

' What direction was she coming from?'

Olivia plunged.

' From the gate leading to the Monk's Path. She nearly always takes her dogs for a run there before tea.'

Inspector Dart made another entry in his notebook. Her heart was beating painfully, but at any rate she'd sounded quite casual and undisturbed.

' Did you notice the time when you got to the Vicarage, Mrs Strode?'

' The church clock was striking the quarter as I turned into Church Lane.'

' How long did it take you to get to the Vicarage from the turning?'

' Oh, about half a minute, I should think.'

' Did you see anyone about in the lane?'

' No one at all.'

She was aware of his steady gaze.

' Are you absolutely sure? There are some houses along there, aren't there? New bungalows, and Church Cottages: Robinsons, Earwakers – he's a gardener up here, I under-stand, Paleys, Lethbridges?'

Olivia's heart gave a particularly painful leap. Sergeant Murch must have briefed this man about the Earwaker situa-tion, and of course he'd freeze on to it. In her anxiety about Barbara she'd forgotten Fred.

' I'm quite positive I didn't see anyone,' she said decisively.

A loud rat-tat came from the door leading to the colonnade.

' That'll be my sergeant.' Dart put away his notebook and

got to his feet, towering over her. 'We'll be taking a look at the deceased lady's rooms now, but that shouldn't disturb you or your patients. You've given me some helpful information, Mrs Strode.'

Chapter Eight

Inspector Dart walked across to the window of Sister Roach's sitting-room and jerked the curtain over it.

'Got all those statements signed?' he asked Sergeant Metcalfe, also of the Highcastle C.I.D.

'Yes, sir, Mr and Mrs Ainsworths', the matron's, the cook's and the two German girls'. Tie up nicely, don't they?'

'We've nothing yet from the two chaps who brought the team over, nor from the games master belonging to this place.' Dart was ultra-cautious, and Metcalfe, young and ambitious, found him damping to work with. 'All the same,' Dart went on, 'it looks as though the whole lot were having their tea when Roach went out, and if we can prove it, it'll save no end of time.'

'There's a Mr Garnish who's very anxious to see you, sir. He's the chap who owns the whole place, and uses the matching bit to this for week-ends and so on.'

'I'll see him when I'm ready. The next job is to go through these rooms of Roach's, and see if there's any clue about what she went out for yesterday afternoon. A diary, or a letter, for instance. And anything that fills in the picture a bit. She's been here a year, but doesn't seem to have any close friends.'

'Dark horse, perhaps?' suggested Sergeant Metcalfe.

'Could be. What we want is evidence though, not speculation.

You get cracking here, while I go over and see what this Garnish wants.'

Left alone, Sergeant Metcalfe spent a few minutes getting the feel of the room, an activity which his superior officer would have scorned. Like a room in an hotel, he thought. Nicely done up and furnished, but bleak all the same. Impersonal. Not a photograph or anything that looked as though it belonged to the occupant, barring a workbasket and yesterday's paper. A cagey sort of room. He went out quietly to explore the bedroom next door.

Roy Garnish in slacks and sweater still managed to radiate a great deal of money and the confidence that goes with it. He was clearly not in the best of tempers.

' Getting mixed up in this business is a bloody nuisance for me,' he told Dart. ' I've got a top-level board meeting of one of my companies on Tuesday morning, and the hell of a lot of work to do beforehand. We'd planned to get away from here as soon as it's light tomorrow, so I hope there's no question of wanting me to hang around to answer questions. The only thing I can tell you is that I got soaked to the skin helping Ainsworth search the grounds last night. My wife and I were in Polharbour the whole afternoon, and didn't get back here till after six.'

' We've no wish to inconvenience anyone where it isn't necessary, sir,' Dart replied. ' Perhaps you and Mrs Garnish would make a formal statement of your whereabouts yesterday afternoon now, while I'm here? You'll understand that in a case of this kind routine enquiries have to be made.'

' Fair enough, I suppose. It's your job – paid for by the taxpayers. What do you want to know? We left here by car about quarter past twelve. Did you notice the exact time, Pam – if it matters?'

Pamela Garnish was lying back in an armchair, smoking a cigarette. Downright ugly woman, thought Dart, taking in her

thinness, lavish make-up and blood-red nails. In his opinion her
with-it clothes and diamond rings made her even more of a
sight.

'I did, as it happens,' she said, with a bored glance at her
husband. 'I set my watch by that.' She indicated the electric
clock on the mantelpiece with a nod. 'And it was just on twenty
past twelve. You were outside in the car, yelling at me to get
a move on.'

It appeared that they had overtaken John Ainsworth in the
drive, and some boys who were carrying benches down to the
games pitch. On arriving in Polharbour shortly before one
o'clock they saw from the hoardings that the West End hit *The
Mousetrap*, was on at the Esplanade Theatre. As it looked like
being a wet afternoon they decided to ring up for seats from
the Zenith-Excelsior, where they always ate when in Polharbour.
After lunch they had driven to the theatre, picked up their
tickets, and spent the afternoon at the play, having tea brought
to them in the second interval.

As he jotted down these particulars Dart reflected that they
would be extremely easy to check, in the unlikely event of this
being necessary.

'We had a filthy drive home,' Roy Garnish went on. 'Patchy
drizzling mist. Not a hope of getting up any speed on these
roads of yours. It took us over an hour. As I said just now,
we didn't get in till after six, and we'd barely got our coats
off when Ainsworth rang through. I finally got in just before
half-past eight, plastered with mud and wet through. That's all.
Does it satisfy you?'

'No good getting it in your hair, Roy,' Pamela adjured him,
yawning, 'I'm sure the Inspector understands it's urgent for
you to get back.'

Dart replied coldly that there was no obstacle in the way of
their departure.

'Just one or two points about the search of the grounds last
night, sir,' he added.

Roy gave him the information he wanted with hardly concealed impatience.

'Is that all?' he demanded. 'We want to go out and get a meal. This place has been like a morgue all day. No objection, I suppose?'

'None whatever, sir.' Dart rose to go. 'I must ask for the loan of the boots you were wearing for the search of the grounds last night. We are trying to get prints sorted out. I'll give you a receipt for them.'

'Christ!' exclaimed Roy Garnish. 'Perhaps one of your chaps'd like to clean 'em?'

'Inside the lining,' Sergeant Metcalfe said, indicating a suitcase with an air of suppressed triumph. 'She'd made a slit here, see? Neatish job. I got 'em out with tweezers.'

Dart grunted and pulled a chair up to the table. Three foolscap envelopes were lying on it. The first was inscribed

> F.E.
> Oct. 7th ?
> Oct. 14th ——
> Oct. 15th E.E. ! ! !

The final entry had been scored with such violence that the ball pen used had torn the paper. The envelope itself was empty, unlike the second one which contained a sizeable wad of treasury notes. It carried the inscription

> B.W.
> Oct. 27th ?
> Nov. 3rd £25

The third envelope was both blank and empty.

'Looks as though she won't be missed in some quarters,' commented Sergeant Metcalfe.

'Maybe, but it's our job to find out who did her, blackmailer or not. F.E. could be that chap Fred Earwaker, Murch was talking about. Said to have had an affair with one of the foreign girls up here, and his wife's left him.' Dart referred to his notes. ' He's a gardener here.'

' Perhaps Roach tried it on and he wouldn't pay up.'

' Possible. She could've blown the gaff to the wife if the initials are right, and enjoyed doing it if those exclamation marks are anything to go by.'

' Any idea who B.W. is, sir?'

' There was a Mrs Winship around on Saturday afternoon with some dogs,' Dart said thoughtfully. ' Give me that telephone directory. There's a Colonel Winship, MC, DSO, Crossways, Affacombe. Class that takes its dogs for regular walks. What's this?'

Sergeant Metcalfe laid a Post Office Savings Book on the table with the air of a supercilious retriever.

' Found it locked away in a drawer in that desk. Key was hidden under her smalls in the bedroom. Reckon she's been in the game quite a while.'

Dart turned the pages with interest. There had been a number of periods during the past ten years in the course of which regular deposits had been made, each coming to an end when the date stamp showed a move to a fresh place. The amounts varied from one to ten pounds. Not a bad scheme, he thought, not pressing 'em too hard or too long. Opening her mouth a bit wider now.

' Pity she hadn't got round to putting the next victim's initials on this third envelope,' Metcalfe remarked. ' We'd know who to go for, like as not.'

' Doesn't follow,' replied Dart. ' What matters is where we go from here. I don't want to put the wind up this Earwaker chap, and have him making off. You heard Murch say he lived in Church Lane. You go up to the far end and work back, making a genuine house-to-house enquiry which takes him in. Ask 'em all if they were out and about between three forty-five and five-fifteen yesterday, and who they saw. See what sort of an alibi Earwaker puts up, but don't rattle him. While you're doing that I'll try this place Crossways on chance.'

Hugh Winship cleared a pile of nurserymen's catalogues from a chair in his den, and invited Dart to sit down.

'Smoke?' He held out a cigarette box. 'Won't offer you a drink, knowing the drill. You've come about this shocking business, I take it? They're saying in the village she was murdered, poor woman.'

Typical old war-horse, thought Dart. Stuck in a groove, but a decent sort. Not like that Garnish blighter.

'At the moment we're treating it as a case of murder,' he replied, offering a light. 'That's the reason for this house-to-house enquiry. We're hoping someone will be able to give some information.'

'Can't help you m'self, I'm afraid. Spent the whole afternoon in the garden burning up rubbish. You can't see the road at all. No one came near the place either.'

'Do you remember what time you knocked off, sir?'

'About twenty past four, when m'wife got back with the dogs. We didn't go out again: rain was just starting.'

'Perhaps I could have a word with Mrs Winship, then, if she was out?'

A worried look came over Hugh Winship's rather impassive weatherbeaten face.

'Afraid you'd suggest that. She's upset by it all. She was along that path with the dogs, you see. Not very pleasant to think it might have been her. Another of these sex maniacs, I suppose?'

'I quite understand how she feels, sir, but I'm afraid I'll have to get her statement at first hand. Matter of regulations.'

'Yes, yes. Not your fault. No point in it, though. She didn't see a soul. Told me so. Keep it as short as you can. She's only just over 'flu.'

Dart's instant reaction to Barbara Winship was satisfaction. He had not expected to find her so much younger than her husband. A good-looker, and what you'd call elegant, too. Easy to fit a spot of blackmail into the picture. Tall and well-built. Physically quite capable of knocking out a small woman like Roach, and heaving her over that rail. She certainly looked a bit under the weather, but there could be a lot more to that than the 'flu.

He proceeded cautiously, apologizing for troubling her when she had been unwell, and stressing the routine nature of the enquiry.

' I understand you were exercising your dogs along the Monk's Path yesterday afternoon, madam,' he said, his eyes on her restless hands. 'Can you remember when you started off from here?'

Barbara gave a slight shudder.

'Not exactly,' she said. 'About half-past three, I think.'

'Did you go far along the path?'

'Roughly half-way.'

Dart took out his notebook and opened it carefully at a clean page.

' I wonder if you could draw me a very simple map to show where the path begins and ends, and about how far you went?' he asked. 'It would help to get the picture clear in my mind.'

' I'll try, if you like,' she replied, sounding faintly surprised as she took the notebook from him.

' Ordnance map any use?' enquired Hugh Winship, who had taken up a defensive stance at his wife's side.

' Thank you, sir, but I'm all right on the general lie of the land. It's just this bit of detail. Thank you, madam, that's fine. I gathered from Mr Ainsworth that the path's a public right of way. Did you meet anyone on it yesterday?'

' No one at all,' Barbara answered flatly.

' Are you absolutely sure? It's very important. And I include anyone near the path as well as actually on it, of course.'

She looked straight at him, with a curious mixture of fear and confidence in her blue eyes which he found puzzling.

' On the way out I could see people drifting towards the school after the match. By the time I came back they'd all disappeared. Apart from them I didn't see a soul the whole time.'

Dart tried another tack.

'Forget about people now. I want you to think back your whole walk. Did you see or hear anything at all that struck you as unusual?'

Her hands clasped and unclasped in her lap as she frowned in concentration.

'Nothing whatever, I'm afraid,' she said finally.

Hugh Winship ostentatiously cleared his throat.

'Just one more question,' Dart said. 'Did you notice the time when you arrived home?'

'I remember the church clock striking the quarter just after I came out on to the road. A friend saw me, and we waved. A Mrs Strode. So I must have got in two or three minutes later.'

'Near enough,' said her husband. 'I heard the quarter while I was collecting up m'tools. You came along just afterwards.'

Dart picked up his notebook and turned over the page.

'May I have your full name for my report, madam?'

'Barbara Jane Winship,' she told him.

He stood up, thanking her politely for her help. At the door he glanced back and saw her with her face in her hands.

On learning from Sergeant Metcalfe that Fred Earwaker claimed to have spent the whole of Saturday afternoon watching Grandstand, alone in his cottage, Dart's satisfaction expressed itself in unusual communicativeness.

'Half-past six,' he remarked, as they drove towards High-castle. 'We could've done a lot worse. Gave his wife's name as Ethel, did he? Looks as though we've got Roach's two clients nicely lined up, and neither of 'em with an alibi. If Winship's dabs are on those treasury notes, it clinches it where she's concerned. You got Earwaker's, of course?'

'Got 'em on my card.'

'What's he like?'

'Great hefty chap. Truculent at first. If I hadn't got my foot in I reckon he'd've slammed the door on me.'

Dart grunted, and relapsed into silence for the rest of the journey. He liked a case where there were some facts to go on right from the start, good solid leads to follow up.

On arrival at police headquarters he found plenty to occupy him. After a brief conference with the Chief Constable and Detective-Superintendent Martin, there was the coroner to contact and arrangements to be made for the inquest. A report had come through from Lewisham. Mrs Grant, the next-of-kin, was an elderly arthritic widow, a half-sister of the deceased. She had stated that there had been little contact between them of recent years, although she had brought up Sister Roach after the death of the parents, and got her into her hospital training. Mrs Grant had not appeared upset by the news, merely remarking that her half-sister had obviously got into bad company.

Dart felt a sudden unexpected sympathy for Sister Roach. Perhaps an unhappy childhood and adolescence was at the bottom of it all. Dismissing this aspect of the case from his mind, he considered the checking of the Garnishes' alibi, and rang the Super at Polharbour.

The fingerprint and photographic experts who had come on ahead had little of value to show him. After a night of heavy rain there were no distinguishable prints on the iron railing at the Leap. The rain, following the trampling of John Ainsworth and Roy Garnish, had also obliterated any possible footprints. Consigning the two men to perdition Dart stared disgustedly at a photograph of a large pool of water with muddy margins.

'Ruddy lake,' he remarked. 'Get anything on the notes?'

This was more encouraging. Both Sister Roach's and Barbara Winship's prints had been found on the treasury notes. Microscopic examination of some threads caught on the iron bar had shown that they came from Sister Roach's coat. On the other hand, the most exhaustive search had failed to find any clues near a patch of trodden grass behind bushes across the path at the Leap, with the exception of a small part of a heel print. A plaster cast had been made of this. Dart looked at it doubtfully. Beyond the fact that it had not been made by the boots handed over by John Ainsworth and Roy Garnish it told him nothing. He decided to send it to the forensic laboratory in case something could be deduced from it.

Finally Dart settled down to consider the various statements taken at the Priory. The first essential was to fix the time when Sister Roach had left the school kitchen with her tea tray, as this seemed to be the last occasion on which she had been seen, other than by the murderer. There was no problem here. Three members of the domestic staff had been on duty. They were Mrs Tonkin, the assistant cook, and two German girls, Elsa Schmidt and Maria Bauer, and their statements agreed in every particular. As soon as there were sounds of people returning from the match, Elsa had gone into the boys' dining-room, and received the plates of food from the other two through the serving hatch. The electric tea urns had already been switched on. She had stood waiting until the hands of the clock reached 3.45, when she rang the tea bell. Meanwhile Maria Bauer had wheeled a trolley of eatables to the drawing-room, and returned to the kitchen as the bell was ringing to fetch a second trolley with the tea and hot water. As she came into the room, Sister Roach had entered by the opposite door, picked up her tray, nodded to Mrs Tonkin and departed again. Say 3.46, thought Dart.

The next job was to check up on the whereabouts of all adults known to be on the premises from 3.46 onwards. The three domestics had retired to their own dining-room to enjoy their tea, and had sat over it until they heard the boys dispersing about half-past four. From then on they had been busy clearing and washing up until after five. Mrs Claythorpe and Sheila Wills had had tea with the boys, and been about afterwards keeping an eye on the common-rooms where the visitors were being entertained. Dart, always cautious, considered the possibility of their having been in league and covered up for each other, but decided that it was too far-fetched to be worth following up for the present.

He next turned his attention to the tea party in the drawing-room. According to the statements of the two Ainsworths it had consisted of five people, themselves, the headmaster of St Hector's, and the games masters of both schools. They had all been present when tea was brought in, and no one had gone out of the room until the gathering broke up at about a quarter to five. The visiting team had then been rounded up, and their coach cheered off just before five o'clock. Bob Notley, the Priory games master, had then stayed chatting to the Ainsworths about the match before driving off in his car at a quarter past.

Dart made a note to get Polharbour to check with St. Hector's, and to see Bob Notley himself. It certainly looked pretty watertight. Mrs Claythorpe said it was 'about quarter past five' when she took a boy to the East Wing, and found Sister Roach absent.

He spread out a large-scale map and began to consider distances and times in the light of his interview with Barbara Winship. Suppose Roach had gone straight back to her own quarters from the kitchen, having left a kettle on? She certainly hadn't made the tea before she went to get the tray, because she'd used the cup from the latter. This was an important point. She'd got to make it, and presumably drink it, and it would have been piping hot. A booster before going to meet her victim? A cuppa! Almost pathetic, if you could think of a blackmailer as a human being. What was the earliest she could possibly have got to the Leap? Dart scratched his head as he stared at the map. Well, certainly not before four o'clock. And how long would it have taken Barbara Winship to get from the Leap to the place where Mrs Strode saw her?

After some careful measurements, using the scale line and a piece of fine string, Dart decided that it could have been done in five or six minutes by anyone stepping out. Winship wasn't the athletic type, but having committed a murder was enough to get anybody moving. If there'd been an appointment for four, and the whole thing was premeditated it looked as though there could have been time for the job. It depended on the state of

79

the path, of course. He'd have to go over the ground himself the next day. Then there was this Fred Earwaker, very likely suspecting – or even knowing – that Roach had given him away to his wife. Murch had said that he'd cut himself off from everybody out of working hours since she'd gone, taking the kid with her. He'd have brooded over it all, and got so worked up against Roach that he might very well have gone off the deep end on meeting her in a deserted place. On the face of it, it looked much more like a man's crime, too. Anyway, tomorrow he'd tax both Winship and Earwaker with having been blackmailed by Roach, and see how they reacted. With the right sort of handling there was a reasonable prospect of one of 'em tripping up or cracking.

As he gathered up his papers and prepared to go home Dart conceded that some useful headway had already been made in the case.

Chapter Nine

John Dalby and Richard Miles, the two boys in bed with colds, were showing signs of boredom and restlessness. As Olivia sat reading to them she heard the detectives come out of Sister Roach's sitting-room and leave the East Wing by the door on to the colonnade. She intercepted a meaning glance between the boys, and hurried on with *The Red-Headed League* in the hope of averting awkward questions. A few moments later there came the sound of a car starting up and driving away.

Behind the red-polled throng in Pope's Court, and the scratching of Jabez Wilson's pen over the sheets of foolscap, she was acutely conscious of her own anxieties struggling for precedence. Would the Ainsworths be faced with a mass withdrawal of boys by horrified parents? Barbara in an unhappily compromising situation...surely she wouldn't be such a fool as to deny having been on the Monk's Path yesterday afternoon? Ought I to have tried to warn her about the C.I.D. man, Olivia thought? Then there was Fred Earwaker: they were obviously on to him already.

She stumbled over her reading, and made a great effort to concentrate on the story.

At last there were footsteps, and Mrs Claythorpe appeared to announce that she had come to take over, and that Mrs Ainsworth would be glad if Mrs Strode would look in before she went home.

In the drawing-room Olivia found the two Ainsworths in anxious conclave with Simon and Jane Fairhall. Faith broke away from the group as she came in, and seized her hand in both her own, her eyes suspiciously bright.

'Olivia darling, it's no good even trying to say what you're being to us.'

John Ainsworth, red round the eyes with exhaustion, pulled up a chair for her.

'Come and join the party,' he said. 'Among other things we're worried stiff about that fool Earwaker. Murch has obviously passed on the whole history of the family bust-up to Dart, who's been asking me endless questions about Fred's work, and what have you. It looks as though they think Sister may have been the person who blew the gaff to Ethel, and that Fred's an obvious suspect. Let's face it: if they can prove it was Sister, things don't look too healthy for him. We've simply got to get Ethel back in case they start hounding him and he does a bunk, or something equally mad. I absolutely refuse to believe that he's a murderer.'

'The point is,' Simon Fairhall took up, 'we all think you're about the only person with a hope of persuading Ethel that Fred really is in a spot, Olivia. Jane and I went to see her last week to try and smooth things over, but it was like talking to a brick wall. And Faith and John can't very well leave here at the moment.'

'You mean you want me to go in to Highcastle tonight?' Olivia was unable to keep a note of dismay out of her voice. Increasingly uneasy about Barbara Winship and possible repercussions affecting David and Julian, she had already decided to go straight to Crossways on leaving the school. She realized with discomfiture that the others were looking at her.

Faith burst out unhappily.

'I know you're simply worn out after all you've done for

us today! We seem to be living in some ghastly nightmare – '

'I'm not in the least tired,' Olivia said hastily. 'It's just that I'm not at all hopeful of pulling it off. I've dropped in a note asking Fred to come down and do various jobs in the garden since Ethel went, and he's just ignored it, knowing quite well that I should tackle him about the whole business. But I agree that we ought to try and get her back, and of course I'll go.'

After the Fairhalls had hurried off to Evensong, she waited to ask John how the parents were reacting.

'I've managed to contact all but four by phone,' he said wearily. 'God, I never want to make another call as long as I live. They're taking it quite calmly on the whole. Worried, of course, but reassured by hearing that the police are posting a man here pro. tem. Only two are coming straight over to take their boys home.'

'Their boys won't thank them,' replied Olivia. 'The two in the East Wing are absolutely agog. How *do* children manage to nose out things in the way they do? Anyway, it's very reassuring about the parents, and I'm awfully glad. I suppose there's no hope that it will turn out to have been an accident after all? There can't have been a proper post mortem yet, surely?'

'Dart was cagey, but apparently she was dead before she went into the water, and had been coshed on the side of the head.'

'She was last seen about four o'clock, wasn't she?' asked Olivia, in an attempt to reassure herself.

'Quarter to, or a minute after. Tonkin and Maria are prepared to swear that's when she came into the kitchen and collected her tray.'

'I hadn't realized it was as early as that.' Olivia felt chilled.

A few minutes later she parked outside the gate of Crossways, and walked quietly up the drive. An empty police car was drawn up at the front door.

I suppose they came straight on here, she thought, wondering how long her mission to Highcastle would take her as she quietly withdrew.

Ethel Earwaker herself opened the door of her mother's council house.

'Why, it's Mrs Strode!' she exclaimed.

Olivia looked at her steadily.

'Will you come and sit in my car for a few minutes, Ethel?' she asked, and without waiting for an answer turned and led the way down the path. To her relief Ethel followed, if inauspiciously, slumping down into the passenger's seat and maintaining an obstinate silence. Olivia decided on shock tactics.

'I've come to tell you about Fred,' she said. 'The police will probably arrest him tomorrow.'

'Why, whatever's 'e done?' gasped Ethel, slewing round.

'The charge would be murder,' replied Olivia bluntly. 'Sister Roach was killed and thrown over the Monk's Leap yesterday afternoon. It was Sister who told you about Fred and the German girl, wasn't it?'

'The letter wurn't signed, but I said all along 'twas 'er as wrote it, the dirty bitch, but Fred, 'e never –' She burst into sobs which Olivia made no attempt to check. Presently she fumbled for the door handle, saying that she'd have Tommy and their things ready inside of ten minutes, if Mrs Strode could wait.

On the way home, when five-year-old Tommy Earwaker had dropped off to sleep, Olivia probed further.

'Why did you think that Sister Roach had written the letter?' she asked.

Ethel, unusually silent since they left Highcastle, became voluble.

'A real nasty snooper, she was, Mrs Strode, for all she's dead and gone. None of us women could stick 'er. A proper creepy-crawly. You'd never 'ear 'er comin', an' there she'd be alongside o' you. I told Mrs Ainsworth I wasn't cleanin' in the East Wing, not if she paid me double. Went pokin' round the place o' nights, what's more.'

' Where, Ethel?'

' Out in the grounds, like, Mrs Strode. Fred seed 'er. Back last spring, 'twas, when Blake wur down with the 'flu. Fred wur worried about they greenuses, not bein' used to 'em, an' went up late to see everythin' wur right, an' saw 'er come creepin' round the side o' the 'ouse, flat up against the wall. She didn't see 'im. That German slut 'adn't come then, so Fred wurn't after 'er,' Ethel added realistically. ' When 'e come 'ome I arst 'im if 'e'd called in at the Arms, when 'e told me about 'er. For a joke, like...' Her voice broke off into a sob.

' You and Fred will have lots more jokes together,' said Olivia kindly. ' He's going to be in a much better position now you've come home. I'm sure you'll tell him to be absolutely truthful with the police, won't you? It's no use trying to hide things – they always find out, and it makes them suspect you. Not that he's anything to hide, I'm sure,' she added, trying to sound convincing. She was finding the odd little story of Sister Roach's nocturnal activity disturbing. It was easy to imagine Fred dwelling on what he had seen as he sat alone in his cottage during the long, solitary evenings when Ethel was in Highcastle, his suspicion and anger slowly building up.

Back at Poldens Olivia felt too tired to face a meal, and made some strong coffee to brace herself up for a call at Crossways. As she sat drinking it, she tried to visualize the situation she would find there. Nearly half-past nine. Julian would be back from London by now, poor darling. What on earth would Barbara be like after that heavy-footed Inspector's visit? Would he have let on that she (Olivia) had admitted to seeing Barbara coming away from the Monk's Path, and if he had, would Barbara be violently hostile? Didn't the police usually talk about ' information received '?

Her thoughts reverted to the incredible fact of the murder itself. If one firmly put aside appalling and fantastic possibilities, who *could* have killed Sister Roach? Surely it could only have been one of these dreadful mentally-deranged creatures that seemed to crop up so often these days?

Preparing to start off on foot, Olivia suddenly regretted having put away the car. The village street was unlighted, the drive at Crossways dark and shut in by trees. It's absurd, she thought angrily. I've never been nervous in Affacombe in my life. But she walked swiftly, swinging the beam of her electric torch from side to side, and was glad to reach the front door and press the bell-push vigorously. A chorus of barking broke out, and Julian's light step sounded in the hall. The next moment the porch light came on, and the Jack Russells tumbled out to nose round her ankles.

Julian exclaimed with surprise and pleasure.

'Only David,' she said, kissing Olivia affectionately, 'would have been more welcome, if that isn't rude.'

With the heightened perception arising from tension Olivia looked at her with interest, sensing unaccustomed confidence. Something's happened to her, she thought. Can they have been to bed?

'I should have been here long ago,' she said, pulling herself together, 'but the most urgent thing in this dreadful business seemed to be to get Ethel Earwaker to come home. I'll explain presently. How's Barbara?' she asked, in a lower tone.

'Not nearly as upset as you expect – so far. Pops says she was splendid over the C.I.D. man. Do come into the drawing-room.'

The room was empty, and in spite of the weight on her mind Olivia felt a quick thrill of pleasure at its lovely proportions, white panelling and pale green and gold. Flames flickered tranquilly on the hearth, and bronze chrysanthemums smouldered in great masses, filling the air with sharp fragrance.

'I know it's awful of me,' Julian was saying, as they stood facing the fire, 'but life's so marvellous at the moment that I don't seem able to take it in. About poor Sister Roach, I mean. Of course I'm sorry and all that – '

'Ju, you must. That man who was here. He'll come back tomorrow. He'll arrest me.'

Barbara's whisper, harsh and sibilant, made them both spin round aghast. She was standing just inside the doorway, very still, her eyes fearful and fixed on Julian. Her long housecoat of pale grey swept to the ground, and in a brief moment of fantasy Olivia saw her as a classic symbol of doom. Then, without apparent arrival, Hugh Winship was at her side, poised to intervene.

'They'll try me at the Highcastle Assizes – '

'Rubbish, Babs. Never heard such tommy rot in m'life. You're overwrought.'

His words dispelled the general paralysis. Firmly seizing Barbara's arm he led her towards the sofa. Julian ran forward to arrange the cushions. Olivia sat down on the nearest chair, instinctively husbanding her strength for an imminent crisis.

'Olivia,' Barbara said, still in a whisper, 'you've been up there. When did they last see her?'

'At a quarter to four, or a minute later,' Olivia replied calmly.

Over Barbara's face came the expression of one who has arrived at the end of the road, to find it a cul-de-sac.

'I didn't kill her,' she said wildly. 'Oh, yes, she was blackmailing me. It's no good trying to hide it any more. That policeman's bound to find out. But I didn't kill her. I swear I didn't.'

There was an appalled silence. Olivia felt herself go cold from the shock of the sudden illumination. Hugh Winship stood staring at his wife with a stunned expression. After what seemed an eternity Julian, with an oddly determined look on her face, dropped on to her knees and took Barbara's hand.

'Not to worry, Mummy,' she said firmly. 'You see, I've known since yesterday that you aren't my real mother.'

Every vestige of colour drained slowly away from Barbara Winship's face.

'It was in the ambulance,' she said, and would have slipped to the floor if they had not caught and held her.

They had regrouped. Barbara lay on the sofa which had been drawn nearer to the fire. Hugh occupied a low chair at her side, his left arm resting lightly round her shoulders. In his right hand was a glass containing brandy, from which she took an occasional sip. A faint colour had crept back into her cheeks. Olivia and Julian sat together on the opposite side of the hearth, with the dogs curled up asleep at their feet. On Julian's lap was the faded photograph of a young naval officer, and the face looking out of it might have been her own. She was talking, pausing between sentences, a small furrow of a frown suggesting concentration and gravity rather than anxiety.

'Sir Arthur Pridcott is my trustee,' she explained to Olivia. 'My grandfather left the letter and photograph with him, to be given to me when I married, or on my twenty-fifth birthday. No one else knows what is in the letter. I feel I don't want to show it to anyone except David, but as things have turned out I'm going to say briefly what was in it.' She paused again, as if selecting her material.

'It worried Grandfather,' she went on, 'that I was so absolutely unlike the Wrey family, and yours too, Mummy. We – we needn't go into what he sometimes wondered, need we? Then quite by chance, just before Daddy came on the scene, he read something in a newspaper about a case in which one baby had been substituted for another, and it made him think about Cousin Ruth and her baby. He couldn't get it out of his mind, and after a bit he went to a top firm of private detectives in London. It took them ages, but in the end they got hold of this photograph.'

'Why didn't he tax me with it? I knew quite well that he disliked me and didn't trust me.' Barbara's voice quivered. Hugh Winship's arm tightened round her shoulders, and he put the glass of brandy to her lips.

'He explains that in his letter,' Julian said gently. 'He was a proud old boy, wasn't he? He couldn't face letting the whole

88

world know about it. And he had got very fond of me, hadn't he? My real father had gone down with his ship on an Arctic convoy, and I'd no near relations left. Grandfather hadn't, either, and wanted to leave me his money. So he jumped at an excuse to adopt me when you married Daddy, so that I had at any rate a legal relationship with him.'

Hugh Winship glanced up quickly, with an expression of relief.

'But how did that damned woman get on to it?' he demanded.

Suddenly and unexpectedly Julian burst into tears.

'I'm sure it was all my fault,' she sobbed, struggling to control herself. 'It was when I got stung by a wasp at the Ainsworths' party, and she took me up to the surgery to put something on it. I was trying to be friendly, and when she said she'd come from Midstead I nattered on about having been born there on the day of the Baedeker raid, and how your cousin and her baby had been killed. Oh, Mummy!'

'Ju, darling, don't. As if you've got anything in the world to reproach yourself with.'

'But it was that, wasn't it?' persisted Julian through her tears.

'Well, yes, it was. She was quite young in 1942, waiting to go for her proper hospital training, and just helping generally at the nursing home. She didn't remember me at all, and told me that she hadn't recognized me, but she had helped to wash and dress my baby after it was born, and remembered that the top joint of one of the fingers of its left hand was missing, and that we had both survived. You can understand how the nurses who weren't killed must have talked about the raid and the casualties. Darling, please don't cry. It was so terribly wrong of me. I think the absolute horror of the home being hit must have unhinged me for a time, and afterwards I was too terrified to admit what I'd done.'

'No need to dig it all up. Put it behind you for good and all, poor little girl,' murmured Hugh Winship soothingly.

' But they can send me to prison anyway, for saying Ju's my child. I let her be registered as Richard Wrey's and mine – '

Julian dried her eyes.

' David knows all about this,' she said, ' and of course the legal aspect interested him. He told me that the Registrar-General could take proceedings if it ever came out, but he didn't see why it should, especially as I was legally adopted by Grandfather, which scotches any claim to the money by some long-lost Wrey relation.'

' But suppose the police find out that she was blackmailing me? That's what frightens me so?'

' I can reassure you there,' said Olivia, resolutely suppressing her feelings of near-panic at Barbara's disclosures. ' David once told me that the police can't insist on people telling them what they are being blackmailed about.'

' Mummy,' said Julian suddenly, ' I'm sorry if it distresses you to talk about it, but I want to know exactly what happened at the time. Then we need never think about it any more. It doesn't make one scrap of difference to David and me, but I'd like to know – '

Barbara cut short Hugh's protest.

' I'd much rather you all did know. I've longed and longed to share the awful weight of it over the years, and the feeling of always playing a part has been so ghastly.'

John Wrey's reaction to the death of his adored only son had been a violent possessiveness towards his unborn grandchild. Brushing aside the suggestion that Barbara should return to her parents for her confinement, he arranged for her to go to an expensive nursing home in the small town of Midstead, not far from where he lived, and scheduled as a ' safe ' area. It was fantastic, he declared even to consider the vulnerable northern industrial town where Barbara's father was a parish priest.

As Olivia listened, she began to understand Barbara's early background: the big, bleak vicarage in the drab town, and the

90

cramping shortage of money from which she had escaped to join the W.R.A.F. and meet and marry Richard Wrey, a rich man's son. A young widow, her alternatives to falling in with John Wrey's wishes were a return to her parents, or a struggle to rear her child in penurious independence. She had accepted both the nursing home and all her father-in-law's plans for her future.

Owing to the uncertainties of wartime travel and the difficulty of leaving a delicate husband, it was decided that Barbara's mother should not come south until after the baby was born. Ruth Maitland, a cousin and the wife of a naval officer, was expecting her first child at the same time, and Barbara, already in receipt of a generous allowance from her father-in-law, offered to help with the fees of the Midstead nursing home so that they could be together. Here, in the small hours of a spring morning, Ruth gave birth to Julian. Barbara's labour had already started, and her baby, also a girl, was born on the following afternoon.

'It was absolute heaven just lying peacefully in bed when it was all over,' Barbara said abstractedly, her eyes unseeing. 'I drowsed, too tired to worry about John Wrey being angry because it wasn't a boy. I didn't bother a scrap when the siren went: it so often did when the German planes were going to bomb Midland industrial towns, or South Wales. Then without the slightest warning the whole world just fell to pieces. I can't explain what it was like. The noise was solid. The ceiling and the walls seemed to be heeling over and the dust – I was coughing and choking...'

Hugh muttered inaudibly, his face a stiff mask of distress.

'Someone was trying to force the door open,' Barbara went on, ' and a nurse burst in with two babies in her arms: you, Ju, and mine. You both had labels tied round your wrists with pink ribbon. Before I could ask her anything she'd stuffed you both into my arms and dashed off again. There were more frightful explosions farther away, and shouting and ambulance and fire sirens. Then a lot of the ceiling came down, some of it on the bed. I was terrified, and tried to hide you both under the clothes. Then two men came in with a stretcher and got us downstairs somehow through all the wreckage. It was just as we were being lifted into an ambulance that I chanced to turn my head. I saw that the wing where Ruth's room was . . . well, simply wasn't there.'

Julian exclaimed with horror and pity.

' Yes, your real mother.' Barbara averted her face for a moment. ' We were left in the ambulance for what seemed like hours. There was another awful crash which must have been some more of the buildings coming down, and more shouting and confusion. I think I must have fainted. When I came round we were still alone, and it was then that I saw my baby was dead. I heard afterwards that it was the blast and dust.'

' So you changed over the labels?' asked Julian softly.

' Yes. I suddenly felt I couldn't face – nothing. Richard had gone, and the life together we'd planned, and Ruth, and now my baby, and with her all the security John Wrey had offered us. It was like a bottomless abyss opening in front of me. I saw the way out in a sudden flash, and something just snapped inside me. My hands shook so badly that I could hardly manage the little bows. And the moment I'd done it the door was flung open and they brought in a terribly hurt woman. There was a Red Cross worker who came with us all the way to the hospital at Wynfordham where we were taken. She came to me to see how I was, and I saw that she'd realized my baby was dead. She said I'd be more comfortable just holding my own – you, Ju – and took it away. I never saw the poor little darling again. That's all, except that I never had the courage to say what I'd done.' She turned her head away again, tears running down her cheeks.

But you've had the determination to carry it through for nearly twenty-five years, thought Olivia, appalled. Doubt and fear too strong to be brushed aside rose up and assailed her.

Chapter Ten

'Motive?' Dart said, in response to an opening gambit from Metcalfe, 'the case is lousy with it. Anything to do with a blackmailer always is. We haven't a clue what other poor devils Roach was bleeding. Somebody we haven't even heard of may have done the job. Meantime all we can do is to check up on Winship and Earwaker. I'm going to time the walk down from the Monk's Leap to the road myself: it may turn out to be crucial. You'd better carry on with the house-to-house enquiries. A line on Earwaker would change the whole look of things. Not that we're likely to get one.'

His faint optimism of the night before having evaporated, Dart sat gloomily in the police car meditating on the full P.M. report which had come in before they left Highcastle. Calling in at Leeford they learnt from Sergeant Murch that the constable posted at the Priory overnight had been relieved after an uneventful vigil. The Garnishes had driven off at half-past seven, and Fred Earwaker was at work as usual. Enquiries about any strangers seen during the week-end were already under way at the outlying farms. The C.I.D. men drove on to Affacombe, where Dart dropped Metcalfe at the Church Lane turning, going himself to a convenient parking place just inside the Priory gates. From here he walked to the beginning of the Monk's Path.

For the first hundred yards or so this followed the hedge, and then ran close to the Sinnel. It was rough and muddy. Picking his way Dart wondered who would be responsible for maintaining a public right of way which ran through private property. A rum arrangement, come to think of it, and of course no landowner would want to encourage people to come tramping through his place. On the park side of the path there were intermittent clumps of brambles and other bushes. Through the gaps Dart could see the goal posts on the games pitches mentioned by Barbara Winship. From time to time he made a short detour into the park to avoid a particularly boggy patch. Numerous heavy footprints suggested the stretcher party which had brought Sister Roach's body down to the road this way. Lost in thought he almost came a cropper over a snaky tree root and swore aloud, putting up a blackbird which flew off scolding hysterically.

It was being borne in on him that the rough going would inevitably slow down a woman of Barbara Winship's type, and this became even more obvious on the steep rise to the Monk's Leap with its loose stones. At the top the path broadened to include the small level space overlooking the river, where a seat had been placed, facing downstream to get the view. A railing had been erected as a safeguard, a single iron bar supported by wooden posts at about three feet from the ground. Dart eyed its inadequacy with disapproval; it bore out his impression that the path was little used by the general public. All the same, the feet of those who had paused to admire the view over the years had worn a shallow depression in front of the railing, and it was here that the rainwater had collected and infuriatingly obliterated possible footprints. There was still quite a large puddle. Dart stood back a little, and surveyed the scene with narrowed eyes. The seat was dirty and damp, with patches of green mould: you couldn't imagine women sitting on it and risking stains on their clothes. Anyway, the full P.M. report which had come in overnight specified a heavy downward blow delivered by a taller, right-handed person, standing in front of, and slightly to the left of Roach. She must have been standing talking to her murderer close to the railing, so that her body fell across the iron bar, threads from her coat catching in its rough surface. There wouldn't have been any difficulty about lifting it: a good heave would have toppled it over and down the sheer thirty feet or so to the water.

Dart stepped across the puddle and stood resting his hands on the bar. The Sinnel, still running quite high, was surprisingly colourful, the golden peat-stained water creaming white over the boulder of the legend, and in quieter stretches mirroring the morning blue of the sky with astonishing vividness. At the foot of the Leap it ran still and silent, engaged in its immemorial task of undercutting the cliff. The strong current had swirled the body along with it, and wedged it under the projecting bank a short distance downstream.

As he returned to the path it struck Dart anew what a very secluded spot the Monk's Leap was, despite the fact that it was on a public path and almost within hailing distance of a house. Upstream the path soon vanished round a corner. The direction from which he had come was cut off by the convex slope of the rising ground. Across the Sinnel were some marshy fields, not even carrying stock at this season, and the great emptiness of Sinneldon. On the Priory side of the path the clump of bushes where the heel print had been found formed an effective screen. You could be half a dozen miles from anywhere, he thought, going over to examine the carefully marked spot where someone – surely the murderer? – had stood for some time. But if it was Winship who had hidden there it didn't look like an appointment with Roach, unless she'd got there too early, and was afraid someone else might come along. Or had she spotted Roach coming up to the Leap for an innocent breather, and simply acted on impulse? He must ask for whatever she'd been wearing on her feet, but she'd probably have several pairs with Monk's Path mud on 'em.

He walked on through the ruins to the edge of their comparatively level site, and ran his eye along the back of the Priory.

The windows of the West Wing and its garage were all shut. The school windows were hygienically open, and the sudden shrill ringing of an electric bell was followed by a babel of talking and laughter and a fusillade of banging desk lids. Dart's gaze moved on to the back of the East Wing. It had a door giving on to the flagged space at the back of the buildings. Roach would have come out that way, he thought, and wondered what route she would have taken to the Leap. Walking in an easterly direction he came on a faint but discernible track going up the slope towards the ruins, and leading out on to the Monk's Path quite near the Leap. All the same, he decided, if she'd had that cuppa before starting she couldn't have arrived there before four at the very earliest. More likely a minute or two later.

Reminding himself that the going wouldn't have been so slippery before Saturday night's rain, he set out for the road, stopwatch in hand, at what seemed a reasonable pace for a woman like Barbara Winship who had just committed a violent murder. He found himself emerging on to the road exactly six minutes later.

Back in the car he lit a cigarette and settled down to review his findings, unhappily aware that they were inconclusive. Suppose the two women had met at four, the earliest possible moment as far as he could see, whether by appointment or not. It seemed pretty certain to assume that Winship would have got a conversation going in order to take Roach unawares. Say 4.3 or 4.4 for the actual murder, and another couple of minutes for heaving the body over the railing, and looking round for any possible traces. There was the question of the weapon, so unhelpfully described by the autopsy as a blunt instrument. Winship could have started off at 4.5 or 4.6 then, making the arrival in the road 4.11 or 4.12. Perhaps a few seconds more to the point where Mrs Strode saw her at 4.15. That left a margin of three or four minutes.

Dart frowned as he drew on his cigarette. It was just possible, but damn tight. You could hear Counsel for the Defence inviting the jury to study photographs of the Monk's Path...a charge

96

was out of the question unless the blackmail could be established beyond doubt, and Roach's hold shown to be pretty deadly. Winship would deny it, and then he'd spring the evidence of her dabs on the notes on her. That was the moment when she'd give herself away...if she were guilty. There was still Earwaker to consider. Coshing and chucking over a cliff was much more a man's crime on the face of it, and it seemed safe to assume that Roach had tried to blackmail him, and had then given him away to his wife. A motive there, all right. But so far there was no evidence whatever that he'd been anywhere near the Monk's Path on the afternoon of the murder, whereas Winship admitted having been there at the probable time when it happened. Dart, who disliked what he called hanging about, came down in favour of going to Crossways first.

There was a static element in Dart's thinking of which he was unaware. He always expected to go on from where he had left off, and an unexpected change in a situation was apt to put him off his stroke. He was disconcerted to find Barbara Winship more composed than on the previous evening, and her husband more the old soldier accustomed to authority than merely a nice old buffer. Moreover he was showing a tiresome tendency to stick.

'Some additional information of a private nature has come to our knowledge,' Dart said, taking refuge in officialese. 'I should prefer to discuss it with Mrs Winship in private.'

'I wish my husband to be present, Inspector. Shall we sit down?' Elegant, if a little drawn, Barbara took a chair and indicated another to Dart.

'No point in beating about the bush,' Hugh Winship suddenly barked. 'M'wife's told me the woman was blackmailing her, and everything about it.'

His carefully-planned procedure for the interview collapsing in ruins, Dart hastily improvised.

'It's very sensible of you to be so frank, madam,' he said,

taking out his notebook. 'I'm afraid I must ask you a number of questions, all the same. I must explain that if you wish you are entitled to have your solicitor present.'

'Cautioning her?' demanded Hugh.

'A police caution has to be perfectly explicit, as I'm sure you know, sir,' replied Dart. 'I'm merely explaining to Mrs Winship that she's entitled to have her solicitor present if she wishes.'

'I can hardly decide about that until I know what kind of question you want to ask me, Inspector.'

'Very well, madam, I'll go ahead. How long have you been paying blackmail to the late Sister Roach?'

'I have only paid it once. A week ago today.'

'Had further demands been made?' asked Dart in some surprise.

'Yes. I was to pay her £25 on the 23rd of each month.'

'How did she approach you in the first place?'

'I got an anonymous letter, printed in capitals. It came by post, on the 27th of October. I was to take the dogs for their usual walk a week later, bringing the money to the Monk's Leap at four o'clock. If I didn't, or went to the police she was going to send some – information to my husband.'

'You realized who had written the letter, of course?'

'Not at once.' For the first time Barbara hesitated. 'Then I remembered something that had happened a short time ago, and realized it must be Sister Roach.'

Dart decided to probe.

'How long had you known her?'

'I didn't know her at all. As far as I know I'd only spoken to her once.'

'Then, as she only arrived in Affacombe just over a year ago, I take it that the subject of the blackmail is a recent occurrence?'

'Police can't insist on the disclosure of a subject of blackmail.' Hugh Winship was as staccato as a machine gun.

'I'm well aware of the regulations governing police procedure, sir,' retorted Dart, nettled.

'I'm prepared to say that it was actually something which happened many years ago, when I was a girl. It was the merest chance which reminded Sister Roach about it. I didn't recognize her when she came to the school, and she didn't place me until quite recently.'

Suspecting an attempt to lead him up the garden path, Dart became more forthright.

'This is a very odd story, Mrs Winship. Sister Roach knew something about your past which you were willing to pay her £25 a month to keep quiet, and yet you tell me that you both lived in this small village for a year without recognizing each other? Are you sure you wouldn't like to reconsider this part of your statement?'

'It happens to be the truth,' she told him.

'Bear it out,' interjected Hugh.

Dart ignored him pointedly.

'We'll return to the events of last Saturday, then. I put it to you that the real object of taking your dogs along the Monk's Path was to keep an appointment with Sister Roach, made at your request.'

'That isn't true. No appointment had been made.'

'So you met her by accident, then?'

'I didn't meet her, or see a sign of her, as I told you yesterday.'

'Four o'clock at the Monk's Leap was the time and place where you handed over the money on November 3rd, wasn't it?'

'Yes.'

'Rather curious, surely, Mrs Winship, that you chose to revisit a place with such unpleasant associations at exactly the same time of day?'

'I take the dogs along there practically every afternoon before tea, if I'm at home. You can ask anybody in the village.'

Feeling that he was getting nowhere, Dart tried an abrupt switch.

'When the anonymous letter arrived, did you show it to your husband?'

' No, I burnt it.'

' Why did you tell him about it subsequently, then?'

Barbara Winship met his eyes steadily. He noticed that her hands were tightly clenched, but they showed none of the nervous twisting of the evening before.

' Because of Sister Roach's murder. I was naturally very frightened. As you can see, I had a strong motive for – well, getting rid of her. And by almost incredible bad luck I had been near the Monk's Leap at the time when it could have happened.'

' How did you know when it could have happened?' Dart cut in sharply.

' Mrs Strode, who is doing Sister Roach's work temporarily came in to see us last night, and told us that no one at the school had seen Sister after about a quarter to four,' Barbara replied without hesitation.

Some time later Dart left Crossways with Barbara Winship's signed statement in his pocket, having once more failed to shake her in her account of her actions on Saturday afternoon. Before going to find Sergeant Metcalfe he sat for a few minutes in the car. An illegitimate kid would fit in with Roach being a nurse, of course. Not that finding out about it would help on the case much. A deep one, Winship, to have covered up whatever lapse she'd had all these years. Not so easy in her walk of life. For all that she was so drooping and lah-di-dah there must be real toughness underneath. But on the other hand, there was that bloody path and the timing...

He started up the engine and cruised down the village street. Metcalfe conveniently emerged from a cottage and hurried over to join him.

' Priory,' said Dart, moving over into the passenger's seat. ' We'll take Earwaker next. Got on to anything?'

' Not much, I'm afraid, sir. Nothing on Earwaker. Half of 'em seem to have been in Polharbour between one and six,

100

blowing the wages packet. The shopkeeper thought he could remember all his customers, and I've checked up on the whole lot. He saw Mrs Strode going up the street soon after four. A few places were shut down with everybody out to work. I got a complete list of the people living in the place from the List of Electors in the church porch.'

' Anyone seen a stranger around?'

' I asked everyone that question. The only lead I got was from an old girl called Ellen Labbitt, who lives opposite Mrs Strode. She went on about a man with a beard and dark glasses who called on Mrs S. a week last Saturday and stayed about an hour. Then she saw him go up the street. Friendly they were, she said, but not to suggest any goings-on, Mrs Strode being a real lady, for all that she was fair mazed about what happened hundreds of years ago. I let the old thing natter on a bit, and it turns out that Mrs Strode's son's engaged to Mrs Winship's daughter by her first marriage, who had a fortune left her by her granddad.'

Dart looked up sharply.

' The devil he is,' he exclaimed, uncomfortably aware of not having known that Barbara Winship had a daughter, and proceeded to give Metcalfe a summary of his recent visit to Crossways and subsequent reflections.

Metcalfe listened with keen interest as they drove past the main front door of the Priory and parked outside the West Wing.

' It sounds as though you've got something there, sir,' he said tactfully. ' I mean, if there's a lot of lolly in it, and Roach knew the girl was a bastard she'd have Winship on toast.'

' Hell of a job to prove it now, if she was. However, it's a lead of a sort. We'd better get hold of Earwaker, and try to collect something you can call evidence.'

' I forgot to mention that his wife's back, sir. Mrs Strode went over to Highcastle last night and fetched her home.'

' Mrs Strode? That blasted woman keeps cropping up at every turn. She wants watching.'

'Interested party all right,' said Metcalfe thoughtfully.

'Interested to get Winship into the clear all right. Quite a lot hangs on the time they met on Saturday afternoon, for instance. Five minutes later would make a big difference.'

'Strode got to the Vicarage at the time she said. I've checked with the Vicar and his missis.'

Dart gave a snort compounded of irritation and frustration and extracted himself from the car.

The Priory School book-room which John Ainsworth had assigned to the detectives as an office was inconveniently small for three men, two of whom were over six feet. It smelt overpoweringly of old books, and after the arrival of Fred Earwaker of earth and sweat as well. Dart managed to force up the window over the small table at which they were sitting.

'That's a bit better,' he said. 'Now then, Earwaker, we want to ask you a few questions connected with the murder of Sister Roach last Saturday. If you wish you're entitled to have a solicitor present, and we can wait till you've got hold of one.'

'I don't want no solicitor,' replied Fred Earwaker, wiping his brow with the back of an enormous hand. 'You'm after what I wur doin' all afternoon, I takes it? Wal, I wur in me 'ouse watchin' the telly, an' no man livin' can prove I wurn't, seein' I wur.'

'It would be useful if you could bring forward a witness, you know. It's a long time for a man to stick at home on his own.'

Fred Earwaker eyed Dart with shrewd complacency.

'Try ter find summun 'oo seed me out an' about, then. I don't 'ave ter prove me innercence. The lor 'olds a man innercent till 'e's proved guilty.'

'We're not trying to prove anyone guilty,' said Dart patiently, reflecting that the inhabitants of Affacombe seemed to have an unusual grasp of their legal rights. 'The job of the police who are enquiring into a crime is to collect facts, and we're asking

102

you to help us. What time did you have your dinner on Saturday? Let's start from there...'

It emerged that Fred had worked on the pitch on Saturday morning, in preparation for the match. He had knocked off at twelve, had a quick pint at the Arms, and gone home and fried up for his dinner. Then he'd settled down for an afternoon of watching Grandstand. Questioned by Sergeant Metcalfe he gave a reasonably accurate account of the events featured, but, as both detectives well knew, he could have gleaned a good deal from the Radio Times and repeats in later programmes. No one had called at the house until Metcalfe himself just after six. He'd heard nothing of his neighbours until the two families had returned from their weekly outing to Polharbour shortly afterwards. Then he'd scratched round for a bit of tea.

Dart adjudged that the psychological moment had arrived.

'A chap fending for himself's a poor sort of thing,' he remarked easily. 'You had it in for Sister Roach, hadn't you, for splitting on you to your wife?'

To his amazement and chagrin Fred nodded agreement.

'That's right,' he said, adding a string of unprintable epithets. 'Comin' between a man an' wife. But 'twurn't me sent 'er wur she berlonged, fer all that.'

'Your wife had an anonymous letter, I understand,' said Dart. 'How did you know Sister Roach had written it?'

He listened to much the same account of Sister Roach's snooping tendencies that Ethel Earwaker had given to Olivia Strode. In addition Fred admitted an occasion when he and Luisa had been disturbed while having a bit of fun in the bushes. He had crept out to see Sister Roach hurrying off in the direction of the house. It was after this that she had tried to blackmail him.

'I couldn't swear on the Bible as I knows she wrote 'un,' he concluded, 'but if 'twur me last word I'd say she did, an' allus will.'

'Well, if you've nothing more to tell us,' Dart said after a pause, 'Sergeant Metcalfe here will type out a statement and give it to you to read. If you agree that it's a true record of what you've told us, he'll ask you to sign it. And if you can think of anybody who could have seen or heard that you were in your house between four and five on Saturday, the sooner you get on to us about it the better.'

He got up and squeezed out of the cramped little room with difficulty, dislodging some copies of *The Merchant of Venice* in the process. As he crossed the front hall Faith Ainsworth darted out of a door and intercepted him.'

'I've a message for you, Inspector,' she said, clasping and reclasping her hands in a worried way. 'It's from Mrs Strode who's helping us in the East Wing – the sanatorium, that is. She says that she wants to see you as soon as possible, and that it's important.'

Chapter Eleven

It was after midnight on Sunday when Olivia Strode left Crossways. Julian insisted on getting out the car and running her home. They sat outside Poldens in the intimacy of shared anxiety, their voices unconsciously lowered in the enfolding silence of the sleeping village.

'Julian, do you mind?' Olivia asked. 'About your early history, I mean?'

'No. Actually, it's a relief. Even when I was quite small I knew somehow that Mummy didn't mean to me what other children's mothers did to them. I've always felt guilty about it. That's over now: it's a kind of liberation. I think I must have known all along in some instinctive way.'

'Perhaps you sensed it telepathically from Barbara. What are you going to do about David and this business of the murder?'

'Ring him very early tomorrow, being cagey, of course. Even with S.T.D. people might be able to listen in...I shall simply tell him to look at the papers and get down here as soon as he possibly can. I – I suppose our solicitors in Highcastle really are competent?' Her voice quivered a little.

'Merrydew and Drake? I've always heard they're a first-class firm,' Olivia said bracingly.

Olivia slept very little, and got up at half-past seven to discover how exhausted the strain of the past thirty-six hours had left her. As she bathed and breakfasted she wondered how long it would be before the Ainsworths managed to get at any rate a temporary replacement for Sister Roach. Glad though she was to help them, the unaccustomed work in the East Wing was extremely tiring. Poldens, too, was beginning to look neglected, while the Parish History seemed to belong to a different world.

She had hardly taken over at nine o'clock when the occupational hazards of institutional life started crowding in on her. The woman from the village who did the cleaning in the East Wing was off sick, and her substitute, uncertain of what had to be done, bumbled about in an ineffective and maddening manner. A lavatory cistern suddenly began to overflow torrentially, and a telephone call to the school secretary's office produced the information that the handyman had just been sent in to Leeford. John Dalby and Richard Miles were up and dressed, awaiting discharge by Dr Coppin, when he paid his routine visit after his morning surgery. They had already fallen foul of Mrs Claythorpe, and as Olivia struggled to tie up the arm of the ballcock, she was startled by a violent thud against the door of their ward, accompanied by yells of 'Wham! Gotcher!'

Opening the door with difficulty, for there was a pillow on the floor just inside, she was confronted by a Dalek, draped in an eiderdown through which the handles of two toothbrushes were gripped so as to form the two thin projecting arms. In the far corner John Dalby's tousled head appeared over the wire mattress of a bed on its side. The pillows of all the other beds together with various other movable objects had been gathered to form a heap of ammunition.

'Please, Mrs Strode, can we have our elevenses in case Dr Coppin's late and we miss them over at school?' he enquired with a beaming smile.

The Dalek glided forward, moving the toothbrushes up and down in a suppliant gesture.

' Be-a-sport-Mrs Strode,' it intoned hollowly.

' You're very naughty boys,' Olivia said sternly, trying to conceal her amusement. ' Anyone would think you were six instead of ten. The ward's in a disgraceful state. Take off that eiderdown at once. Richard...oh, look, now you've dropped the toothbrushes on the floor! Pick them up and rinse them under the tap. You certainly won't have any elevenses until everything's been put straight again. I shall come and see presently.'

She managed to retire in good order, and repaired to the pantry where she set about preparing two mugs of cocoa and some bread and jam. A glance at the clock showed her that it was nearly ten. With any luck Dr Coppin would arrive in about half an hour, and she'd send those two little wretches packing... If there weren't any in-patients, perhaps she could go back to Poldens and just be on call.

The telephone rang, breaking in on this pleasing thought.

' Mrs Coppin speaking,' said a brisk voice. ' Oh, it's you, Olivia! My dear, what a tower of strength you're being to the poor Ainsworths. I've rung to say that Bill's had to dash off to Higher Cragtor Farm: there's been a bad accident with the tractor. He won't be able to get along to you until after lunch, as he's got one or two other rather urgent cases. My dear, do tell me...'

When Sonia Coppin rang off, Olivia sat for a moment with closed eyes, mustering her reserves of energy. Then she put through a call on the house telephone to the school secretary, who commiserated and undertook to have the boys' dinners sent over to the East Wing. Returning to the kitchen she heated the cocoa again and took the tray of elevenses to the ward. It had been tidied in a rough and ready fashion, and the boys rose politely to their feet as she came in.

' Now, listen,' she said. ' Dr Coppin's been called out to an accident on one of the farms, and won't be coming until after lunch, so you can't go back to school till then. And please understand that I don't want any more nonsense from either of you.'

107

'No, Mrs Strode,' they agreed virtuously, their eyes on the tray.

'What about settling down to a jigsaw?' she suggested. 'They're splendid things for making the time go quickly. I'll get you one from the games cupboard if you like.'

Rather to her surprise the idea was well received.

Peace descended on the East Wing, so all-embracing that Olivia's suspicions were presently aroused. Leaving the linen which she was sorting she went quietly along the passage, and saw that the door of the boys' ward was ajar. She had maligned them: they were sitting side by side at a table, absorbed by the puzzle.

'It *is* a car!' exclaimed John Dalby. 'Look, here's a bit of the windscreen with the licence.'

'Here's a bit of the number plate. Wonder what make it is?'

'Could be a Mercedes, like Tycoon Roy Garnish's smasher.'

'I say! You saw them go off this morning, didn't you, when I was in the loo? Was it old Roy this time, or Ma Garnish's boy-friend?'

'Boy-friend?' John Dalby's voice rose to an incredulous squeak. 'But she's *old*! About forty, I should think.'

'She brings a boy-friend along when Pa Garnish doesn't come,' Richard Miles asserted confidently. 'Tim Ferrars found out.'

'Don't believe it! How?'

'He did a Round-the-World one night when he was in with pink-eye before half-term. He told me. He's a sort of cousin of mine.'

'Lummy! Was he copped?'

'Not him! He's as fly as they come. He waited till Cockroach put out his light and he heard her telly going, and then oozed out of the window. He was on his own because pink-eye's catching.'

'Which way round did he go?'

'Round the back and the West Wing. That's when he saw

them – Ma Garnish and a chap, having supper with lots of drinks in the kitchen. It was a jolly warm night, and they'd got the window up at the bottom, and the curtains were swinging in the draught.'

' I bet the chap was R.G. all the time.'

' Oh yeah? Listen to the rest of it, fathead. Tim thought it was him until they started talking about him. About Pa Garnish, I mean. The chap said he wondered how old Roy was getting on, and they sat and laughed themselves sick. So the chap couldn't have been him. Q.E.D. And next morning Tim watched 'em drive off, and the chap had a whacking great muffler half-hiding his ugly mug. Laugh that off!'

Olivia realized that it was her hand which was hurting her, and relaxed her unconscious grip of the door-post. She listened avidly, hardly daring to breathe; but with the inconsequence of small boys they had suddenly lost interest in the subject and reverted to the jigsaw. She withdrew as noiselessly as she could, and went to the surgery. With hands which shook slightly she took from a drawer a book labelled Register of In-patients.

A careful record had been kept ever since the opening of the school. There were columns headed ' Name ', ' Age ', ' Date of Admission ', ' Complaint ', and ' Doctor's Remarks ', the entries under the last of these being almost wholly illegible. Olivia ran her finger down the first column for the current term. She learnt that Timothy Ferrars, aged eleven years four months, had been admitted on Monday, October 27th, suffering from conjunctivitis, and discharged again on the following Saturday, November 1st.

Monday, October 27th, had been the day of the Revel meeting, when Barbara Winship had received the blackmailing letter and had a nervous collapse in the evening. It was on the afternoon of Tuesday, October 28th, that she herself saw the Garnishes' car passing Poldens in the late afternoon, and had the brief telephone conversations, first with Pamela, and then, ostensibly, with Roy who was hoarse and unrecognizable with a bad cold.

Olivia felt muzzy with tiredness. She rested her head on her hands and struggled to think clearly. Unless both Fred and Ethel Earwaker were lying, which seemed unlikely, Sister Roach had been seen creeping furtively round the back of the Priory one night last spring. If Timothy Ferrars, out on an illicit Round-the-World, had seen and heard a man with Pamela who wasn't Roy, surely the odds were that a purposeful snooper like Sister Roach would have got on to it too? Of course it could have been the one and only time that Pamela had risked it...

Quite suddenly Olivia's mind leapt forward so violently that she seemed to experience a physical shock. What about that very first time that she'd rung the West Wing? The time when Roy hadn't been able to come and speak to her because he was in his bath, and Pamela had quickly brushed aside her offer to ring again at a more convenient time, and insisted on acting as a messenger? In retrospect Olivia remembered that she had thought it slightly odd, but had put it down to the Garnishes' well-known aversion to getting embroiled with the village.

Suppose that Sister Roach had been blackmailing Pamela? For a moment far-reaching implications darted into Olivia's mind, but her excitement subsided as she remembered that both Garnishes had spent last Saturday afternoon and early evening in Polharbour. Or had they? No, she was being idiotic. Pamela would hardly have enlisted her husband's help in disposing of a blackmailer who was bleeding her on the grounds of her infidelity to him. Besides, could that thin-looking woman really have had the physical strength to carry out this particular murder? It seemed doubtful, to say the least of it. No, she really was being dim. Pamela would have turned to her lover, of course. Couldn't he have kept an appointment made with Sister Roach, while Pamela established a cast-iron alibi for herself in Polharbour?

Olivia's thoughts raced furiously. If this man had been in Affacombe on Saturday afternoon, surely someone must have noticed him? She smothered an exclamation as she remembered the match. It was an accepted thing that parents and friends often turned up to watch matches and take boys out afterwards. On these occasions strangers were taken for granted and attracted little interest.

The whole baffling situation seemed to be taking on a new significance. Her weariness forgotten, Olivia hurried to the house telephone, and asked if Inspector Dart were still on the premises. On learning that he was, she left an urgent message asking him to come over to the East Wing as soon as possible. Stuffy and tiresome though he is, she thought, he can't flatly refuse to listen to me, surely?

Getting no answer to his knock, Dart opened the door of the East Wing and walked in. As he paused in the passage he heard a woman's voice in the distance, apparently engaged in a tele- phone conversation. A door near at hand opened quietly, and a boy's head emerged.

' I say, Super, will you give us your autograph?'

A second head followed the first.

' Oh, please do, sir!'

Amused, his exasperation with Olivia Strode abating, Dart stood in the doorway, looking down on two eager faces.

' It's been the lousiest luck, sir, being shut up here while there's a murder hunt going on in school.'

' You see, if we had your autograph we'd be able to slap down the other chaps when we go back. I say, you haven't given it to anyone else, have you?' Richard Miles' intelligent, cheeky face momentarily clouded over with anxiety.

' No, not yet,' Dart said, taking a ball pen from his pocket and accepting a couple of grubby envelopes. ' But I'm not a Super, you know. I'm a Detective-Inspector.'

' P'raps you'll be promoted, sir, if you track down the mur- derer. Are you and your sergeant hot on the trail?'

' You must never question police officers, you know,' Dart told them with solemnity. ' Here you are.'

111

'Detective-Inspector J. F. Dart, C.I.D.,' Richard read aloud. 'Thanks most awfully, sir.'

Dart turned as Olivia Strode came into the room, feeling slightly self-conscious. Inevitably they exchanged an amused glance, and felt a perceptible lessening of the tension between them.

'I'm so sorry,' she said. 'A parent rang up about a chicken-pox quarantine problem. How kind of you to give the boys your autograph. Now listen, you two. Your dinners will be coming over from school in about half an hour. Just stay in here out of the way while Inspector Dart has another look round.'

'Please, Mrs Strode,' pleaded John, 'couldn't we just have one or two biscuits to keep us going?'

'You need an awful lot of calories when you're a growing boy, my Mum says,' Richard told her.

Disregarding the ethics of bribery in the interests of peace and quiet, Olivia fetched a liberal supply of biscuits from the pantry, which was received with astonished gratification.

'Jolly little blighters,' Dart remarked, as he followed her to the ward where he had interviewed her before.

'They're irresistible, really,' she agreed, as they sat down in front of an electric fire. 'All the same, I must confess I'm beginning to find them a bit wearing. They're perfectly fit again and ought to have been discharged this morning, but the doctor was called out to an accident case, and can't get here until after lunch. As a matter of fact it's something to do with them that I feel I ought to report to you. About half an hour ago they were so quiet that I thought they must be up to something. I went along to see, and found that the ward door was ajar. I peeped in, and they were sitting with their backs to me doing a jigsaw puzzle, and having a conversation about a night during the week beginning Monday, October 27th. It wasn't clear which one. Shall I go on?'

'Please do, Mrs Strode,' Dart replied, his surprise tinged with a touch of scepticism about Olivia's motives. 'I'll interrupt if necessary.'

112

' I think,' she said slowly, ' I'd better go back to the afternoon of Tuesday, October 28th, which is where I come in myself. No doubt ' – Dart was aware of a shrewd glance – ' you think it's very odd the way I keep cropping up in this case, Inspector, but it's through no choice of my own, I can assure you. Anyway, soon after four on that afternoon I was drawing the curtains in my sitting-room, and from the window overlooking the village street I saw the Garnishes' car heading up the hill in this direction.'

Dart listened in growing bewilderment as Olivia described her first meeting with Roy and Pamela Garnish, and the reason for her telephone call to the former on the evening of October 28th.

' Did it strike you at the time that the man who spoke to you didn't sound like Mr. Garnish?' he broke in.

' Not for a single moment. The speaker was very hoarse and catarrhal, as you would expect someone with a bad cold to be, and anyway, I wasn't familiar with Mr Garnish's speaking voice, having only met him once before.'

' Carry on then, please.'

Olivia had a good memory and managed to give him an almost verbatim report of the boys' conversation about Timothy Ferrars' alleged exploit. Dart, who had a temperamental aversion to anything bordering on the fantastic, listened with increasing annoyance and some dismay. Preposterous though the whole story was, his professional experience warned him that it would be unwise to disregard it entirely. To gain time he made no comment when Olivia finished, and let her go on to Ethel Earwaker's account of how Fred claimed to have seen Sister Roach behaving suspiciously one night during the spring. He noted that the facts tallied with those given by Fred himself.

' What sort of boy is this young Ferrars?' he asked abruptly.

' I don't even know him by sight, I'm afraid,' Olivia said. ' Normally I hardly ever come into contact with the boys, apart from getting invitations to school plays and concerts.'

This at any rate was an indication that there was some truth in the story, Dart thought. If she'd simply invented it as a red herring to divert him from Winship, she'd have built up Ferrars as a thoroughly reliable boy.

'You've a son of your own, haven't you, Mrs Strode?' he asked, trying out another tack. 'What was your reaction to those two boys this morning? Was Ferrars' cousin trying to lead the other boy up the garden path, do you think? He looked a bit of a lad to me, and kids have rum ideas of humour.'

'I'm pretty certain he wasn't,' Olivia replied thoughtfully. 'For one thing they're both too intelligent. I mean, Richard Miles, who told the story, would know better than to waste his time trying to fool a boy like John Dalby, even if he might try it on with someone rather dim and gullible if he felt like ragging. And there was something very natural and convincing in the way they suddenly got bored with it all and began to talk about something else in the disconnected way children do. And in the first place I can't see Richard Miles being led up the garden path by his cousin, who's very little older.'

Dart sat and considered. The more he thought about this new development the less clearly could he see his way ahead Why, even the most tentative questioning of Ferrars would have the story all over the school in no time, and it could easily get round to the Garnishes. Suppose there really was something in it? He realized belatedly that Olivia Strode was speaking.

' ...Ferrars was right, and the man he saw was someone Mrs Garnish had brought down and was passing off as her husband, it's a very curious and suggestive situation, surely, Inspector?'

'I'm not sure that I follow you, Mrs Strode,' he replied rather coldly as his suspicion of her returned.

'Well,' she said deliberately, 'if I had brought a man down here in my husband's absence and without his knowledge, and somebody found out and tried to blackmail me, I'd certainly discuss possible ways of getting out of the mess with the man.'

Dart showed his annoyance at what he considered was an attempt to teach him his job by bringing the interview to an abrupt end.

'I'm sure you realize the importance of absolute discretion in an enquiry of this sort, Mrs Strode,' he said as he got to his feet. ' I must warn you that repeating what you have told me this morning to anyone – anyone at all – might have the most serious consequences.'

Outside in the colonnade Dart stood for a few minutes debating whether to seek out John Ainsworth and get an opinion on Timothy Ferrars. Sooner or later something must be done to check up on the story. Finally the memory of Faith Ainsworth, intense and agitated, tipped the scales in favour of a prior consultation with his superiors. At the back of his mind the weak points of his case against Barbara Winship and the problem of Fred Earwaker's alibi were lurking disquietingly. He made a sudden decision and walked across the gravel sweep to the police car in which Sergeant Metcalfe was sitting patiently.

' Highcastle,' he said briefly as he got in. ' We'll have some grub there.'

Chapter Twelve

'Ever heard of a place called Affacombe?' asked Chief Detective-Superintendent Crowe of New Scotland Yard.

'No, sir,' replied Chief Detective-Inspector Tom Pollard.

Crowe favoured him with his characteristic bird-like stare.

'Well, it'll soon be written on your heart, like Calais on Bloody Mary's. Someone's chucked a nurse over a precipice down there, and you're the lucky little chap who's going along to find out whodunnit. It happened forty-eight hours ago, just long enough for the trail to have cooled off nicely. Their C.C. rang us last night to ask for some enquiries to be made, but it took them until a couple of hours ago to decide to call us in.'

'West Country, isn't it?' asked Pollard.

'Yeah. Twenty miles from Highcastle. They've taken the usual line: more on their plates at the moment than they can cope with. Another murder on the far side of the county, and a big drugs hunt on at Overport. Also there's a possibility that it isn't a local job. Fag?'

'Thank you, sir.' Pollard took a cigarette from the box thrust across the desk, and offered his Chief a light.

'I'll tell you all they gave us, and a few things we've unearthed since yesterday,' Crowe went on. 'You'll have time to get the 7.15 from Paddington, and their Inspector Dart who's been in charge up to now'll meet you, and hand over when he's briefed you. The inquest's out at Affacombe at ten tomorrow, and there'll be an adjournment after establishment of identity. By then you'll have got the hang of things.'

Crowe tilted back his white head and watched a perfect smoke ring wreathe and disintegrate. Although he was on the brink of retirement his memory was as phenomenally retentive as ever.

'Ever heard of Countrywide Properties?' he resumed.

'Frequently,' ventured Pollard.

'That's something, anyway. A bit of general knowledge helps in our job. The bloke behind 'em is Roy Garnish, a highly successful tycoon on a medium scale. He owns Bagnall and Mayhew's, too, the posh estate agency with its head office in West Audley Street. They deal in houses and so on all over the country, not just in the commuter belt. About fifteen years ago Countrywide Properties bought up Affacombe Priory, a smallish stately home. Garnish seems to have taken a fancy to it, without losing his eye to the main chance. He modernized it, kept a wing as a week-end retreat for himself and his wife, and let off the rest to a boys' prep school. It's the school nurse who's had it.'

'A bit far for week-ends. I suppose he lives up here?'

'Luxury flat in Kensington. Anyone at his level can afford to take time off when they feel like it, and run the sort of cars that make distance look silly without shaking the guts out of you. Returning to the nurse, she was a petty blackmailer. Been at it for years, apparently – they've found her Post Office book. Two of the locals, a retired colonel's wife and one of the school gardeners admit to have been among the victims, and neither has a satisfactory alibi, according to Highcastle. In fact the lady doesn't deny having been at the scene of the murder just about the time when it probably happened. It appears there are snags about charging her, though.'

'Local bigwigs?' asked Pollard.

'Could be. I gather there's something about timing, too.

You'll soon find out. Garnish and his wife were down there at the week-end, but have a cast-iron alibi in Polharbour over the time of the murder, and left to come back here early this morning. Since then a rather odd story has come out through a couple of kids at the school, and it's vouched for to some extent by a woman who lives in the village and writes history books. Funny how these school cases seem to come your way, Pollard. You'll be teaching yourself soon, if you aren't careful, God help the new recruits. The story is that Mrs Garnish has been bringing down a boy-friend and passing him off as her husband. If it's true by any chance, it's a possible lead. Never theorize ahead of your data, though, as I may have said before.'

' Do I take it, sir, that Mrs Garnish's private life will be looked into up here, while I go down and get on with the field-work?'

' That's the idea. And as soon as you let us have some dope about the nurse, we'll try and dig up her past. Blackmailers usually leave a trail. Well, you better push off and do a spot of work after sitting on your backside all the week-end. Nothing like being put on a robbery which doesn't come off.'

' Anything more come in on it, sir?'

' Nix. The call-off reported by Henderson's contact was obviously genuine, not the double-cross we suspected. Get cracking, if you're catching that train. You want Toye, I suppose?'

' I'd be jolly glad to have him if he can be spared.'

' Right. Good hunting then.' Crowe picked up some papers. ' Here, come back,' he called, as Pollard reached the door. ' If you chance to go along the cliff road from Polharbour to High-castle, you'll see a decent little bungalow called Sunset View. I've bought it for my retirement. I'm changing the name to Crow's Nest,' he added with a touch of coyness.

Blimey, thought Pollard, making his exit. If I pull off this job, do I make the grade, I wonder?

Chief-Detective-Inspector Pollard and Detective-Sergeant Toye read the London evening papers in the train. The Affacombe murder had been a bonanza in a period unusually poor in sensational human interest. There were screaming headlines, and colourful accounts of Sister Roach's disappearance, the search of the grounds and the discovery of the body by Sergeant Harry Murch of the Westshire Constabulary. The *Evening Record* had an interview with Tycoon Roy Garnish of Countrywide Properties, owner of Affacombe Priory, in his London home, and a photograph of the Monk's Leap entitled The Death Drop. Mr Garnish had agreed with the *Record* that the murder was a shocking business. Headmaster John Ainsworth, ex-Rugger Blue, was obviously less experienced in dealing with the Press, and the *Late News* credited him with a number of statements of outstanding banality. This journal had gone to town on the legend of the Monk's Leap, and invested the ruins with a traditionally sinister atmosphere, introducing Mr Andrew Pethybridge (87), who stated that as a nipper he had been thrashed by his father for venturing along the Monk's Path after dark.

Pollard flung down the newspapers and stretched.

'I'm for a nap,' he said. 'We shall be up most of the night mugging away at the file.'

Sergeant Toye agreed, and settled down in his corner.

Inspector Dart, heavily gloomy at first, brightened up in face of Pollard's and Toye's friendliness and lack of what he had anticipated as Yard Lah-di-dah. He admitted frankly that he was glad to pass over the case.

'Fact is,' he said, 'we don't get a lot of homicides in this part of the world, and those we do are pretty straightforward as a rule. Drunks slugged in fights, or some young thug coshing an old biddy behind a counter a bit too hard. This Affacombe affair's different. It's got fancy touches, like one of those detective novels people write. And I shan't be surprised if it's an outside job – right outside our area, I mean. Deceased had moved round quite a bit, blackmailing as she went, from the look of it.'

'Blackmail can have dashed long roots,' Pollard agreed. 'Her past could very well give us the lead we're looking for. This large-scale map of yours is fine for giving us an idea of the lie of the land. I know everything's in your report, but an outline recap of the whole show up to date would be an enormous help, if you can spare the time.'

Dart's careful, methodical mind duly produced a clear narrative of events, from the time when Sister Roach's absence was first noticed to the decision by the Highcastle authorities to call in the Yard. When it came to getting across the personalities concerned, however, Pollard noted that he was much less successful. At the end of the account the three men sat smoking in silence.

'At present, then,' Pollard said thoughtfully after a lengthy pause, 'the only evidence for the existence of Mrs Garnish's boy-friend is the unsupported statement of this Mrs Strode, whose son is engaged to Mrs Winship's daughter by her first marriage, who inherited a packet from her grandfather?'

'That's right,' replied Dart in a gratified tone. 'It struck me, too, that it looked a bit fishy, but the Super and the C.C. weren't keen on risking the balloon going up by questioning the kids, especially as you chaps were taking over the case.'

'I'm thankful they haven't been questioned: you can't shut kids' mouths, and of course there could be something in it. But Mrs Strode must be an utter fool if she thinks she can make up a yarn like that and get away with it. Is she, do you think?'

'No, I wouldn't say that. She's writing a book about Affacombe, and gives talks on TV about what happened around here in the Year One. Bit too clever, if you ask me. Why, she had the nerve to tell me in a roundabout sort of way that the boy-friend might be the murderer.'

'She fancies herself as an amateur sleuth, I expect,' Pollard said soothingly. 'So many people do. What are the young couple like?'

120

' I haven't seen either of 'em. The girl's been working at the General Hospital here, Sergeant Murch of Leeford says, though the Lord knows why. She can't need the cash. She's just given up the job and gone home to get ready for the wedding. January it's fixed for.'

' Where were they both last Saturday afternoon?'

' I couldn't say,' replied Dart, looking slightly embarrassed. ' There was no sign of the girl when I interviewed her mother on Sunday evening.'

He's missed out on this altogether, Pollard thought with surprise. If the blackmail was something to do with the girl, in theory she and young Strode might have been involved in the murder. Suppose Roach knew she was illegitimate and threatened to let on? Would it affect the grandfather's will? Better get it looked up at Somerset House.

' Excuse me, sir,' Toye was saying, ' I think the Inspector said something about an unknown man calling on Mrs Strode recently?'

' That's right,' said Dart, sounding relieved at the change of subject. ' That dame keeps cropping up wherever you turn in the case. We didn't get on to it before you people were called in, I'm afraid.'

' You managed to get the hell of a lot done in forty-eight hours,' Pollard said truthfully. ' We're dashed grateful to find so much already lined up. Now I suppose the best thing is for us to push off to our pub, and chew over your report and the statements.'

After a short discussion about transport and arrangements for the inquest on the following morning, Pollard and Toye were conducted to the Southgate, Highcastle's largest hotel, situated conveniently near the police headquarters. They were received with undisguised interest by the night porter, who undertook to bring up a supply of sandwiches and beer to Pollard's room.

121

For a couple of hours there was virtual silence, apart from the turning of pages and an occasional comment and exchange of papers. It was finally broken by Toye in the small hours of Tuesday morning.

'It's the first time I've been on a case with you, sir, that you haven't set about tabulating facts and drawing up timetables from the word go.'

'There's bloody little to tabulate so far, let's face it,' said Pollard, splitting the last bottle of beer between them. 'For one thing, there are no contradictory statements. People freely admit being blackmailed, and even to being on the scene of the murder at the critical time. Then, apart from motive, the evidence against Barbara Winship is purely circumstantial, and not at all conclusive at that. Of course we'll vet that path and Dart's timing, but I don't see how anything definite can emerge when it's a matter of minutes. And slugging and chucking over a cliff isn't a characteristically feminine method of committing murder, although one can't argue from that, of course, as Roach seems to have been a small woman and Winship well-built and tall. As to the gardener chap, he's got a motive, assuming that he wanted to get his wife back instead of being grateful to Roach for her departure, but there's not even circumstantial evidence against him at present. It's entirely up to us to prove that he wasn't in his cottage all the afternoon, and so far there hasn't been a soul who claims to have seen him out and about.'

Toye turned back some pages.

'There are still a few houses where enquiries haven't been made yet.'

'True. We'll have to check up on those, although I expect it'll be more cases of the Saturday afternoon Polharbour shopping spree. Then we've got the principals of the cast to work through: the Woman with the Guilty Secret, the Young Couple with a Fortune at Stake, the Ubiquitous Woman Writer and Broadcaster – the lot.'

'Not to mention those boys,' said Toye dubiously.

'I'm inclined to give those a miss for the moment. We'll be

on much firmer ground over the boy-friend if the Yard can get on to something about Mrs Garnish's love-life... God, look at the time! We'd better turn in. I don't believe in drawing up a rigid list of priorities when a situation's as fluid as this one: you could miss an important lead that way.'

The news that Scotland Yard had been called in filtered through to Affacombe in the course of Monday evening, and was received with satisfaction. The move was felt to elevate Sister Roach's murder to an event of national importance, and also to indicate that it had been committed by a foreigner, in the local sense of someone unconnected with the village.

The bar of the Priory Arms did a roaring trade, as good as a fine August Bank Holiday or Election night, Ted Cummings the landlord told one of the newspaper men. A group of these was waiting about on the chance of seeing the Scotland Yard men arrive that night, and would be at the inquest on the following morning in case there were unexpected developments. Inside the pub the noise was terrific and the air thick with smoke. Outside parked cars, scooters and bicycles stretched up and down the street.

The awkwardness of the Earwaker marital situation had been conveniently forgotten in the general excitement over the murder. In the bar, his status and popularity re-established, Fred was being the not unwilling target of sly digs about his affair with Luisa. His unsupported alibi for Saturday afternoon was discussed vigorously in terms of the Englishman's rights before the Law.

' T'ain't up ter you, Fred. It be up ter them, see?'

' Trust 'em to pick on a workin' man, the boogers.'

It did not escape notice, however, that Fred left for home well before closing time, and there were some good-natured bawdy comments about the price of getting Ethel back.

Hugh Winship learnt about Scotland Yard from a fellow member of the County Council Parks Committee which was meeting in Highcastle on Monday afternoon. He hurried away as soon as he possibly could, and managed to catch his solicitor at his office. James Merrydew was non-committal about the implications of the new move. Sometimes a police authority was reluctant to bring a charge against people of standing in the neighbourhood. On the other hand it was to be hoped that the arrival of the Yard meant that a non-local lead had been discovered, which would result in an arrest being made, and Mrs Winship being delivered from her unfortunately invidious position.

Hugh drove home feeling depressed and worried. Seeing a light in Olivia's sitting-room, he stopped his car and called in to tell her the news. On hearing it she resolutely suppressed her excitement, but felt justified in saying that it looked very much as though the police could have got on to something in Sister Roach's past. Greatly cheered, for he had a high opinion of Olivia's sagacity, Hugh went on home, where he broke the news to Barbara and Julian. Watching his wife he saw her go tense, and hastened to be reassuring.

'Out of a different stable, these fellows from the Yard,' he told her. 'It must mean they've got on to something in the woman's past.'

After supper Julian went down to Poldens to let Olivia know that David was paying them a flying visit the next day.

'He rang me again this evening. The senior partners are being most awfully decent, he says, and he'll turn up as soon as he can make it, although he'll probably be pretty late. It's a purely personal visit, of course – James Merrydew and professional etiquette, and so forth.' She gazed at Olivia, starry-eyed, yet with a slightly guilty expression. 'It's awful of me, but I keep realizing that I've forgotten *why* he's coming, and can only remember that he *is*!'

'Not awful at all,' Olivia said decisively. 'It's some natural law in operation. The human race would have died out long ago if the young weren't able to reach out for the future from a sticky present.'

At the Priory School John Ainsworth had adopted the slogan 'Business as Usual', and started rehearsing the Christmas pantomime, having hastily excised all references to Sister Roach and the East Wing from the script. He was enjoying himself so much that he was irritated by a well-meant telephone call from Hugh Winship to tell him about Scotland Yard.

'The Lord God Almighty can come and take over the case as far as I'm concerned,' he said, 'as long as it's cleared up and the school can get on with its job again.'

Shortly before closing time the rumour that Sergeant Murch was outside percolated through the packed bar of the Priory Arms, and lent invaluable support to Ted Cummings when it came to clearing out his customers. When the noise of the departing cars and scooters had died away, and the wash of the headlights over granite and cob had yielded to darkness once more, deep silence enfolded the village, broken only by the hunting owls and the immemorial running commentary of the Sinnel.

Chapter Thirteen

Before leaving for Affacombe on the following morning Pollard rang the Yard and put enquiries in train relating to Julian Wrey's birth certificate and the provisions of her grandfather's will. He also allowed time for a visit to the police station at Leeford *en route*, and introduced Toye and himself to a gratified Sergeant Murch. While stoutly maintaining that the murderer must be an outsider, the latter produced some useful sidelines on the inhabitants of the village. Mr and Mrs Ainsworth were a very nice couple, and everybody was sorry that all this trouble had come on them. The school was well-run, and of course it meant jobs for Affacombe people, and even for one or two from Leeford. But it would be better without the foreign girls, who made for upsets with the village lads, and even with a married man now and again, like Fred Earwaker, though that business seemed to have blown over now that Ethel was back. No, in Murch's opinion, Fred never did the murder. He wasn't a man for what you might call delayed action like that.

Mrs Winship? Well, there was no denying that she had a motive, and had happened to be along the Monk's Path that afternoon, but for all that it didn't ring true. Altogether too – well – energetic. The lazy, comfort-loving sort, Mrs Winship: she'd never stand if she could sit, never mind if other folk were on their feet. Always pleasant-spoken to you, though, even if a bit too much the lady for some. Now the Colonel, he was a different cup of tea. Bluff in his way of speaking, but a real good friend to anyone who was up against it. He'd stand by his wife whatever came out, if it ever did. You'd never credit that she was that sort now, but she must have been a pretty young girl, and maybe tripped up when the war was on, and everything at sixes and sevens. It looked as though that was where Roach must have come in, didn't it? Bit of real bad luck for Mrs Winship, her turning up in a little place like Affacombe.

Miss Wrey? Everyone had a good word for her. Much more like her stepfather than her mother. A very popular match, her and young Mr Strode, who was almost Affacombe born, and a lawyer up in London now. His father and mother had come there on their honeymoon, and taken such a liking to the place that they'd bought Poldens, where Mrs Strode was living now. Very much liked and well-thought-of, Mrs Strode. Clever, too, and people liked seeing her on the telly, even if half of 'em didn't rightly know what she was talking about. Why, she was dependable all right. Anything that came from her could be taken as gospel.

'All this has been a tremendous help,' Pollard said. 'I'm dashed grateful to you, Sergeant. I hope you don't mind our parking ourselves on you like this? I've told the Yard to contact me here during the day.'

Sergeant Murch, overcome at the prospect of direct contact with the higher powers, muttered that it was an honour, and the Inspector had only got to say . . .

'Knows his job,' Inspector Dart muttered grudgingly to Pollard in the Village Hall at Affacombe, as the coroner opened and adjourned the inquest on Sister Roach in record time. Evidence of identity had been given by John Ainsworth as the deceased's employer, since Mrs. Grant of Lewisham, her half-sister, was an elderly invalid, unequal to making the journey.

After signing the burial certificate and briefly conferring with

Pollard and Dart, the coroner, a busy Polharbour solicitor, hurried to his car and drove off at speed. Affacombe residents of the less sophisticated type, who had looked forward to a morning of sensational disclosures, melted away, and the journalists closed in on the policemen.

'Have a heart,' said Pollard. 'I've only just arrived. You all know a lot more about the set-up than I do.'

Managing to satisfy them temporarily with some non-committal statements, he at last shook them off, and strolled with Dart towards the latter's car.

'Well, I suppose I'd better be getting along,' Dart said. 'Good luck to you. Let us know if you want any help. Perhaps you'll be looking in?' he added, unexpectedly wistful.

'You bet I shall,' replied Pollard heartily. 'You'll all be sick of the sight of me before I'm through. You can get on to me through the Leeford station if anything comes from the Yard about the boy-friend. And I'd like to know if you get a report on that heel-print. I'll be in tonight, if and when I get away from here.'

Remarking that the lab boys would have to be bloody wizards to make anything of it, Dart boarded his car and went off. Pollard turned to wink at Toye, but seeing that the latter's face had become suddenly expressionless, hastily composed his features.

'There's a lady here who'd like a word with you, sir,' Toye told him, and stepped aside to reveal a figure in a long tubular burberry and horizontal felt hat with a pudding-basin crown.

Pollard had a flashback of himself arranging the two-by-two procession of animals on the dining-room table, with Mr and Mrs Noah standing at the threshold of the Ark to usher it inside.

The wearer of these evocative garments advanced with hand outstretched.

'Rainbird. Miss Hilda,' she announced.

Pollard shook the hand and introduced himself and Toye.

'I shall be very glad to hear anything you have to tell me

128

which has a bearing on the case, Miss Rainbird,' he said.

' This way, then.' She set off so briskly that Pollard had to lengthen his stride. ' Only a stone's throw to the church.'

'You're a resident of Affacombe, I take it?' he asked her, wondering what she could conceivably have to tell him which involved the church. Or perhaps she thought it was a suitable *milieu* for making a statement to the police?

' Certainly,' she replied in answer to his question. ' Corbel Cottage. Fourth on the right after the turning. The Vicar will vouch for my character. I have carried out the duties of verger and sacristan since 1956, when old Malachy Twitchen died in harness. Oil-fired central heating made it possible. Not the grave-digging, of course. A little group of the men see to that. Here we are.'

As they turned in at the lychgate Pollard registered the row of cottages immediately opposite, and shot a quick look at Toye, who nodded. The path sloped up gently to the south porch, which was protected by an outer door of wire netting.

' Birds,' remarked Hilda Rainbird succinctly, pushing it open.

' Last Saturday afternoon I was standing here at 4.15 precisely. I – '

' Just one minute, Miss Rainbird,' Pollard broke in. ' I'd like to have a little background, if I may. Are you usually here at that time? Suppose we sit down?'

She subsided on to one of the stone seats flanking the interior of the porch, and planted her feet in front of her. Pollard and Toye sat down on the opposite side.

' Yes,' she said, ' I am. The Vicar ' – she lowered her voice slightly, imparting an esoteric flavour to the statement – ' is in Church from 2.30 to 3.30 on Saturday afternoon. Unless there is a wedding. Then he is there, too, of course, but for a different purpose.'

' Quite,' said Pollard, one of whose aunts was an ardent Anglo-Catholic.

' So I have to come later in the afternoon to get ready for

129

Sunday,' pursued Miss Rainbird. 'And to clear up. We have a Flower Rota. People must be drawn in, but some have very little idea. They slop water, or else forget to fill up their vases. Or even to come at all.'

'So normally you come along soon after half-past three and stay for about half an hour?' suggested Pollard.

'At least. It depends on whose week it is on the Flower Rota. One soon gets to know. Shall I go on telling you about last Saturday now?'

'Please do.'

Toye unobtrusively took out his notebook.

'It was smoke. It came quite suddenly out of the Earwakers' chimney. Someone had made up the kitchen fire.'

'Are you quite sure that it was the Earwakers' chimney, and not one of the others?' asked Pollard, getting up and standing in the doorway. 'There are four cottages and four chimneys across the road, aren't there?'

'Quite certain. It's that second one from the left. I looked hard.'

'Why were you so interested?'

'I hoped it might mean that Ethel Earwaker had come back. I'm sure you know all about the trouble over there.'

'Miss Rainbird,' Pollard said, turning and facing her, 'this is very important. Are you prepared to swear that you saw smoke suddenly come out of that chimney at four-fifteen last Saturday afternoon?'

'On the Bible,' she replied without hesitation, the old-fashioned phrase conveying an unshakeable assurance.

'How is it that you are so certain of the exact time?'

'The clock chimed the quarter just as I came out to lock up, and it was then that I saw the smoke. I stood on the step looking at it.'

Pollard considered, and then shot an abrupt question at her.

'Have you mentioned this matter of the smoke to Fred Earwaker?'

Hilda Rainbird faced him squarely, her grey eyes shrewd in

130

her weather-beaten country face, and her roughened hands clasped before her.

'No, Inspector, I haven't. I'll swear that on the Bible too, if you like.'

'Did you see anyone go past while you were watching the smoke?' he asked her, casually this time.

'Only Mrs Strode. She lives at Poldens, down at the bottom of the village. She was going to tea at the Vicarage, I expect. She didn't see me, though. She'd have waved if she had. Always so nice and friendly, Mrs Strode, although she's wonderfully clever, you know.'

'Bang goes Earwaker, sir?' asked Toye as they walked back to their car.

'I think so. Sea-green incorruptible, that old girl. We'll go along and have a bash at the chap now. He'll be working up at the school, so that means a call on the headmaster. Politeness always pays.'

John Ainsworth was engaged with some prospective parents, but his secretary assured Pollard that every facility was to be made available to him. She directed them to the vegetable garden where Fred Earwaker was working. This lay beyond the West Wing which they eyed with interest as they walked past. Pollard pointed out a second, and apparently unused drive stretching to the north-west. On entering the walled garden they saw a tall fair-headed man digging vigorously in his shirtsleeves. As they came up to him he straightened up, planted his right foot on the spade and stared at them belligerently, red in the face from his exertions.

'Brought the 'andcuffs all the way from Lunnon?' he asked with heavy sarcasm.

'Mr Fred Earwaker?' enquired Pollard.

'That's me name. I arst if you'd brought the 'andcuffs?'

'No,' Pollard replied. 'I believe in travelling light. I've come to ask you a simple question about last Saturday afternoon.'

Fred Earwaker stated forcibly that he had already told the police where and how he had spent last Saturday afternoon.

'There's one thing you didn't tell Inspector Dart, though.'

'Wot's that?'

'If you made up the fire during the afternoon?'

'Wot if I did? Free country, ain't it?'

'Did you?'

'Orl right, I did. Though wot the 'ell – '

'Did you put the light on when you made it up?'

A faint glimmer of comprehension dawned in Fred Earwaker's face, and he became less truculent.

'That's right. Kitchen's dark of an evenin'. Faces south-east. I switched on the electric fer a coupla minits.'

'Did you happen to notice the time when you put the light on?'

'Matter o' fact I did, thinkin' to get out me copy coupong fer the pools results. Quarter after four, it wur.'

'One more question,' said Pollard. 'When did you last have a conversation with Miss Hilda Rainbird?'

Fred gaped at him.

'With the 'Oly 'En? Cor lumme, mister, I dunno. Not to say passin' the time o' day when us meets in Church Lane. Parish Noo Year Party, could be.'

'Thanks,' said Pollard. 'That's all. Off the record, you're in a better position than you were as far as this enquiry goes.'

Stymied for words Fred gave an abrupt nod and resumed his digging.

'Looks as though he's clear, doesn't it, sir?' Toye asked when they were out of earshot.

'Yes. And if Dart's correct in concluding that Roach couldn't have got to the Monk's Leap before four, Earwaker couldn't have murdered her and got home by 4.15 to make up his fire without overtaking Mrs Winship on the path. I refuse to believe that he risked sprinting or bicycling down the front drive, even if he could have done it in the time. I'm sure that we can rule out any idea that he went up to the place after

4.15. Roach went out hurriedly, without her proper tea which she'd taken the trouble to collect from the kitchen. She wouldn't have hung about up at the Leap for half on hour or so on a drizzling November evening. Besides I'm quite certain that she was murdered before dark.'

'Yes,' agreed Toye. 'And I suppose any idea of Earwaker getting a pal to make up his fire can be ruled out. A bit too risky.'

'Quite. Well, exit one of our two suspects. Still, as Inspector Beakbane remarked when I was rockbottom at Meldon, you've got to clear the ground before you can really get started on a case... Let's go and visit the scene of the crime.'

They had no difficulty in finding the track which led up the slope behind the Priory, and on through the ruins to the Monk's Path. At the Leap they spent a little time reconstructing the murder, and then stood for a few moments by the railing looking at the view. It was a still day, flooded with pale November sunlight. Pollard gazed longingly at the smouldering autumnal bronze of Sinneldon. To be up there with Jane... One day they'd have a walking holiday on Crownmoor. Stay at a decent little pub somewhere. The thought of his wife brought back the possibility of his promotion and the sharp urgency of the present. He wheeled round and stared at the clump of bushes on the far side of the path where the heel-print had been found.

'Got your bearings from that map we saw last night?' he asked Toye. 'There – straight ahead – is the house and the drive, leading down to the lodge and the road. If you turn left at the lodge you pass the small gate on to this path, and go down the village street out on to the Highcastle–Polharbour road. If you turn right, you gradually bear right round the west side of the park, and pass the lodge and gates of that second drive we saw just now, and presumably another wicket gate at the far end of this path we're on. Then the road climbs a steep hill with some sharp bends, and eventually rejoins the main road a bit nearer Polharbour.'

Toye nodded.

' Okay, sir,' he said. ' I'm with you.'

' Anything strike you?'

' The Highcastle chaps don't seem to have taken much interest in these other ways of getting here, do they?'

' Just what I've been thinking. You cut along to the right, and go round and see what the set-up at the second lodge is like, and if the gates are open, anyway for pedestrians. Keep your eyes skinned generally, although I don't quite know what for. While you're gone, I'll ferret about round here.'

As Toye's footsteps died away Pollard crossed the path and subjected the bushes to a careful scrutiny. The patch of trampled grass had recovered by now, and only the pegs inserted by the Highcastle CID indicated its position. Deciding that he was most unlikely to come on any clue in an area which had been so meticulously searched, he walked on into the ruins. Jane would want to paint them, he thought. Shafts of sunlight and late autumnal scatters of scarlet and gold lightened the sombreness of broken grey walls and dank undergrowth. The sense of remoteness which had been commented on by Dart also struck Pollard forcibly, and he went on further to confirm the surprising nearness of the Priory. As he looked down on it a blend of domestic and scholastic sounds floated up, together with a smell of cooking. His eye fell on the back of the West Wing with its closed windows. Roy Garnish had provided himself with the amenity of an integral garage, unobtrusively built out so as to be invisible from the front of the house, while his tenant would have to make do with the various outbuildings away to the left. That garage, Pollard thought with interest, is the nearest building to the Monk's Leap, for what it's worth.

He made his way down the slope to have a closer look. The garage was a brick-built rectangle with a modern tilting door, secured by a Yale lock. It had no windows and was entirely unremarkable. A short drive coming round the side of the West Wing linked it to the gravel sweep in front of the Priory. He followed this, pausing to peer in through the kitchen window, thinking of Timothy Ferrars and the alleged supper party.

The room was lavishly equipped, with a dining area near the window. If the latter had been open at the bottom conversation could easily have been overheard by someone listening outside.

Pollard went back to the garage door. Anybody coming out of it could have been seen from the back windows of the school, he thought. On the other hand, in an institution which functioned with a regular rhythm there would be times when the risk of anyone looking out on that side would be minimal. For instance, during a match down on the games pitches, with the kitchen staff engrossed in preparations for tea. Realizing that he was theorizing not so much ahead of his data, but virtually in the absence of any data at all, he strolled on, intending to locate the windows of the boys' dining-room, but stopped short in front of a red plastic dustbin at the back door of the West Wing, which stood aloof from a row of the plebeian galvanized iron variety outside the school. It was provided with the refinement of a foot-operated pedal for raising the lid. For the first time Pollard felt a faint stirring of excitement. What about the safest place of concealment being the most obvious? Dragging the river for the weapon was a predictable police reaction, so what about dumping it in a handy dustbin, from which with any luck it would be removed in the normal rubbish collection before anyone thought of looking for it there?

Suddenly remembering that he had noticed dustbins standing outside the houses in the village that morning, Pollard took a quick look round, seized the red one in his arms and carried it up into the seclusion of the ruins. He depressed the pedal and the lid flew back, disclosing a bundle of newspapers which had been put in on the top of the rest of the debris. He spread some of these on the ground and began the unappetising task of sorting the contents of the bin.

Mrs Garnish was clearly unfamiliar with the practice of wrapping up her kitchen refuse in hygienic parcels. Soggy tea leaves and coffee grounds had filtered through everything. With a grimace Pollard removed a quantity of eggshells and various

135

opened tins and grapefruit skins. Underneath these were some nauseating left-overs and torn-up circulars. Then came a lot of damp biscuits, of a well-known make sold by good grocers, and the tin from which they had come.

Must have gone soft, he thought, throwing some crumbs to a companionable robin watching him from a nearby bush. The paper wrapping round the tin was oddly discoloured. He sniffed at it and realized that it had been scorched. Puzzled, he covered his hand with a piece of paper and removed the lid. Inside was some charred material which gave off a pungent smell. Sniffing again he identified the antiseptic astringence of Dettol, and sat back on his haunches wondering if this curious find could possibly have any connection with the case. Finally he put the tin carefully aside, and worked down through more unsavoury layers to the final horror of a very high chicken carcass.

'Having a picnic, sir?' enquired Toye decorously.

'Damn your eyes,' replied Pollard. 'Help me get this stinking muck back into the bin, and then if the coast's clear you can nip down and park it outside the back door of the West Wing again.'

By the time Toye returned Pollard had cautiously shaken a few of the burnt fragments from the tin on to a sheet of newspaper, and was examining them through a powerful lense.

'I'll swear it's bandages,' he said. 'There are some tacky bits which could be bloody. Rum, isn't it?'

'Most likely they're all-electric in there, and haven't any means of burning stuff?' suggested Toye.

'It doesn't hang together, though,' said Pollard thoughtfully. 'Why should people who are so filthy with their household rubbish be squeamish about chucking soiled bandages into a dustbin? D'you know, I think we'll send it up to the lab boys? Anyway, it'll look as though we're being diligent little detectives, won't it? Did you happen on anything?' he asked, tipping the fragments back into the tin and wrapping it in paper.

'The North Lodge, as it was called on that map, doesn't exist

136

any longer. It's been demolished, right down to the foundations. The gates are locked, and at first sight look as though they haven't been opened for years, but I took a sniff at the keyhole, and then shoved in a bit of blotting paper. Luckily there's a sample in my diary.' Toye took out an envelope and extracted a strip of white blotting paper soiled at one end.

Pollard inhaled.

'Oil, all right,' he said. 'Fairly recent, I'd say, from the amount soaked up. We'll send this too, while we're about it. I suppose it might be a handy way in for the village lads visiting the foreign girls after hours. They could by-pass the inhabited lodge this way. Let's drop in on the headmaster, and ask him if that gate's ever used officially.'

John Ainsworth was fetched from the class he was teaching, and arrived in his study in a state of barely-controlled exasperation.

'The North Gate? Good lord, it hasn't been opened for ages. The last time was when a big tree on that side of the grounds had to be taken down, and we didn't want heavy lorries chawing up the front drive. Must be about five years ago. There's a key somewhere.'

He rummaged in a drawer and produced it.

'Thanks,' said Pollard. 'We may want to take a look around there. Sorry we're having to be such a confounded nuisance.'

John Ainsworth suddenly recovered his good humour and grinned.

'Apologies for getting a bit steamed up! This business is damn all in the middle of term, even if the parents are making surprisingly little stink about it. Anything else I can tell you?'

'When was the North Lodge taken down?' Pollard asked him.

'Before we moved here in 1953, anyway. According to Garnish it was derelict and not worth putting in order. But there seems to have been some feeling about it in the village. Housing was still pretty difficult from the war years. He'd spent a packet on modernization, though, and I suppose there was a limit, even for him.'

'Do they come down much? It's a goodish way from town.'

'Quite often in the summer, just for a few nights. Not much at this time of year, although as a matter of fact they've turned up twice during the last couple of weeks.'

'I wonder if by any chance you've got a photograph of them? We'll have to check their Polharbour alibi for last Saturday as a matter of routine, and it would speed things up.'

'We have as it happens.' John Ainsworth got up and unhooked a framed photograph from a wall. 'He gave away the prizes the first year we were here. Once and for all, he said. They make a point of keeping clear of local commitments. That's Garnish, and that's his wife. Let me have it back: it's interesting to have a record of things.'

Pollard thanked him, and insisted on giving a receipt. He went on to the subject of Sister Roach.

'My wife would be a lot better on her than I am,' replied John Ainsworth. 'Look here, what about my sending you in some lunch on a couple of trays? We could all have coffee together afterwards.'

There was no question at all about Sister Roach's professional competence and reliability.

'We've never had anyone so good,' Faith Ainsworth assured Pollard. 'She knew her job, and was absolutely dependable. Most conscientious.'

'What was she like as a colleague?' he asked.

'Oh, most helpful. She didn't mind lending a hand anywhere if she hadn't got patients to see to. And always so anxious to do the right thing.'

'But in a more personal sense?' Pollard persisted.

'Well,' Faith hesitated slightly, 'she was certainly rather reserved and didn't make any close friends. But she never quarrelled with people or made trouble.'

' How did she get on with the domestic staff?'

' They disliked her,' said John Ainsworth bluntly. ' They thought she used to snoop to see if they were doing their work properly.'

' That was mostly Ethel Earwaker, John. She's a bit too independent.'

' Have you any reason to suppose that she ever did snoop, apart from the incident of Fred Earwaker and his girl-friend?' asked Pollard. ' I think I must tell you that a second person in the village has admitted being blackmailed by her.'

The two Ainsworths looked appalled.

' How *could* she do such dreadful things?' Faith burst out, flushed and tearful. ' She seemed such a quiet harmless little person.'

' I think she probably felt terribly insecure,' Pollard replied.

' Insecure?' repeated John Ainsworth in a baffled tone. ' Why on earth? She had a good job here, and nurses are on a seller's market if anyone is.'

' Not economically insecure, perhaps. Insecure as a person because for some reason she'd not been able to form satisfactory human relationships. So she may have tried to compensate through her blackmailing strangleholds on people.'

' Poor woman,' said Faith, drying her eyes. ' And this is such an easy friendly place. The present staff are a particularly nice lot.'

' I'm afraid,' Pollard told her, ' that she came to you too late. Where did she go in the holidays? She doesn't appear to have seen much of her half-sister in Lewisham.'

' She was reticent about her own affairs, but it somehow got out that she took temporary jobs, and that they were very paying. Like looking after rich old ladies while their companions had holidays.'

' I see,' said Pollard thoughtfully.

' I wish to God we'd never imported her,' John Ainsworth remarked gloomily. ' Her references were perfectly okay. She'd

139

certainly moved round a bit, but then some people do. I remember saying at the time that she didn't look like a stayer. Of course we'd have sacked her on the spot if we'd had the slightest idea of what she was really like. It's true that the daily women complained that she snooped, but you know what a lot of gossip goes on in a place like this, and we just didn't take it seriously, did we?'

Faith shook her head unhappily.

'Perhaps we ought to have – John, I've just thought of the boys' name for her.'

'Cockroach, according to Inspector Dart's report, I think?' said Pollard.

'Her full nickname was The Curious Cockroach,' John Ainsworth told him.

'Did you take it to mean that they thought her a bit of an oddity?'

'That's how it struck us, yes.'

'Interesting. I think, you know, that with the perspicacity of the young they were using the word curious in its more usual sense.'

Chapter Fourteen

' In here, if you don't mind.'

Hugh Winship waited for Pollard to enter his study. Following him in, he shut the door, and stood with his back to it, very erect.

' Never cared for shillyshalling, Chief Inspector,' he said. ' Are you here to charge m'wife with this murder?'

' No, sir,' replied Pollard, meeting the older man's straight look with one equally direct. ' I don't consider that present evidence would justify such a step. But Mrs Winship freely admits being at the Monk's Leap within a very short time of the crime, and I still feel it's possible that she unconsciously noticed something connected with it. That's why I'm asking to see her.'

' Can't prevent a man doing his job, I suppose. She's resting upstairs. I'll go and ask her to come down. Drawing-room's this way.'

As they came in a girl sitting in the window looked up from a newspaper. She was small and slight, with dark hair and an attractive, rather thoughtful face. Two Jack Russell terriers ran forward, and whimpered as they nosed the turn-ups of Pollard's trousers.

' Chief Inspector Pollard, m'dear,' said Hugh Winship. ' M'stepdaughter, Miss Julian Wrey. I'll go up and have a word with m'wife. Down, sirs! Don't let 'em be a nuisance.'

He went out of the room.

'Won't you sit down?' invited Julian, putting the newspaper aside.

'Thank you, Miss Wrey.'

Pollard sat down and gave a quick appreciative glance round the room and back to the girl herself. Not pretty in the conventional sense, he thought, but extraordinarily pleasing. And a lot of character.

'This is a lovely house,' he said warmly.

Julian Wrey looked slightly surprised at this opening gambit.

'Queen Anne,' she told him. 'The best of all periods for domestic architecture, to my mind.'

'And mine,' he answered. 'You've been living in Highcastle lately, though, haven't you?'

'Yes. Until last Friday,' she told him. 'I've come home now to get ready for my wedding in January.'

'May I wish you joy?' he said, noting the challenge in her voice. 'I'm sorry to have to bother you with tiresome routine questions when you must have a good deal on hand.'

'Thank you.' Julian replied, looking at him steadily, without returning his smile.

'Well, here's the first question. Were you in Affacombe last Saturday?'

She shook her head.

'I was in London with my fiancé. I went up from work on Friday evening, and didn't get back here until nearly nine on Sunday evening. Shall I give you his name and address?'

'Please.' Pollard took out his notebook.

'The flat is really the top floor of the house, which belongs to a Mr and Mrs Hopewell. They could confirm that we were there.'

Point shrewdly taken, thought Pollard.

'Mr Strode's mother lives in Affacombe, I believe?' he remarked.

'Yes. And he's coming down tonight on a flying visit.' There was a note in her voice which all the anxiety of the present could not stifle. Her face suddenly lighted up with irrepressible happiness. Pollard found the upward curve of the corners of her mouth enchanting.

'I'm glad to hear that,' he said, wondering if the young man were coming in a partly professional capacity on his prospective mother-in-law's account.

Julian turned towards him with a quick decisive movement.

'Chief Inspector, there's something I'd like to tell you – if you won't let on that I have. It's a small thing really, but it explains a lot. I'm afraid that sounds rather muddly.'

'Please tell me about it, Miss Wrey, however small a matter it seems to you. I'll respect your confidence if I possibly can, but I can't give you an absolute undertaking about it, I'm afraid.'

'No, I quite realize that,' she answered, meeting his eyes squarely. 'The thing is, it's all my fault that Mummy was blackmailed. It happened like this. I know it sounds incredible, but Sister Roach really had been at the Priory for over a year without either of them realizing who the other one was. It wasn't until Sister Roach treated a wasp sting that I got at a party last September, and I made polite conversation about a – a place, that she cottoned on to who I was, and realized that she and Mummy had met before, ages ago. Then things – well – linked up in her mind. It's the truth,' she added with sudden urgency. 'I'd state it on oath.'

Pollard made a rapid mental calculation. Julian Wrey looked in her early twenties. Born in the early nineteen-forties, say. Roach would have been rather young to have nursed Barbara Winship through a hushed-up confinement. Still, she could have easily been involved in it in some way.

'You know,' he said aloud. 'I think this may be important –' He broke off as the door opened to admit Barbara Winship, followed by her husband, and stood up, keyed to the highest pitch of alertness.

His immediate reaction was astonishment that mother and daughter could be so unalike physically. This was a tall, well-built and elegant blonde, who must have been a very pretty girl. In spite of unmistakable signs of strain under her careful make-up she was still decidedly easy on the eye.

'You want to see me, Chief Inspector?' she asked, in a quiet, rather languid voice, when Hugh Winship had introduced him.

'Please, Mrs Winship,' he replied. 'And privately, if you don't mind.'

'Certainly,' she said decisively, without looking at her husband and Julian. The ensuing silence was electric with their astonished dismay. She's going to talk, thought Pollard. He turned to Hugh Winship.

'You have no reason to worry, sir. I'm well aware of the extent of my authority, and Mrs Winship is perfectly free to decline to answer any of my questions unless her solicitor is present.'

Hugh stared unhappily at Barbara, muttering something inarticulate which included the word 'unwise'. Receiving no response from her, he turned abruptly on his heel and walked out of the room. Julian, who had been putting some logs on the fire, touched Barbara lightly on the shoulder and followed him. The dogs, uneasy at the dispersal of the family, stood in the middle of the room making small distressed noises.

'Will this do?' Barbara subsided into one corner of the sofa, automatically adjusting cushions to give herself greater comfort.

Pollard took the opposite corner, crossed his legs and studied her. Keen on the good things of life, he thought, just starting to put on a bit of weight. But unless I'm greatly mistaken, there's something pretty tough under this façade of elegant languor.

'Since you talked to Inspector Dart, Mrs Winship,' he began without preamble , 'have you been able to remember anything further that you noticed on your walk along the Monk's Path last Saturday?'

She looked at him, anxiety in her big blue eyes.

144

' I simply can't. I've thought and thought, but it's hopeless. You see, I was thinking about my – my worries most of the time, and didn't really notice anything much.'

' It's amazing what one's subconscious mind retains,' Pollard said easily. 'I know this will be very tedious, but we'll try various lines on that walk of yours, and see if anything comes to the surface. I've just come from the Monk's Path myself, so the lie of the land's quite clear in my mind.'

Over the next ten minutes he tried all the evocative approaches he could think of : near and distant visual impressions, sounds, smells, the topography of the path itself, the aesthetic, but without getting any new reaction. If she's hiding anything, he thought, she's damn clever.

' Are you a fast walker?' he asked her suddenly.

' No. I'm very unathletic. Physically rather lazy, in fact.'

' What about last Saturday afternoon? Would you say that you walked at your normal – perhaps rather below average – pace?'

For the first time Barbara Winship showed signs of agitation, twisting her hands together.

' Not for the last bit. I expect it tells against me, but I hurried, and I'm telling you I did. It was just starting to rain, and I hate getting wet.'

' You hurried down from near the Monk's Leap itself? Is that what you mean by the last bit of your walk?'

' Yes,' she said faintly.

' If you often take the dogs there, Mrs Winship, I expect you know pretty well how long it takes you to get home from the Leap. What would you reckon is your normal time?'

' Just under ten minutes.'

' And on Saturday?'

' Well, say eight. It's awfully difficult to be exact.' She spoke almost appealingly. 'I mean, I wasn't bothering about time at all.'

Pollard did some quick thinking. His own and Toye's timing of the walk to the road from the Leap had borne out Dart's

145

six minutes to the gate. Say a couple more to get back here. He deliberately allowed the pause to elongate, and then plunged abruptly.

'You know, Mrs Winship' – he sensed her stiffen – 'there's one thing in your statement to Inspector Dart that I find very puzzling.'

'The time I got home?' she suggested unconvincingly.

'Nothing to do with time. I mean your claim that you and Sister Roach had lived in this small village for over a year before she discovered some earlier contact with you which enabled her to blackmail you. Meanwhile you say you hadn't recognized her either. Would you care to amend your statement about this matter?'

'I can't.' She twisted her hands nervously. 'It happens to be the truth.'

'Well, will you add some explanation of this very remarkable situation? I have no authority to insist on your telling me the grounds of Sister Roach's blackmail, but I think that you should consider whether it wouldn't be to your advantage to clear up this point we are discussing.'

Barbara Winship turned her head so that he could not see her face. There was another long pause. Then she spoke in so low a voice that Pollard leant forward to catch what she was saying.

'Would I be prosecuted now for something I did nearly twenty-five years ago? It wasn't anything really dreadful like – like murder. Or blackmail.'

'You must know,' Pollard told her, 'that if you choose to tell me about it, I can't give you any undertaking that no action will be taken against you. On the other hand, unless it's a case of a serious crime or of someone still living having been wronged, there's a reasonable chance that the matter would be allowed to rest. The police don't go around looking for trouble.'

She glanced at him, quickly averting her eyes again.

'Suppose I could convince you that we hadn't recognized

146

each other? Would that help to clear me as far as her death goes?'

'It won't alter the fact that there exists some circumstantial evidence against you,' Pollard replied unequivocally. 'It would certainly remove from my mind the suspicion that you are not being frank about your acquaintance with her.'

With a swift movement Barbara Winship turned and faced him. He saw that her languor had dropped from her like a discarded disguise.

'I'm going to tell you the whole story,' she said abruptly. 'Even if it all comes out it's better than facing a murder charge. It's quite simple. Julian isn't illegitimate, as I'm sure you're thinking. She isn't my child at all. I made a false registration of her birth. Sister Roach was at the nursing home where she was born, and discovered what had happened by pure accident one day last September. Then she realized who I was, although she had completely forgotten me, and even then didn't "recognize" me in the ordinary sense of the word.'

'I see,' said Pollard, illumination flooding in.

'It's a long story, I'm afraid.'

'Please take your time, Mrs Winship. And don't be put off if I make a note from time to time.'

This is her real self, Pollard thought, as the complicated sequence of events unfolded. He resolutely thrust aside his natural compassion. Here was a woman who knew what she wanted of life so clearly that when the incredible eleventh-hour chance came to salvage it from the wreckage, she could make a split-second decision and substitute another child for her own dead baby. And then, when she'd carried through the deceit for nearly twenty-five years, up bobs Roach. Wouldn't she have grabbed at a chance to silence Roach for good and all? Motive and opportunity reinforced by temperament.

He watched Barbara, her long narrative at an end, sink back wearily against the cushions, as though resuming the lazy grace which had become her habitual bearing.

'I suppose you think I'm a very wicked woman?' she asked him.

'As you yourself realize,' he said gravely, 'you acted most illegally. I shall want confirmation of what you have told me. For instance, that your late father-in-law was morally certain that Miss Wrey was not his grandchild when he adopted her. That will involve my asking her to show me the letter you spoke of.'

'I'm certain Julian will agree to that. She and my husband know everything. At first I meant to pay that woman to keep it from them, but after she was murdered I was too frightened to go on alone. I was sure the police would find out she'd been blackmailing me and suspect me. Shall I fetch Julian?'

Pollard thought quickly. He felt disposed to accept Barbara Winship's story for the moment as Julian Wrey had confirmed it in part. His immediate job was to find Sister Roach's murderer.

'Not just now, thank you,' he answered. 'I shall be seeing Miss Wrey later.'

He started to get up, attracting the attention of the Jack Russells who came pattering across from the hearthrug. One of them stood up on its hind legs and pawed his knee, wagging an abbreviated tail.

'Jolly little chaps,' he said, glad of an opening to end the interview on an easier note. 'What are they called?'

'Rather sweet, aren't they?' she replied. 'This one's Flash, and the one trying to jump up on you is Streak. They can go like lightning, you see.'

'Want to come up, old man?' asked Pollard, picking up Streak.

A piercing yelp of pain rang through the room.

'Good God, I'm most frightfully sorry!' he exclaimed. 'What on earth did I do to him?'

'I wonder if he hurt himself somehow on Saturday?' Barbara, startled into sitting erect, stared at Streak with a puzzled frown. 'I've just remembered. They both suddenly dashed into the ruins, and the next minute one of them gave a yelp just like that. I thought they'd gone after one of the school cats and called to them. They came running out and seemed all right then.'

'Where did this happen?' Pollard tried to keep the interest out of his voice.

'I'd just passed the Leap on the way back. How extraordinary. I'd completely forgotten about it till this moment.'

'Shall we have a look at him?'

Streak was coaxed on to the sofa, and Pollard gently parted his coat.

'Look,' he said. 'A nasty bruise, just behind the shoulder.' He explored delicately. 'I don't think anything's broken, though.'

Barbara looked, and exclaimed in dismay.

'But how extraordinary,' she said again. 'I suppose he fell and caught himself against one of the old walls or something.'

She relapsed back into her corner, fondling Streak. Pollard realized that she was genuinely exhausted, and that the possible significance of the dog's injury had not occurred to her.

Toye was waiting patiently in the car outside the drive gate. Getting in, Pollard gave him a condensed account of his interview with Barbara Winship.

'So there you are,' he concluded. 'Death in the blitz, one baby substituted for another, a fortune, and a wasp sting leading to blackmail, and possibly to murder – the lot.'

Toye, who had listened with rapt attention, remarked that it had most films beat.

'We'll have to get it checked, but it can wait for the moment. I must say I'm grateful to that dog. Assuming that Mrs Winship was speaking the truth about the yelp on Saturday, it does seem to bear out that somebody was hanging about in those bushes. I'll swear that bruise was made by a hefty kick.'

149

'From somebody who was mighty anxious not to be discovered, and to drive the dog off,' said Toye. 'Ties up with that heel print, and the trampled grass. Makes things look a bit brighter for Mrs Winship, too, doesn't it?'

'I'd feel a bit brighter myself if there was some news of a stranger seen about last Saturday afternoon after four o'clock. Anyone knowing the ropes could have arrived about 2.30, banking on being taken for a parent who had come to watch the match, but everyone would have cleared off by 3.45, when tea started. Getting away at – say 4.15 – without being noticed by anyone would have been tricky, to say the least of it. Did you have any luck?'

Toye had managed to finish off the house-to-house enquiry in the village, but with entirely negative results. He had also rung Sergeant Murch at the Leeford police station, and reported that no call had come through from the Yard.

'We'll go and call on this Mrs Strode, then,' said Pollard. 'The lady who tried to teach Inspector Dart his job. As far as I'm concerned all contributions will be gratefully received.'

Olivia Strode came to the door of Poldens and greeted Pollard and Toye with composure. She had obviously been expecting them, and led the way to her sitting-room. Uncomplicated and shrewd, thought Pollard with relief as they followed her.

'I realize that Inspector Dart regards me with misgivings,' she remarked with a glint of amusement in her eye, 'but as I'm presumably not a suspect may I offer you some tea?'

Pollard accepted gratefully and she left them to go to the kitchen. He looked round with interest. This was an attractive room, too, but a study rather than a drawing-room, with well-filled bookcases and a filing cabinet. He got up to examine a beautiful old map of the county which hung over the mantelpiece, and tiptoed over to the paper-strewn desk. Here Olivia had been working on the Affacombe churchwardens' accounts for the eighteen-sixties. But there were flowers and photographs in the room, too. The young man must be her son, and Julian Wrey's fiancé.

'Egghead,' Toye mouthed at him, looking impressed.

Pollard suppressed a smile as the door opened to admit Olivia and a tea-tray. He watched her as she poured out, interested as always in humanity's limitless variety. Barbara Winship was pretty, elegant, and rather limited and humourless. A self-indulgent woman, yet with remarkable determination and tenacity of purpose. Olivia Strode clearly possessed these two latter qualities too, but there the resemblance ended. She had an intelligent sensible face and physical robustness, but no pretensions to good looks or elegance. Certainly a nice sense of humour, and a directness. As soon as they were supplied with tea and cake he found her glancing at him enquiringly.

'May I begin?' he asked. 'I don't want to take up more of your time than I must.'

'Please do.' She sat back in her chair, relaxed and attentive.

Pollard consulted his notebook.

'You'll understand that we're interested in any strangers who have been seen in the village lately. We have had a report that a man with a beard and wearing dark glasses called at this house a week ago last Saturday.'

He looked up to see her smiling.

'Dear old Ellen Labbitt. My caller was Professor Plowright of Highcastle University, Chief Inspector. He's an archaeologist, with an almost obsessive interest in the site of the Saxon victory over the Britons somewhere here in the West Country in 608, according to the Anglo-Saxon Chronicle. He's walking Crownmoor section by section, looking for somewhere geographically and strategically convincing.'

'Do you know,' Pollard replied, making a brief note, 'I had a hunch that it would turn out to be a fellow-worker of yours. Now, I'm afraid this is going to be rather tedious, but it's only by sifting and resifting statements in a case like this that one gets to what is really significant. Can you think back to the moment when you left here last Saturday afternoon to go to tea at the vicarage?'

As he expected, she was an excellent witness, clear and unhurried. Her account of her progress up the village street and brief glimpse of Barbara Winship was identical in every detail with that already given to Inspector Dart. Had she noticed anything in the least unusual about Mrs Winship on catching sight of her? No, nothing whatever. Pollard listened with interest to the frank admission that she had been glad to avoid stopping and getting involved in conversation: Mrs Winship had been very nervy and upset as a result of the blackmail.

'There's no point in my trying to conceal the fact that I know all about it,' she said. 'You see, I was at Crossways on Sunday evening when Mrs Winship told her husband and Julian Wrey and myself the whole story.'

Pollard decided that he could not properly assume that she knew Julian Wrey's history, and turned to another topic.

'May we go back now to your visit to the Priory last Saturday night?' he asked. 'I understand that Mrs Ainsworth rang you about eight o'clock, and asked if you could go up as a crisis had developed?'

'Yes. When she was short-staffed as a result of the German girl going off and the Earwaker upset, I told her I would gladly help out in any difficult situation. I imagined that there had been some major domestic upheaval, like all the foreign girls walking out.'

'You drove yourself up, I imagine?'

'Yes. By that time it was pouring with rain.'

'Just go ahead, Mrs Strode, and describe your arrival and what happened afterwards. The more detail the better: one doesn't always realize the significance of things at the time.'

Olivia Strode shut her eyes, frowning in the effort of recollection.

'I ran up the steps and opened the hall door. The light dazzled me for a moment after the awful night outside. Then I was astonished to see John Ainsworth and Mr Garnish sitting on the big settle that's just inside, struggling out of wet muddy Wellington boots. Particularly Mr Garnish, of course.'

'Why?' asked Pollard.

152

'Because the Garnishes keep very much to themselves, and seldom contact even the Ainsworths when they come down. They let it be known that they came to Affacombe to get a complete break from the rat race, and didn't want to get involved in social contacts. I remember now that the sight of Mr Garnish gave me a shock: I realized that something serious must have happened. Mrs Ainsworth was carrying wet macintoshes towards the downstairs cloakroom at the back of the hall. Both the men looked rather exhausted and worried. John thanked me for coming, in an automatic sort of way. Then we all started making for the drawing-room, on the tacit assumption that we couldn't discuss things in the hall.'

'Was anyone else about who might have heard?'

'Not actually in the hall – at least I didn't see anyone – but the boys were going to bed upstairs, and some of them sleep on the first floor. There was a good deal of running about on the landing, and doors slamming and so on. Supper would have been over and cleared away by then. I remember noticing a strong smell of baked beans on toast, mixed with damp clothes and Dettol.'

Pollard was silent for so long that she opened her eyes and looked at him.

'Dettol?' he repeated, as casually as he could.

'Yes. Potent, isn't it? A nice clean smell, though.'

'And then you all went into the drawing-room, I think you said?'

'Yes. John Ainsworth produced drinks and cigarettes, and told me that Sister Roach seemed to have disappeared, and that he and Mr Garnish had been searching the grounds. After we'd discussed the pros and cons he finally decided to ring the police at Leeford.'

'Did they seem worried about Sister Roach?'

'Mrs Ainsworth certainly did. She's a sensitive, rather highly-strung person. John Ainsworth was worried too, but thinking about the adverse effect publicity might have on the school as well. Mr Garnish agreed that it was sensible to contact the police, but seemed sure that Sister Roach would turn up with some perfectly good explanation. He was obviously a bit exasperated at having got involved.'

'One can hardly blame him,' said Pollard. 'Searching the grounds on a night like that can't have been exactly a picnic. Hence the Dettol, I expect. Did you notice it in the drawing-room?'

Olivia gave him a sharp puzzled look.

'Now you come to mention it, I did.'

'I'd like to talk to you now about that conversation between the two boys which you overheard, Mrs Strode,' Pollard resumed. 'I gather that you thought it had an authentic ring.'

'I'm quite sure that it was authentic as far as Richard Miles was concerned. I'm sure he was passing on a story which he'd had from Timothy Ferrars. I don't know Timothy, so I can't say if it was a leg-pull on his part, but as I told Inspector Dart, Richard isn't the sort of boy who's led up the garden path very easily.'

'Yes, I see,' said Pollard, turning the pages of his notebook. 'I want to be quite sure about these dates. Ferrars was admitted to the sick bay on Monday, October 27th, wasn't he? And discharged on Saturday, November 1st? The Garnishes' car was seen by you arriving in the village on the 28th, and Mrs Garnish left by car accompanied by a male passenger on the morning after Ferrars' alleged nocturnal outing?'

'That's quite correct. But I can't tell you which morning that was, except that it couldn't have been later than November 1st, when Ferrars was discharged. He probably wasn't feeling too good when he first came in, so his Round-the-World – assuming he really did one – was more likely to have been at the end of the week, I think.'

'I agree, having had a go of pink-eye myself. And it was on the evening of Tuesday, October 28th, that you rang Mr Garnish about going up to see him and he spoke to you, but put you off because he had a bad cold?'

'Yes.' For the first time Olivia sounded hesitant.

'What's in your mind, Mrs Strode?' Pollard asked.

'This is where I was slapped down by Inspector Dart, you know,' she told him with a smile. 'All the same, the more I think about it, the more I feel there's been something odd about my contacts with the Garnishes. You know all about October 28th. Then there was my first telephone call on September 20th, when Mrs Garnish said her husband was having a bath. It was about nine in the evening. When I suggested ringing again at a more convenient time she wouldn't hear of it, and insisted on taking a message and bringing back an answer.'

'Do you know if they had just arrived?'

'No, they hadn't. Their car went up the drive towards the West Wing about four that afternoon. I was at a garden party which the Ainsworths were giving, and saw it.'

'Did you see who was in the car?'

'No. It shot up at a terrific speed – John Ainsworth was standing near me and remarked on it – and we weren't very near the drive in any case.'

Pollard considered for a few moments.

'You had another contact, didn't you? When you visited them to discuss some papers about the Priory?'

'Yes. To my surprise Mr Garnish rang me from London a week later, and invited me up to the West Wing for drinks on the following Saturday – the fourth of October – to see the papers which he had found.'

'Did anything strike you as odd on this occasion?'

'No, not really,' Olivia said doubtfully, 'but there was a moment when I saw that he could be rather formidable. Everything went quite normally and pleasantly at first, and he seemed really interested in the Parish History I'm writing, and naïvely pleased that the Priory was going to feature quite prominently in it. On the strength of all this I decided to broach the question of an archaeological excavation of the ruins behind the present house. Of course, I suppose I may have imagined it, but he suddenly stamped on the idea – and talked about strangers digging up the place. And Mrs Garnish teamed up with him in a flash, saying that they really had to consider their tenants. I backed down at once, taking the line that local historians were apt to get carried away, and that I quite appreciated his point of view. Then we suddenly seemed to be back in square one, and he was perfectly pleasant again and admitting his lack of education, and swinging right round to the idea on snob grounds. But he made it quite clear that any excavation would be organized by him – in a big way.'

Pollard was aware that for some reason Olivia's narrative had disquieted him, but before he could analyse his reaction there was the sound of a car drawing up outside the cottage, followed by a series of toots on its horn.

'Why, that's my son!' she exclaimed, starting to her feet. 'Will you excuse me a moment? I wasn't expecting him until later.'

The two detectives rose politely as she hurried from the room, and stood looking at each other.

'When we've passed the time of day with young Strode,' Pollard said, 'I think we'll make for Highcastle. I feel an urge to do a bit of tabulating.'

Sergeant Toye's serious face lighted up in a broad grin.

Chapter Fifteen

After escorting Pollard and Toye to the front door David Strode came back to the sitting-room. Olivia realized with a pang that he was looking older. Almost middle-aged, she thought.

'I told Julian I shouldn't be down till later because I simply had to see you first,' he said, slumping down into a chair. 'I can't tell you what hell it's been not knowing the facts properly, and not being able to discuss it over the phone. I take it that Barbara hasn't been charged?'

'No,' replied Olivia, sitting down on the opposite side of the hearth, 'and I personally don't think she will be as things stand at present. The woman was blackmailing her, of course, so there's an obvious motive, but apart from that there's only inconclusive circumstantial evidence against her.'

'An absolutely bloody situation,' David commented gloomily. 'Unless they can establish beyond doubt that somebody else did it, suspicion will hang around her for the rest of her natural life. So jolly pleasant for Julian. What exactly is this circumstantial evidence?'

'Sister Roach's last-known appearance was in the school kitchen at 3.46 p.m. on Saturday, when she collected her tea tray. The church clock was just striking quarter past four as I turned into Church Lane on the way to the Vicarage, and saw

Barbara coming away from the Monk's Path. She freely admits that she had been taking the dogs for a run there. Sister had apparently made herself a cup of tea with a strainer, using the cup from the tray, if you follow me. Then she'd got to get up to the Leap from the East Wing.'

'Barely possible for Barbara to have murdered her,' David said thoughtfully. 'Not demonstrably impossible, though. What's your honest opinion?'

'I think it's a psychological possibility,' Olivia replied after a pause, 'knowing as we do the full story of the substitution of Julian for Barbara's own baby. Julian will tell you the details. It was a split-second decision in an ambulance. So Barbara's obviously capable of sudden drastic decision and action, although I certainly shouldn't have thought so before all this came out. But I don't believe it's a physical possibility for her to have committed the murder in the time.'

'Rotten for you to have got involved, especially at a key moment like that. I'm frightfully sorry.'

'Don't worry about me, my dear boy, or Julian either, for that matter. Something's happened to her, you know. She's riding the storm almost triumphantly. I think it's a combination of her subconscious doubts about her parentage being resolved, and being head over heels in love.'

A cloud lifted suddenly from David's face.

'Damn it, I can't wait to see her! What the hell does it matter what Barbara's done? It's *our* lives.'

He began to get up from his chair.

'Wait a minute,' Olivia interposed hastily. 'There's something else I want to talk about. The Highcastle Inspector said I wasn't to mention it to anybody, but after all you're a lawyer, and I can talk to you in professional confidence, can't I? You may be able to make sense of it. I got involved this time through overhearing a conversation between two of the Priory boys...'

David subsided reluctantly, but was soon listening with the keenest interest to the complicated story of Tim Ferrars' alleged

158

Round-the-World, and Olivia's various contacts with the west wing.

'Something's been going on below the surface, without any doubt,' he said when she had finished, 'though whether it's got any connection with the murder's another matter. There's no proof that Roach extended her spying to the Garnishes, although I agree it's highly probable.'

He sat thinking for some moments.

'Let's assume for purposes of argument,' he went on, 'that Pamela Garnish had started bringing a boy-friend down and passing him off as her husband. Not difficult at this end: the whole set-up at the West Wing might have been designed for it. All the guff about not wanting to get socially involved with the village, for instance. If she had him there on September 20th, she obviously couldn't let you speak to him when you rang up. That phone call of yours must have given them a nasty jolt. Hence the bath explanation, and the delaying tactics. I wonder now –' He broke off.

'Wonder what?' asked Olivia.

'Whether that car which wouldn't pass me on the way down the night before could possibly have had anything to do with it? The boy-friend could have been dropped off by a pal where the village road comes out on the main road again. Suppose he'd come on ahead for some reason? She could have given him a key to the North Gate and the West Wing, where he could have gone to ground till she turned up the next day. A bit far-fetched, perhaps. Anyway, to keep to the point, you rang up on October 28th entirely off your own bat, didn't you say?'

'Entirely. Until I saw the car go past here I'd no idea they were coming down.'

'Then it looks as though the cold and the hoarseness could have been thought out beforehand, in case you butted in on a boy-friend visit again, doesn't it? And if young Ferrars really put out that yarn to his cousin and was speaking the truth, he actually saw and heard the B.F. in the West Wing kitchen, and saw a muffled chap drive off with Pamela the next morning. I suppose the man you met at the Priory on the night of the murder really was the genuine Roy Garnish?'

Olivia hesitated.

'Yes,' she said at last, 'I'm quite certain it was. A question like that is a bit unnerving. It makes you feel you can't be sure who anyone is because of preconceived ideas and so on. But it's no good being too theoretical about things. In the context of ordinary life I'm positive it was the same man I'd had drinks with in the West Wing.'

'Right. Well, then, if Roy Garnish was in residence during the week-end of the murder, presumably the B.F. wasn't. Pamela could have had a blackmailing letter from Roach arising out of the visit of the week before. It could have told her to turn up at the Leap at a specified time on the following Saturday afternoon with the lolly – or else. Suppose she handed it over to the B.F. who undertook to keep the appointment. He'd have to get there and get away again. I imagine the police have done the obvious thing and combed the neighbourhood for reports of strangers? You know what this place is like. You've hardly set foot in it before everybody knows you're here.'

'True enough,' agreed Olivia, 'but it was Saturday afternoon, of course, and there'd been the usual exodus. You don't think,' she continued doubtfully, 'that the Garnishes could possibly have doubled back somehow, and done the murder and then gone off again?'

'Because of the Polharbour alibi? The most convincing alibis sometimes turn out to be bustable, and I bet Pollard'll have a good go at this one. But I don't think the idea will wash on other grounds. You see, either Roy Garnish doesn't mind his wife living with another man, and she can afford simply to snap her fingers at Roach, or he's an old-fashioned type, and she daren't let on. I can't see them teaming up to murder Roach just to maintain the fiction that their marriage is a howling success. Blast the whole business, anyway,' he concluded, suddenly leaping to his feet. 'I'm off to Julian.'

'You'll be bound to see Barbara sooner or later,' said Olivia

160

anxiously. 'It really is an appalling situation. What can you say to her?'

'God knows, darling,' David replied, apparently little concerned. 'None of the etiquette manuals I've read seem to deal with this particular problem.'

He waved to her from the door and vanished.

Two minutes later he was roaring up the village street in his mini. If he honked loudly enough as he turned into the drive perhaps Julian would hear and come out to meet him. He honked again with exaggerated caution as he rounded the curve and Crossways came in sight. Jamming on the brake he almost fell out of the car as Julian came running down a shaft of light from the open door of the house.

'Nothing of all this mess-up matters to you and me in the slightest,' he said a few minutes later, his voice muffled in her hair.

'It's funny,' she told him. 'In spite of everything I feel so safe – so absolutely secure. For the first time in my life.'

'Not a bit funny.'

It was cold in the drive, and presently he propelled her gently into the house. Hugh Winship emerged from his study.

'Thought I heard your car, m'boy. Glad to see you.'

'Glad I could get down, sir.'

They shook hands self-consciously, aware of volumes unspoken.

'M'wife's in the drawing-room.'

David was astonished to hear himself asking if he might go along. Without waiting for an answer he walked across the hall and went in, his mind still a complete blank.

Barbara Winship was in her usual chair by the fire. As he came towards her she raised her head and met his eyes without speaking. He stood looking down at her, slowly becoming aware of a kind of detached understanding and compassion.

'If it hadn't happened all that time ago,' he said, 'Julian and

161

I would never have met... Anyway, it's old hat now. And not to worry about this case, either.'

He held out a hand to her.

In the small inner office at Leeford police station, distance telescoped as Pollard dialled his London flat and talked briefly with Jane.

'Fairly heavy traffic on the roads down here,' he told her, using their code for developments in a case he was working on. 'Makes it a bit difficult to hit on the right turning when you aren't sure of the way. I might be back tomorrow—too soon to say.'

Cheered by the sound of her voice he put down the receiver, debated for a moment and looked up the Poldens number.

'Pollard here, Mrs Strode,' he said, when Olivia answered. 'I've been thinking about that invitation you had for October 4th. If another comes along, I suggest you consult me before accepting it.'

There was a brief silence in which he could sense her surprise.

'Well, certainly, if you wish. Not that I think there's the remotest chance of my getting one.'

'Thank you,' he said. 'And don't make a lot of deductions, will you? Just a passing thought of mine. Good – '

'Inspector, can you spare a moment?' she cut in hurriedly. 'My son – he's just left for Crossways – reminded me of something after you'd gone. It was on the night of Friday the nineteenth of September, while he was driving down here for the week-end.'

As Pollard listened he experienced for the second time in the case a faint tremor of excitement. He broke in on a half-deprecating remark of Olivia's.

'You know, Mrs Strode, only time will show what's relevant and what isn't. I'm grateful to you for mentioning this, and please don't hesitate to contact me – here or at the Highcastle station – if anything else occurs to you.'

He rang off and dialled a Yard number, his notebook lying open on the table in front of him. On being put through to his Chief's office he learnt that Crowe was out, but had left a message for him. It was typically laconic, to the effect that a lead was being followed up, and asking him to remain in close touch. In his turn Pollard asked for particular attention to be paid to the night of Friday, September 19th, and the rest of the week-end, and the period October 28th to November 1st. He reported that some suggestive, but at present unrelated facts had come to light during the day.

He sat on for some minutes, doodling absently on the blotter. He had unconsciously executed quite a creditable terrier head before getting up and rejoining Sergeants Murch and Toye.

Murch, asked if anyone in his area owned a large powerful saloon car of a dark colour, scratched his head and relapsed into thought. Finally it appeared not, apart from an elderly Rolls belonging to an arthritic elderly lady. Nor could he think of anyone in the neighbourhood likely to be up to funny business in the middle of the night, unless it was campers in the summer, but they'd have cleared off by the nineteenth of September. Any-one after sheep up to the Moor would use a van.

' What are the chances,' Pollard asked him, ' of finding out if anyone round here saw a car of that sort on the Highcastle–Pol-harbour road about midnight on that night?'

Murch clearly thought they were about nil. There wouldn't be regular traffic about at that time of night, and folk went to bed early in these parts. Still, there were a couple of villages on the road between Affacombe and Polharbour, and the odd house here and there. Did the Chief Inspector want some en-quiries made?

' I know it's a pretty forlorn hope,' Pollard said, ' but this is anything but a straightforward case, and we're rather clutching at straws at the moment. There's another point, too. Are there any houses on what I think you call the Affacombe village road, beyond the entrance to the Priory drive and before it joins the main road again? If so, I'd like enquiries made about anyone hearing a car on it at the same time, or someone going along it on foot.'

Here again, Murch was pessimistic. There was only the one farm, Fogworthy, Ted Docking's place, and it stood well back from the road. Still, they'd have a go. He'd contact his superiors about it.

In the car outside Pollard told Toye about his call to the Yard.

'It looks like postponing our tabulating,' he said. 'With the Chief making a point about keeping in touch, it's a hundred to one they're on to something and we could quite well be hauled back to discuss it tomorrow. So what? Polharbour, don't you think?'

'The Garnish alibi, sir?' asked Toye.

'What's really on my mind is Dettol. I even fancy I keep smelling the damn stuff: you haven't anointed yourself with it, by any chance? Those burnt bandages stank of it. I swear the watcher in the bushes landed Streak that kick, but could it have been in self-defence? Had the dog been startled by coming on him lurking there and given him a nip? Did the bandages stem from this? If so, where did they come from? People don't usually carry round a first-aid kit. At least, hikers sometimes do, but then respectable hikers don't hide in bushes and kick small dogs who chance on them. Then Mrs Strode smelt Dettol in the Priory hall when she arrived on the Saturday evening, and again in the drawing-room, presumably with the door shut, so it doesn't look as though the smell was coming down from the boys' dormitories. Were either of the Ainsworths or Roy Garnish using it on themselves? Quite innocently and legitimately, perhaps. Or on the other hand, perhaps not.'

Toye was silent for a few moments.

'Of course, Mr Ainsworth's alibi between 3.45 and 4.45 rests partly on his wife's statement,' he said thoughtfully, 'but a check was made with the other headmaster, and the teacher he'd brought along with him, wasn't it?'

'True enough, but you never know what'll come out when you go over the ground for yourself. And as you say, there's the Garnish alibi, too. Anyhow, let's go and see if we can get a few more facts to tabulate. At least we'll feel we're doing something.'

Pollard enjoyed night driving on country roads: the exciting sense of being on a tiny moving island in the hidden vastness behind colour-drained two-dimensional hedgerows and trees. There were the fleeting encounters with other islands, and eternally ahead, the unwinding steel ribbon of the road. Now and again, as a reassurance, a bright fragment of the familiar world rushed upon one, and swept past to vanish into the dark once more.

He found such journeys conducive to thought, and while the surface of his mind registered visual impressions he worried away at the problem of integrating the information collected by the enquiry up-to-date. Was it really credible that Pamela Garnish's boy-friend had somehow got into the West Wing after murdering Roach, rifled the medicine cupboard, and in the course of giving himself first-aid had burnt soiled bandages in a biscuit tin after disposing of its contents in the dustbin?

Fantastic, he thought impatiently, it simply isn't on. All that monkeying about under the school windows and fiddling with bandages which could be slipped into his pocket. He abruptly rejected the whole idea, and was beginning to consider a possible case against John Ainsworth when he noticed that they had reached the outskirts of Polharbour, and the road was running along the top of a cliff.

'Here, slow down a bit,' he said to Toye. 'Keep your eyes skinned for a bungalow called Sunset View.'

They came on it almost at once. Toye drew up and looked round enquiringly.

'The name's going to be changed,' Pollard told him. 'To Crow's Nest.'

There was a brief silence during which he could almost hear Toye's careful mind working through the promotions likely to

165

follow Chief Detective-Superintendent Crowe's retirement.

'Is that so, sir?' he said at last in a gratified tone, turning his horn rims on Pollard. 'Very pleasant situation along here.'

The view must be pretty good, Pollard thought, peering out of the window. The cliff fell to Polharbour Bay, above which the moon was riding in a cloudless sky. The big bright scatter of the town rose from the water's edge, and far out at the end of the headland the beams of Pol Light swept rhythmically over the sea.

'Very pleasant indeed,' he agreed as they began to coast downhill. 'Handy for the pub, too,' he added, as they passed an illuminated sign announcing the Flighty Duck, an inviting local. 'It's nearly half-past seven. The show will just be coming on at the theatre, and the Zenith-Excelsior – God, what a name – starting to serve its high-class dinner. Not a good time for calling on either of 'em, but they'll just have to lump it.'

The courtesy visit to the Polharbour police station was quickly and smoothly carried through, and the first port of call was St Hector's School.

'They've had macaroni cheese for supper here,' Pollard muttered to Toye as they were escorted across the hall. 'Not a whiff of Dettol for once, though.'

Kenneth Musgrave, the rather donnish headmaster, and the young games master Paul Travers made no attempt to conceal the fact that they were deeply intrigued by the murder at the Priory School. Just a touch of professional malice, Pollard wondered with amusement, as he introduced the topic of the tea party after the match? But from the point of view of the enquiry the visit was completely unproductive. Both men stated categorically that no one had gone out of the room from the beginning of tea until the gathering broke up at a quarter to five. After that, the Priory people had been about the whole time until the St Hector's coach drove off just before five. In answer to a question from Toye they were emphatic that no one had come into the room during the meal. Parrying offers of refreshment and attempts to discuss police procedure in detective fiction Pollard brought the interview to an end, and after a moment's hesitation decided to take the Esplanade theatre next.

On arriving they found great difficulty in parking, and finally had to produce their credentials, and enlist the help of a constable on duty. They learnt from him that it was the Polharbour Amateur Operatic Society's Week, and that the traffic would be a proper picnic every night until it was over. Huge placards outside the theatre announced a production of *The Gondoliers*, and as they went into the foyer familiar strains came seeping out of the auditorium. There was a surprising amount of excited coming and going, and the manager eventually arrived looking harassed, his dress shirt slightly askew.

'Ruddy shambles,' he remarked with a comprehensive sweep of his hand. 'You should see backstage. I suppose it's this murder case you want. There's the young lady who made the booking: Mrs Young. The police have been round once already. Here, Peggy, my dear, tell these gentlemen anything they want to know when you're free. And now, if you'll excuse me...'

He vanished upstairs again.

Pollard and Toye waited patiently while friends of a member of the cast booked for a large party, arguing interminably over the relative advantages of the seats available on different nights. At last they moved off, and Pollard approached the box office window. The exhausted blonde tried to summon up a welcoming smile.

'We're not the Press, Mrs Young, and we haven't come to book seats,' he told her, producing his official card.

'Coo!' she exclaimed, staring at it. 'My hubby won't be half wild when he hears I've been talking to a real live Scotland Yard Chief Inspector! He's a terrific crime fan. You're on that school murder, I suppose?'

'As we've been asked to take over the Affacombe case,' Pollard explained, 'we like to check up on statements already made as a matter of routine. I'm sorry to bother you at a busy time, but perhaps you'd just run over the booking of the seats for last Saturday's matinee by Mr and Mrs Garnish. This is Ser-

167

geant Toye, who's working with me.'

'Pleased to meet you, I'm sure,' replied Mrs Young. 'Well, it's just as I told the local chap when he came along. It was Mr Garnish rang us, about ten past one. I'd just come on duty. He asked what we'd got for the afternoon, and I offered him a couple of stalls in the third row. A bit far forward, of course, but it was a popular show, and there wasn't much left. He said he supposed it'd have to do, and to hang on to the tickets and they'd pick 'em up after lunch. That's all.'

'Who actually picked them up?'

'She did. Gave the name, and said her husband was parking the car. Paid, and that was that. They'd run it pretty close, and she began to get properly steamed up when he didn't come, and didn't come. He had a job finding a space, most likely: we could do with a car park twice the size. In the end I saw her go out on to the steps, and then they both came hurrying in, and I could hear her going for him, and him giving back as good as he got. Then someone wanted an advance booking, and I never gave them another thought until it all came out in the papers, and said the school belonged to a Mr Garnish, and I wondered if it was them, y'know.'

Pollard produced the photograph which he had borrowed from John Ainsworth.

'That's her!' Mrs Young exclaimed excitedly, jabbing with her finger before he could frame a question. 'Not what you'd call an oil painting, is she? Still, she's married into the money all right: it's written all over her. And that looks like him all right, but I didn't see him so close, of course. Janice is the one you really want. She's the usherette who showed them to their seats and served their tea in one of the intervals. If I pop in and get her now you'll just have time before the end of the act.'

A few moments later the obliging Mrs Young reappeared with a harassed dark woman. She was wearing the usherettes' uniform supplied by the management: a claret-coloured frock with a huge sash, and a headdress with a species of antennae, which

168

in her case seemed to be quivering with agitation.

'I won't keep you more than a minute,' Pollard assured her. 'Do you remember showing a lady and gentleman to seats in the third row of the stalls just before the curtain went up at last Saturday's matinee?'

'I've told the police I did once already. They're on to the last bit of the act now, and I've got to collect my ice-creams.'

'There'll be at least one encore, if I know anything about amateur theatricals. Please look carefully at this photograph, and tell me if you recognize either the lady or the gentleman.'

'That's him, and that's her.' Janice identified both Garnishes without hesitation.

'You must have a very good memory for faces,' Pollard remarked. 'Surely they were behind you when you were leading them down the gangway to their seats?'

'Course they were. But they ordered tea for the second interval, and when the trays passes along you got to look sharp to see the right folk gets 'em. And you takes 'em up again when they've done and has to see the money's right, all before the house lights goes off.'

She gave an anguished exclamation as a roar of applause broke out in the auditorium, and Pollard let her go after ascertaining that she had taken the order for tea during the first interval.

Toye remarked that the forecourt of the Zenith-Excelsior looked like one of the classier bits of the Motor Show. They parked between a gleaming Rolls and a Bentley with a Birmingham registration number, and went up a broad flight of shallow steps to an outsize revolving door. As it decanted them into the reception area the hall porter came forward. Something in his bearing contrived to suggest that they must be under a misapprehension as to the type of clientèle catered for by the hotel.

'Can I help you, gentlemen?' he enquired, his tone implying that such a contingency was unlikely to arise.

' I don't think so, thank you,' Pollard replied, making for the desk, his feet sinking into the lush carpet at every step. Toye followed in his wake, while the porter, taken aback and suddenly unsure of his ground, hovered in the rear.

An elegant young woman engaged in examining her scarlet nails looked up, her expression poised between a welcoming smile and frigid hauteur.

' Good evening,' Pollard said. ' I am Chief Detective-Inspector Pollard of New Scotland Yard, and want to see the manager, please.'

' Excuse me one moment,' she said, looking startled, and vanished through a door behind her in search of reinforcements. Pollard leant an elbow on the desk and contemplated his surroundings. He wondered how it was possible to spend money so lavishly and yet achieve so uninspired a result. Even the massed embankments of chrysanthemums were somehow flat and uninteresting. Through a wide archway he could see a lounge with groups of comfortable chairs round low tables. A waiter carrying a tray of assorted drinks crossed the opening and passed out of sight. The smell of expensive tobacco floated out to him, and blended agreeably with the sharp tang of the chrysanthemums. In the far distance he could hear strains of light music.

' Chief Inspector Pollard?'

He turned at the deep harsh voice, and saw that the receptionist had fetched a smart ugly woman with blue hair and an unattractively underhung jaw. A fairly big gun, he decided.

' Good evening,' he replied. ' As I expect you were told, I have come to see the manager.'

' The manager is engaged,' she told him brusquely. ' He is most unlikely to be free this evening.'

' I have enquiries to make here in connection with the Affacombe case,' he replied, ' and naturally don't wish to embark on questioning his staff without informing him. Would you kindly ask him either to spare me a few minutes or to authorize a deputy to do so? In the meantime my colleague and I can wait in the lounge.'

170

He indicated the archway, and watched her blench.

'Surely it would be more convenient if you had a private room,' she said quickly. 'Please come this way.'

They followed her by a devious route to a bleak little room which Pollard rightly guessed to be a waiting-room for prospective domestic staff.

'Give me the Flighty Duck,' commented Toye as they accommodated themselves on a couple of hard upright chairs.

'Honours easy so far,' said Pollard. 'Now they'll keep us hanging around to show what an important place it is.'

After an interval of ten minutes a sleek young man arrived, and announced himself as the deputy assistant manager. The manager regretted that it was quite impossible for him to see Inspector Pollard. He wished to point out that the police had already made enquiries in the hotel, and could only hope that Inspector Pollard would employ the utmost discretion.

'Who do you want to see?' The young man suddenly became human, having said his piece, and looked at them with undisguised interest.

'The receptionist who saw the arrival of Mr and Mrs Garnish of Affacombe Priory about one o'clock on Saturday, and had some conversation with them, and anyone who served them drinks and was concerned with their lunch. As Scotland Yard has taken over the case, previous statements are being checked as a routine measure,' Pollard patiently explained once again.

'Okay. I'll rustle 'em up for you.'

In a comparatively short time a more senior receptionist arrived, and gave her name as Doris Lanfear. She protested that she had nothing to add to her previous statement, but Pollard was insistent, and took her through it step by step.

Oh, yes, she knew Mr and Mrs Garnish quite well. It wouldn't be much good being in Reception at a place like the Z-E unless you could remember faces and say the right things to them. No, they weren't very frequent guests, but turned up pretty regularly about every month or so. Asked about their time of arrival on Saturday, she replied without hesitation that Mrs Garnish had come in about one o'clock, and crossed over to the desk to say something about being down again for a night or two, and coming over for another lovely lunch. Then she'd said they were thinking of going to see *The Mousetrap*, so she'd better hurry up and order the drinks while her husband was parking the car.

'Did you see Mr Garnish arrive?' asked Pollard.

'Out of the corner of my eye. I was busy with some people who'd come in just before him, but he nodded to me as he went past on the way to the lounge. He seemed in a bit of a hurry. Of course they hadn't much time if they were going to the theatre.'

'Well, they certainly arrived here,' said Pollard when Miss Lanfear had departed. 'Now for their drinks.'

This stage was less definite. It transpired that the Garnishes had not gone to the bar, but a young waiter remembered a tall thin lady sitting down at a table in the lounge and ordering a couple of dry martinis. He had noticed a gentleman join her a bit later, but when confronted with the photograph confessed that he had no idea what he looked like.

Pollard pushed on doggedly with his enquiries. Luigi, the Italian-Swiss head waiter, arrived protesting angrily at being removed from his sphere of influence during the service of dinner in the hotel's Lucullus Restaurant. He treated Pollard to a maddening display of professional mystique in regard to its patrons, their discrimination, and their capacity to appreciate the menus which he, Luigi, composed for them. Certainly he knew Mr and Mrs Garnish, persons of quite exceptional discrimination in gastronomic matters...

With difficulty Pollard at last extracted the information that – quite clearly to Luigi's annoyance – the Garnishes had elected to lunch in the Grill Room on the previous Saturday. Mrs Garnish had, of course, looked in for a word as she passed the door of the Lucullus, explaining that she and her husband were going to the theatre, and to hurry over one of Luigi's luncheons was not to be thought of. Instead they would return to dine at leisure the next night.

172

'And did they?' enquired Pollard with interest.

It appeared that they had, coming in at about eight o'clock.

With a sense of relief at reaching the last lap Pollard demanded the head waiter of the Grill Room, and was pleasantly surprised when a fellow countryman with an underlying Yorkshire accent materialized. On being presented with the photograph he studied it carefully and identified both the Garnishes.

'I understand that they have been coming here for meals for a good many years now,' remarked Pollard. 'I expect you know them quite well?'

The man shook his head.

'No, sir. You see, I only joined the staff here a couple of months ago. To the best of my knowledge I'd never seen the lady and gentleman before last Saturday, but I recognize them clearly. Especially the lady.'

'Why especially the lady?'

'She came in alone, sir, and asked for a table for two, saying she'd give the order as her husband was telephoning and they were in rather a hurry. Later on when I went to enquire if they were finding everything satisfactory the gentleman had joined her.'

'Well,' said Pollard, as he regained the seclusion of the police car with Toye, 'no doubt our two great minds have been struck by a single thought. An unobtrusive chap last Saturday, Mr Roy Garnish. Parking the car while his wife natters to the receptionist and does the head waiter-favoured patron turn with Luigi. Telephoning for theatre tickets while she orders lunch in the Grill Room. Parking the car again while she collects the theatre tickets from the box office.'

Toye agreed.

'All the same, sir, it doesn't make sense, does it? I mean, the idea of the boy-friend being a stand-in over here, while Mr Garnish stops at home to murder Roach, and gets bitten by the dog and bandages himself up and burns the bandages and –'

' Stop, for heaven's sake, unless you're rewriting " The House that Jack Built ". The best idea you've had tonight's the Flighty Duck. Let's go.'

Chapter Sixteen

The map was still a long way off, but Pollard knew that he simply must get to it. With immense efforts he managed to arrive within reading distance and leant forward, peering at it anxiously. If only he could manage to see what places were marked on it he'd know which way to go, but it was so terribly difficult when they kept moving past him all the time. And now the chrysanthemums were being disturbed as if some small animal was rootling about among their stalks...an enormous voice was echoing and booming in his ears 'Down...Down again...Down again.' He fell endlessly and landed soft in the feel of sheets, and a hoarse reiterated 'You're wanted, sir,' accompanied by muffled thumps on the door of his bedroom at the Southgate Hotel.

It was the night porter, bleary-eyed but agog, to tell him that he was wanted on the phone, and that there was an extension along the corridor. Pollard hurried to it, barefooted and in his pyjamas. As he expected it was the Yard, recalling him urgently in view of fresh developments. A brisk voice told him that it was only half-past five, and they'd have plenty of time to get the Sou'wester at six-forty. It had a breakfast car.

'Get you two gennelmen a cuppa?' offered the porter, hovering. 'Things movin'?' he enquired with interest.

'Hope so,' Pollard replied, rubbing his eyes. 'Thanks very

175

much. A cuppa would be just the ticket. I'll go and wake Sergeant Toye while you brew it.'

As the Sou'wester pulled out of Highcastle Station Pollard told Toye to go and get himself a decent breakfast.

'Much the best meal British Railways do,' he said. 'Don't feel like it myself at this ungodly hour, though. I'll settle for a cup of coffee in the buffet car.'

Swallowing it hastily he returned to their compartment, thankful that it was empty, got out the file of the case and settled down to think. He must face the fact that he was worried about his progress up to date, or rather at the lack of it. What had the Yard got on to, he wondered? If they'd managed to establish the existence of Pamela Garnish's boy-friend, that would be a very useful step forward. But it could be something entirely different which he'd missed out on himself.

He shifted his position and lit a cigarette abstractedly. Begin right at the beginning. Somebody had murdered Roach. Ought he to have done more in the way of enquiries about any strangers seen around on Saturday? That blasted shopping bus seemed to have depopulated the whole place. After all, Roach had apparently been carrying on petty blackmail for years. She might have summoned some earlier victim to meet her that afternoon under the useful cover of the school match.

Perhaps it had been a handicap to start off with two such obvious suspects as Fred Earwaker and Barbara Winship, leading one to spend too much time on them at the expense of other lines of enquiry. Pollard re-read the summaries of the evidence against them both which he and Toye had drawn up on returning from Polharbour the night before. Damned unsatisfactory, he thought. Earwaker wasn't cleared, and it was difficult to see how he ever could be as far as his alibi went. Admittedly it was supported by circumstantial evidence but this was far from being conclusive. And if his innocence couldn't be established,

176

neither could Barbara Winship's guilt, because of the sheer impossibility of proving that she had had enough time in which to commit the murder. It was impossible to imagine the D.P.P. giving the green light for proceedings against her as things stood at present.

Presently he came to the conclusion that it was useless to spend any more time on either of them at the moment, and turned his attention to another summary which he and Toye had compiled. Its heading was INDICATIONS OF A POSSIBLE CASE AGAINST A PERSON AT PRESENT UNKNOWN. As he picked up the sheet of paper he had an unpleasant qualm: How would the Old Man react to a string of rather nebulous and seemingly unrelated facts? Gloomily he began to read through them once again.

(1) At about midnight on Friday, September 19th, a powerful dark saloon car driving from Highcastle in the direction of Polharbour was at pains not to overtake a mini. When this latter turned off for Affacombe, the saloon suddenly shot ahead. (See map: the saloon or someone put down by it could have doubled back to the Priory.)

(2) The lock of the north gate of the Priory, said to have been unused for the past five years, has recently been oiled.

(3) Various contacts and alleged contacts with the West Wing of the Priory suggest that the man in residence there from October 28th–November 1st, and purporting to be Roy Garnish, was in fact someone else. There is a similar but less well authenticated suggestion for the week-end of September 19th.

(4) During their investigations on Sunday, November 9th, the Highcastle C.I.D. found a fresh heel print in a clump of bushes immediately opposite the Monk's Leap. It has been confirmed that it was made by a rubber boot, about size nine.

(5) Mrs Winship states that one of her dogs ran into the bushes at this point as she was returning home along the Monk's Path on Saturday afternoon, and yelped with pain. It

has a bad bruise which could have been made by a hard kick or blow.

(6) A tin previously containing biscuits (and the biscuits) were found by me in the dustbin of the West Wing. Inside the tin was charred material, apparently bandages, which has been sent to the forensic laboratory. This material smelt strongly of Dettol.

(7) A Mrs Strode who was with Mr and Mrs Ainsworth and Mr Garnish in the hall and drawing-room of the Priory on Saturday evening, after the search of the grounds for Sister Roach, commented on the smell of Dettol in both these places.

(8) Both the Garnishes claim to have been in Polharbour between roughly 1 p.m. and 5 p.m. on Saturday. There is no reasonable doubt that Mrs Garnish was, but our enquiries have disclosed that her male companion was not seen closely or spoken to by anyone capable of identifying him positively.

Unless something's transpired which alters the whole situation, Pollard thought, I'll go and interview the Garnishes together at the first possible opportunity. I'll try and catch him out on some point about the hotel or the theatre. But if he wasn't there at all, who the hell was impersonating him with his knowledge and consent? Could anyone have done this? Was the man Dart questioned really Garnish?

This was an intriguing idea, and Pollard considered it carefully, but in the end reluctantly rejected it. No impersonation could have stood up to that search of the grounds with John Ainsworth, who must know Garnish pretty well after all the business contacts they'd had over the Priory. Besides, Faith Ainsworth and the quick-witted Olivia Strode had seen the man at close quarters that evening, too.

Pollard stared out of the window at the hedges spinning past in the dreary November dawn like the spokes of a slowly rotating wheel. Was it conceivably possible that Garnish and Ainsworth had been in it together? Unpromising though the idea seemed he extracted the report of his own interview with John Ainsworth from the file, and settled down to read it. He was about half-way through when he gave a sudden exclamation which coincided with the opening of the door from the corridor to admit Toye.

'You've damn well had value for money – or rather, the taxpayers have,' Pollard said. 'Come and read this, and see if anything hits you in the eye.'

Toye slid neatly into his corner and began to read with concentration. Pollard watched him eagerly. All at once he looked up, his eyes alert behind his horn-rims.

'You've got something here, sir,' he said.

'Something to work on, anyway,' Pollard replied, repressing his excitement. 'Let's have another squint. Yes, Ainsworth said categorically that the Garnishes came down quite often in the summer, but not much at this time of year, and commented on the fact that they'd just turned up twice inside a fortnight, as if it were something out of the ordinary. They'd come down twice,' Pollard repeated, vaguely aware of an echo in his mind. 'Now, then, they – or Mrs G and a chap impersonating her husband – came down on September 20th, and again at the week-end of October 4th, when Mrs Strode went along to drinks with them. After that there was a gap until October 28th. They stayed until November 1st, a Saturday, only to reappear on the following Friday. If you remember the weather was rotten all last week, so they weren't lured down to the country by a spell of belated summer. Hell!' he added, as the train glided up the length of a packed platform.

Toye hastily moved across as the compartment began to fill up. As soon as the Sou'wester was moving again they went on talking quietly.

'I can't help feeling that they decided to come down again on November 7th *after* returning to London on the 1st,' Pollard said. 'Otherwise they'd hardly have paid the earlier visit as well. So what sparked them off?'

'Letter?' suggested Toye.

'I think so. It seems to have been Roach's technique to approach prospective victims through the post. Suppose she was out snooping and heard and saw much what young Ferrars' cousin says he did, perhaps on the Friday night – October 31st, I mean. In other words she tumbled to it that the man spending the week-end with Pamela Garnish was not Roy, but someone impersonating him. On the Saturday or Sunday Roach writes to Pamela, threatening to report the matter to her husband unless she turns up with a stipulated amount of cash on the following Saturday. It probably gave her a terrific kick to browbeat a tycoon's wife. With me so far?'

Toye nodded, listening with intent interest.

'Okay. Well, then, if we accept all this provisionally, we've got a situation in which the two Garnishes come down to Affacombe for the express purpose of murdering Roach, and the murder takes place while they – apparently – are in the Esplanade Theatre at Polharbour. And this is where I'm beginning to feel decidedly interested in Roy Garnish's alleged impersonator. You see the possible implication?'

Toye whistled softly.

'An accomplice? A three-man job, in fact?'

'Exactly. Or a two-man-one-woman job. Although I must say that a combined op by a wronged husband, an erring wife and the wife's lover seems rather like a farce turned nasty tragedy, doesn't it? But who was it that had to be prevented from finding out about Pamela's love-life at any cost?'

'The other chap's wife?' propounded Toye doubtfully.

'If so, the lady must be someone pretty dangerous and influential. Maybe she could put a hefty spoke into Garnish's money-making activities.'

They relapsed into silence. The Sou'wester ripped through the air Londonwards. Stations and passing trains swept by in shattering rushes.

'That integral garage!' Pollard said suddenly, bringing his fist down on his knee.

Toye looked at him enquiringly.

180

'Might have been built for the job. We're assuming Number Three's existence. Well, getting him down to Affacombe unobserved was just too easy: on the floor of the back of the car. Then when they've run round to the garage and shut the outer door again, he emerges and goes into the house, and no one's any the wiser. The next day he goes off to Polharbour with Pamela and does a carefully planned impersonation, while Roy keeps hidden at home until it's time to slip out and keep the appointment Roach made with Pamela. And by God, this makes sense of the bandage business and the smell of Dettol Mrs Strode noticed that evening. Snags?'

'Why didn't he just slip the soiled bandages into his pocket?' objected Toye. 'Simple enough, and a lot safer than dumping them in the bin.'

'I've been thinking about that. I believe he was put off his stroke by being bitten by the dog, and rushed into taking unnecessary precautions. One's seen it happen before. He's not a common thug, and committing murder makes even the toughest types edgy. His first reaction was probably to drive the animal off, in case its owner came to see what it was so excited about. Then he'd realize that he'd hurt it quite badly, and mustn't let on that he'd been bitten. It might somehow come out in the enquiry, and get linked up with the dog yelping and the time of the murder. He'd have a compulsive urge to get rid of the evidence – the bandages. You're probably right about the house being all electric. Hence the use of the tin, and the bright idea of putting it out to be carted away on the Monday. I know there was a rubbish collection that day, because I saw bins lined up outside the cottages in the village. It was a gamble which jolly nearly came off incidentally.'

'Daft thing to do, all the same, sir.'

'I'm with you. A text-book example of the careful murderer's single slip-up, if I'm not much mistaken. All the same, Dart might have elected to go over the entire Priory with a toothcomb – Good God, Toye, what fools we're being! The real risk was Number Three being found on the premises.'

181

' The north gate –'

' That poor old bastard Dart!' exclaimed Pollard, struggling to keep his voice down. ' He let them go off to get a meal on the Sunday night! They dined at the Zenith-Excelsior under the aegis of that unspeakable ass Luigi. It was the arrival procedure in reverse! I expect they dropped off Three in Polharbour and he made his way unobtrusively back to Town.'

The Sou'wester was thundering through the outer suburbs, taking one set of points after another. Something similar was happening to Pollard's thinking. Why had it seemed vital to these three people to collaborate in murdering Sister Roach? It could only have been because she was threatening something supremely important to them all. Not the security of Pamela's marriage, as Roach herself thought. No, she was a danger to them because she had found out that Roy was being impersonated – so the impersonation must be a cover for something criminal involving them all.

Pollard surfaced to find the other passengers already on their feet and reaching up to the luggage racks. He turned to Toye and grinned as he stretched himself.

On arriving at the Yard Pollard learnt that Chief Superintendent Crowe wanted to see him immediately. Wishing that he could have had a little time in which to tabulate his new ideas, he took the case file and went along to his Chief's office.

Crowe looked up from his desk.

' Morning,' he said. ' Well, whodunnit?'

' Roy Garnish, I think, sir, with his wife and A. N. Other as accessories.'

Although Crowe's face remained impassive Pollard sensed gratification.

' Let's hear what you've got to say, then.'

Concealing his elation Pollard embarked on his report. It was lengthy, but Crowe followed it with unblinking attention. Only once did he interrupt.

' Hold on,' he said. ' Those boys. Did you question 'em?'

' No, sir. I didn't want any hint that we'd tumbled to the impersonation racket to leak out.'

'Good. Carry on.'

Pollard continued through the intricacies of charred bandages, Dettol, the injury sustained by Streak, and his enquiries at the Zenith-Excelsior and Esplanade Theatre. As he reached the topic of the Garnishes' two recent visits to Affacombe within a fortnight he was aware of an appraising glance.

'My theory is, sir,' he went on, 'that the reason for the Garnishes' visit at the week-end of November 8th was a black-mailing letter from Roach to Pamela Garnish, in which she de-manded a meeting at the Monk's Leap on the Saturday of the murder. Assuming that the boy Ferrars saw and heard what his cousin said he did, it seems reasonable to assume that a profes-sional snooper like Roach would have got on to it as well. She contacted Mrs Winship, and almost certainly Ethel Earwaker by post. The Garnishes – or a couple purporting to be Roy and Pamela Garnish – left Affacombe on Saturday, November 1st. A letter posted in Affacombe that week-end would get to Lon-don on Monday, or Tuesday at latest.'

'So what?' enquired Crowe.

'If we provisionally accept the impersonation, sir, I suggest that the idea behind it wasn't to cover an affair of Pamela's, but to provide cast-iron alibis for Roy Garnish when he was en-gaged in criminal activity elsewhere. Hence Roach's murder. Too much was at stake to risk letting her go on living once she'd rumbled the impersonation racket.'

Crowe lit another cigarette in a leisurely way.

'I should have thought the dates October 31st to November 1st might have rung a bell for you, Pollard,' he remarked drily. 'Large-scale organized crime's a commonplace these days, but that week was rock-bottom. You chaps get absorbed in your own cases. The 31st was the night of the break-in at the Land-chester branch of the Southern Counties Bank, when they got away with a cool £80,000. Usual story. Shop to let next door. You'll be interested to hear that the sole agents were Bagnell and Mayhew, Garnish's high-class estate agency in West Audley

Street. I needn't add that everything about the keys was above reproach. Garnish himself fell over backwards trying to be helpful to the police.'

'Good lord, sir! And the day before was the payroll snatch at Railstone's.'

'Yeah,' replied Crowe. 'People here started getting worked up when you rang about those dates last night.'

'What about the earlier dates? The week-end of September 19th?'

'No big job around here, but on the morning of the 19th there was a sizeable mail van robbery at Bristowe. Lot of registered stuff. Clean getaway, too.'

'If that was a Garnish job by any chance, he could have been in that car late the same night going to ground at Affacombe,' Pollard mused aloud. 'But why should he have wanted a stand-in for the rest of the week-end? It doesn't seem to make – here, wait a bit!' he almost shouted. 'Suppose they sometimes worked it the other way on?'

'What the hell do you mean?' demanded Crowe.

'Sorry, sir. This way. Suppose Garnish and the chap who impersonates him are partners in the organized crime racket? Sometimes one of 'em organizes a job, and sometimes the other. If the impersonator did the mail van hold-up at Bristowe, wouldn't it have been a damn good stunt for him to vanish into thin air by assuming Garnish's identity at Affacombe? Meanwhile Garnish lies low up here, or in one of the handy empty houses on the books of Bagnall and Mayhew.'

'The Garnish woman would have had to come down to Affacombe alone in that case,' objected Crowe.

'I don't think there was much risk there. If she'd been noticed driving off from their flat up here alone, anyone would have assumed she was going to pick up her husband somewhere. Most of the Affacombe people seem to take the weekly bus into Polharbour on Saturday afternoons. If somebody saw her driving up the village alone, it would probably have been assumed that she'd arrived earlier with her husband, and had nipped back

184

to Leeford to get something at the shops. If anyone speculated about it at all, that is.'

Crowe sat silent for a few moments.

' I'm not sure you aren't on to something, Pollard,' he said at last. ' I hope to God you are. There've been too many high-level enquiries about all these unsolved robberies. Last night the A.C. had a conference for the chaps in charge of the Landchester and Railstone cases – that's Reynolds and Blake – and myself. As I said in that message I left for you, there's been a lead of a sort on this alleged impersonation. The Garnishes' flat is in Hunting-ford Court, an extremely expensive block in Knightsbridge. It's ultra-modernized rather than ultra-modern, if you get me, so the tenants have an unusual amount of privacy. There's a hall porter at the main entrance in Gaveney Street. The block's rec-tangular with four street frontages. Service entrance at the back, with a mews opposite where the tenants' garages are. And there are handy side entrances as well, on the two other streets. Where one of these joins Gaveney Street, there's a newsvendor's pitch belonging to an old boy called Reg Platt. We had a stroke of luck here. There'd been a minor car smash at this road junction on October 28th, and Platt had a ringside seat. We sent Nugent along yesterday as an insurance agent making further enquiries. After a bit he made some remark about a Mr Garnish's car having gone out into the main road immediately in front of the one that was in the smash, and suggested that it might have blocked the view. Platt contradicted this at once: said he'd seen both the Garnishes drive off in their Mercedes half an hour earlier. He knew their car well. It was a posh outfit, if ever there was one, and so on. Nugent pretended that he hadn't un-derstood, and after a bit more chat said something implying that Mrs Garnish had been alone in the car. Platt took him up rather impatiently, and then suddenly became reminiscent. Funny thing, he said, but right in the middle of the hullabaloo over the smash he could've sworn he saw Mr Garnish crossing the road. Something about his walk and build – way he had of shoving his left shoulder forward. Then he saw it was a working chap, and anyway it couldn't've been Mr Garnish, seeing he'd cleared off half an hour before. Nugent started another topic, and when he thought they'd had about enough, tipped the old boy and pushed off.'

'Where do we go from here, sir?' asked Pollard after a pause.

'Joint conference with the A.C. on all three cases in an hour's time,' replied Crowe, 'so you'd better have some proposals to make about yours. I'm going to brief him on it now.'

He made a gesture of dismissal. Pollard rose to go. Half way to the door he halted.

'I drew up for a couple of minutes outside a bungalow called Sunset View when I was running into Polharbour, sir.'

'You ought to be damn well ashamed of yourself, wasting your time and the taxpayers' money.' Crowe's bright-eyed stare was broken by the suspicion of a wink.

It was Pollard's first experience of a high-level conference on cases suspected of being interrelated. He found himself the most junior member, but it was the facts he'd unearthed at Affacombe which had first suggested the link between Sister Roach's murder and the robberies. The A.C. was, as usual, incisive beneath surface languor, and the general atmosphere not unfriendly although highly critical. Pollard sensed the need to steer carefully between the Scylla of appearing pleased with himself and the Charybdis of having nothing constructive to put forward. During the cut and thrust of the discussion he tentatively introduced a point which had only struck him within the past ten minutes.

'It did just occur to me, sir,' he ventured, 'that there might be a connection between the Garnishes' trip down to Affacombe last week-end and that eleventh-hour cancellation of the bank robbery we were expecting.'

There was a silence during which three pairs of eyes were focused on him, the A.C's continuing to contemplate the ceiling as he reclined almost horizontally in his chair.

' Could be,' the latter pronounced judicially.

As the conference went on the question of whether Roy Garnish had been the murderer of Sister Roach assumed priority. If he had, there was no question about the existence of his impersonator, and if the latter could be traced the prospects of clearing up the two robberies – and probably others of the same type – would be decidedly more encouraging.

There was agreement that a near relation of Roy Garnish was almost certainly involved. There must surely be a strong physical resemblance to make so successful an impersonation possible. During the investigation of the Landchester bank raid Superintendent Reynolds had looked into Roy's early history. He had emerged from an unknown background in the post-war years, and been borne up on a rising tide of financial success. The War Department reported that he had served unremarkably in North Africa and Italy, and been demobilized in the normal course.

' They gave us his home address, sir,' said Reynolds, consulting his notes. ' It was 73, Worrall Street, Poplar. Next-of-kin, Mrs. Doris Garnish.'

' It will almost certainly turn out to have been flattened in the blitz,' commented the A.C. ' We'll follow it up, of course, and try Somerset House, too, but it looks like a long job.'

Ultimately he turned to Pollard.

' In the first instance this is your murder case. What steps do you propose to take next?'

' I feel I'm at a great disadvantage in not having met either of the two Garnishes, sir,' he replied. ' I'd like to make an appointment to see them both together at their flat. Be rather pedestrian about it, saying it's a routine check of their statements, and so on, and rather dumb when I get there. Play up to them a bit, while keeping my eyes open, of course. And I'd like to take one of the make-up experts along, if I may.'

' To make sure you're dealing with the genuine article, I take it? Not a bad idea, Pollard. I suggest you take Sergeant Bendle.

Well, gentlemen, I propose that we adjourn until the enquiries into the Garnish family have had time to get off the ground, and Chief Inspector Pollard has paid this visit of his.'

Sergeant Henry Bendle of the C.I.D. was a sad-looking man in the fifties whose pale blue eyes gave a misleading impression of vagueness and short sight. In reality his flair for observation of his fellow creatures was phenomenal, and his memory photographic. He was frequently in demand when identifications were wanted, and specialized in the creation of disguises for investigating officers. He had followed the Affacombe case in the papers and listened to Pollard with interest.

' Not to worry, sir,' he said, with complete confidence. ' Why, if the chap was got up so he'd fox his own mother, I'd spot the fake touches all right. And I'll get him taped for future reference all right, too.'

As soon as Bendle had gone off, Pollard rang Jane to report his return and hopes of getting home that evening, and then settled down to review the case. He felt satisfied that his request for an appointment at the Garnishes' flat had not aroused any suspicion. He had rung the head office of Countrywide Properties, and the call, passed progressively upwards, had led to a brief conversation with Roy himself. Careful to be a little routine-bound and implicitly apologetic he had evoked a brusque but matter-of-fact acceptance of the situation, and been asked to come round at five that same evening, when a short time could be made available.

On the way there he'd prime Bendle about playing the red tape touch. Anything remotely resembling a crunch must be avoided like the plague. Then in the meantime the enquiries into Garnish's past would be going on, but that sort of thing took such ages. With a pang of discomfort Pollard visualized some new development in the robbery cases, and one of the two Supers getting in ahead of him. A short cut, that was what was wanted. Something really imaginative. Disconsolately he was forced to admit that his imagination seemed to have gone off the air altogether. The excitement of the early part of the morning had evaporated, too. He decided that a break was called for, and dismissing the entire case from his mind worked at the arrears in his In basket until it was time to go down to the canteen for some lunch.

After an unsatisfactory afternoon which brought him no nearer to any plan of action, he left for Knightsbridge with Sergeant Bendle soon after four, allowing time for a reconnaissance of the outside of Huntingford Court. He stopped to buy an evening paper from Reg Platt. In response to a leading remark, the shabby sharp-eyed little man was voluble about the traffic jams in Gaveney Street, and the dangers of cars coming out of the side roads too fast. While he reminisced about the accident which he had seen right under his nose, Pollard noted the island on which Platt had thought he saw Garnish standing. It was quite near the newspaper pitch, and anyone on it would be clearly visible from the pavement. There must have been quite a decided resemblance, he thought.

'The flat's Number Nine,' he told Bendle as they moved away. 'I think we'll give the impressive front entrance a miss, and go in unobtrusively at the side. Better chance of spying out the land, perhaps.'

A brief inspection showed that Number Nine was on the first floor. They went up a well-carpeted staircase and explored some passages. The front door of the flat was round a comparatively secluded corner, conveniently near the staircase leading down to the side entrance opposite to the one they had used. The whole place seemed deserted and surprisingly quiet.

Roy Garnish himself opened the door in answer to their ring. Pollard's immediate reaction was that his stocky heavy-shouldered figure looked incongruous in city clothes.

'I rang your office this morning, sir,' he said pleasantly. 'Chief Inspector Pollard and Detective-Sergeant Bendle. Good evening.'

'Glad you're on time, at any rate,' Roy Garnish replied, without returning the greeting. 'Straight ahead, first on the right,' he added, shutting the door behind them.

It was a large room with windows on to the side street, furnished with ostentatious luxury, yet somehow giving an impression of emptiness. Lack of personal touches, Pollard decided, in spite of a vague untidiness. No books, hardly any odds and ends, not even a writing desk. A few pictures of the poster type. A tall, unusually thin woman got up and switched off a gigantic television set, a cigarette dangling from the corner of her mouth.

'My wife,' said Roy Garnish briefly. 'Scotland Yard, Pam.' His tone conveyed mock respect. 'Plenty of chairs,' he added, slumping into one himself. Pollard and Bendle waited for Pamela Garnish to resume her seat and then sat down themselves.

'Get cracking, if you don't mind, as I've an appointment at half-past five, and this business has wasted enough of my time already.'

'We shan't need to keep you that long, sir,' Pollard told him, taking out his notebook. 'It's merely a question of checking the statements you and Mrs Garnish have already made. According to the receptionist at the Zenith-Excelsior in Polharbour, Mrs Garnish came in at about one o'clock last Saturday, and spoke to her before going through to the cocktail lounge.'

He turned enquiringly to Pamela, who sat with her head tilted back, watching the smoke from her cigarette wreathing upwards.

'Quite correct, Chief Inspector,' she said sarcastically. 'Actually it was three minutes past, if that helps you. I happened to notice the clock over the reception desk.'

'And then, Mrs Garnish?' he prompted.

'I ordered a couple of drinks. My husband came in and we drank them. Then I went on ahead to the Grill Room to order lunch, while he rang the theatre to find out if they'd got a couple of seats for the show that afternoon.'

As he plodded on, deliberately laborious, Pollard noted how shrewdly Bendle had stationed himself in order to get a view of

190

Roy Garnish with the light from two sets of wall lamps converging on him.

'What the hell's the sense of all this pettifogging detail?' the latter interrupted impatiently.

Pollard registered the watchfulness in the small grey eyes set too close together, and adopted a defensive tone.

'It's official routine to check alibis in a murder case, sir, even when they are apparently quite straightforward. May we go on to your visit to the theatre now?' He speeded up, to give the impression of being anxious to bring the interview to an end. 'Did you both arrive there together?'

'Obviously, since we drove down in the car. My wife went inside to collect the tickets I'd phoned for, while I parked the car. It was later than we thought.'

'Did you meet again in the foyer, then?' asked Pollard.

'God!' exploded Roy Garnish, staring truculently at him. 'Of all the bloody silly nonsense and waste of time! As she was paying for the tickets I found her at the box office. Surprising, wasn't it? And to save any more damn fool questions we went straight in to our seats – third row of the stalls – and sat out the show. Oh, a woman brought us tea in the second interval. Anything else you'd like to know?'

'Thank you, sir,' replied Pollard, watching Pamela Garnish pick up the lighted cigarette which had fallen from her hand on to the carpet, 'that concludes the statements of the theatre staff. I think you told Inspector Dart that it was after six when you arrived back at Affacombe?'

Roy Garnish became more discursive on the subject of searching the Priory grounds in the dark and pouring rain.

'Most unpleasant,' Pollard agreed. 'And I expect you had a trying Sunday, too, with the police in action all over the place?'

'Can't say they bothered us much, did they, Pam? That chap Dart was damn tedious, but it was so obvious – even to him – that we simply weren't in the running that he soon cleared off, and didn't make any difficulty about our going out for a meal and getting away early the next morning. I had a board meeting up here on the Monday afternoon.'

'He had to do his job, I suppose.' With a half-smothered yawn Pamela relegated the police and their activities to an infinitely remote sphere. 'I thought he was quite reasonable, really.'

Pollard put away his notebook and stood up.

'Well, sir, I don't think we need take up any more of your time.'

Roy Garnish heaved himself out of his chair.

'Sorry for Ainsworth, my tenant. This sort of publicity's no good to a school. You fellows don't seem to be making much headway if this is a sample of how you're spending your time.'

'We're doing our best, sir.' Pollard rejected the proffered gambit, hoping to maintain the impression of ineffective perseverance. 'We're grateful for your co-operation this evening, and Mrs Garnish's, too, of course.'

When they were clear of the block of flats Pollard looked enquiringly at Bendle.

The latter shook his head emphatically.

'Nature's own unaided work, Mr Pollard. Not what you'd call one of her best efforts, is it? But whatever funny business there's been, that chap in there wasn't disguised in any way. You can take it from me, sir.'

Presently, as they moved slowly up a rush-hour bus queue, Bendle spoke again.

'That five-foot-ten of skin and grief took a toss all right, didn't she? Cigarette shot right out of her hand.'

'Her husband had just come an almighty cropper without knowing it. I only hope she believes I didn't spot it.'

'Not to worry, sir. You ran on smooth as a Rolls engine in top.'

Chapter Seventeen

The adjourned conference on the Affacombe murder and the two robberies was resumed at noon on the following day. It got off to a depressing start when it transpired that the enquiries about the Garnish family were already bogged down. True to the A.C's forecast, Worrall Street had been wrecked by the Luftwaffe, and subsequently razed to the ground together with much of the surrounding area to make way for an L.C.C. housing development. As Superintendent Reynolds remarked, maximum publicity in the Press and on TV would probably unearth some of the street's former inhabitants, but that technique just wasn't on under the circumstances.

Somerset House had proved rather more productive. Roy Garnish was the illegitimate son of a Doris Wood, and had been registered under his putative father's name. A search for other children of either parent was going on, but so far without result.

'If she made a practice of registering 'em under their father's names, it could take a month of Sundays,' commented Crowe. 'Always assuming she had other kids, of course. Chap could be a first cousin of Garnish's, too. His mum's sister's son, to make it a bit easier to trace, especially if he's another bastard.'

'We're being prodded from on high,' said the A.C., 'delicately, but also insistently. We can't mark time indefinitely with no certainty of tracking down the Garnish family in the end. Equally, we can't afford to put the wind up Garnish himself. I only hope you didn't yesterday evening, Pollard. He's following his normal routine this morning, at any rate. The more I think about it, the more convinced I am that he's up to the neck in the organized crime racket, and that the murder is merely a by-product. I can't imagine a better cover than a property development company combined with an estate agency: a nation-wide network of handy hideouts. Incidentally we're working on a combined map of places he owns and the hi-jacking of lorries with really valuable stuff on board. It's beginning to look quite interesting, but that's beside the point. Then the set-up at Affacombe is extraordinarily neat: made for the job of establishing faked alibis. Installing a school to cast an aura of respectability was a stroke of genius. Which brings me to the point that the *fons et origo* of these deliberations is, after all, Pollard's case. I've no doubt that the conclusion you've arrived at, Pollard, is the right one broadly speaking, but it rests on a pretty insubstantial basis of inference and children's conversation at third hand, and so on. I'm not criticizing you in any way – quite the reverse – but that's the position as I see it. Did you get on to anything fresh yesterday?'

' Again, only by inference, sir.' For the benefit of Superintendents Reynolds and Blake, Pollard briefly summarized his interview with the Garnishes on the previous evening, and Pamela's reaction to the small trap which he had set for Roy.

' What about your next step?' pursued the A.C.

As he went over the top Pollard was borne up by the memory of the small hours, when Jane, roused from sleep, had listened absorbed, sitting up in a blue bedjacket, as they drank one cup of tea after another and ate ginger nuts.

' I'm in favour,' she'd said finally.

' I have thought out a possible line, sir,' he said, ' which I'd like to put forward with your permission.'

' Go ahead, then.'

The A.C. became semi-horizontal with his eyes on the ceiling.

Crowe remained bolt upright, with the expression of a school-master whose promising pupil is up before an external examining board. The other two adopted attitudes of critical neutrality.

Pollard cleared his throat.

'The essence of the plan is shock tactics in order to achieve a short cut, sir. Of course, I admit it's a gamble.'

After breakfast on the Wednesday morning David Strode had called for Julian in his mini. They had driven up to a gateway near Fogworthy Farm, and sat in the car for a final hour together before David started back for London.

'I felt guilty,' Julian said presently, 'because I kept forgetting all about the whole ghastly business, and just thinking of you and me. But when I told your Mamma she said it was a natural law in operation, and quite okay.'

'My Mamma,' David said, 'is sounder than any bell ever cast, in spite of her preoccupation with stone rows and menhirs and chaps like Affa.'

'Was there really a chap called Affa?'

'My darling girl, I must brief you at once. She would be shattered. It might affect the mother-in-law relationship. Affa – or Æffa – was a blue-eyed Saxon invader, who came up the combe in the 7th century with his merry men, and decided to take it over. I expect he took over a small, dark, lightly-built British girl as well. In short, he was the prototype of me.'

Later they told Olivia that they had decided to go ahead with preparations for the wedding as if nothing had happened.

'We think it's essential for Mummy's morale,' Julian said. 'You see, if anything really frightful happened, calling it all off and sending back the presents would be a drop in the ocean anyway.'

'We should simply get a special licence and marry at once,' added David. 'Well, I suppose I'd better be pushing off.'

Both of them robust and resilient, thank goodness, Olivia

thought as she watched them go out of the door. All the same it would be the most enormous relief if somebody other than Barbara could be arrested.

As Wednesday went on the non-appearance of the C.I.D. made for uneasiness in the village. There was a tendency to break off conversations at the sound of a car, and to answer the telephone with a twinge of apprehension. But towards evening tension relaxed. They must surely have gone back to London, and if they had, this meant that the solution of the murder lay there. Or anyway not in Affacombe. It would soon be cleared up and forgotten, and life would go back to normal.

The community was drawing together. It had leaked out that Barbara Winship was exercising the dogs along the Monk's Path on the afternoon of the crime, and that she had, in consequence, been three times questioned by the police. The Winships' friends rallied round in a variety of ways, and an unusual number of invitations were arriving at Crossways. Barbara's daily woman, Mrs Moon of Pear Tree Cottage, was more explicit.

'Proper daft lot, perlice,' she remarked, as she peeled potatoes at the kitchen sink, a bright floral pinafore strained over her ample bosom. 'Why, the 'ole village knows 'ee takes they dogs upalong afternoons. Doan't 'ee let'n worrit 'ee, me dear.'

At another level Fred and Ethel Earwaker found themselves cast for the role of victims of police persecution, and Jim Brent had announced his intention of standing down from the leadership of the barrel party at Revel.

Thursday passed uneventfully. A rumour went round that Sergeant Murch had been asked what had happened to the Yard men, and had replied that for all he knew the earth could've opened and swallered 'em up.

On Friday morning Olivia hurried through her chores and settled down at her desk, hoping for an undisturbed session at her Parish History. She was soon completely absorbed. When she eventually came to, she was astonished to find that it was nearly half-past one and that she was hungry.

196

It was too late to start cooking the lunch she had meant to have, so she knocked up a snack and installed herself comfortably in the kitchen, *The Times* crossword propped up in front of her. It was pleasant to relax with the feeling of a solid block of work behind one. The man's having another bout of Tennyson, she thought, putting in ' porphyry ' for ten across.

Just as she had finished eating the telephone broke in clamorously. With a mutter of annoyance she went to the sitting-room to answer it.

' Leeford 227,' she said.

Someone – a woman – at the other end was incoherent, and in a flash Olivia felt the fears and tension of the past week grip her once more.

' I can't hear you,' she told the speaker, her own voice sharp with alarm. ' Speak up, please. Who is it?'

It was Faith Ainsworth in a state of extreme agitation.

' Olivia…they've come back.'

' Who have?' she demanded, her mind oscillating between Pollard and Toye and the Garnishes.

' The detectives. Only more of them. There must be, because there are *two* cars, parked down beyond the West Wing.'

Olivia was aware of a constricting feeling in her chest.

' Well, surely that's not very surprising, Faith,' she said. ' The case hasn't been cleared up. I mean, they aren't likely to go off leaving it in mid-air, are they?'

' No-o. I suppose not.' Faith gave an unmistakable gulp. ' But it's so – well, sinister, just sitting in their cars as if they're waiting for something to happen. I'd almost rather they came here. If only John weren't away.'

Compunction overwhelmed Olivia.

' My dear, I'd completely forgotten that he'd gone to that H.Ms' meeting in London. How beastly for you. Would you like me to come up, just to have someone on hand?'

' Oh, Olivia, you're the most wonderful friend anyone could have! I just can't tell what it would mean – '

Cutting short these protestations of gratitude, Olivia put down

197

the receiver and stood staring out into the garden. Just what could it mean? Nothing to do with Barbara, obviously, or they'd be at Crossways. Surely the Garnishes weren't coming down again? She shivered suddenly. Faith was right. There was something unnerving having two carloads of police just sitting outside one's house. Bundling her lunch things into the sink, she went upstairs to get her coat and handbag.

In after years Pollard maintained that he had never had a tenser wait than the two hours in a police car outside the West Wing of Affacombe Priory. Toye, and Dart who had joined them at Highcastle with Sergeant Metcalfe, whiled away the time with a series of cat naps, but Pollard found himself unable to relax. He sat with ears cocked for the sound of an approaching car.

From time to time he tried to reassure himself about the strength of the cleft stick into which Roy Garnish had been manoeuvered.

It had been just before 9.30 that morning – a lifetime away – that the call had come through from the detective shadowing Countrywide Properties House, reporting the arrival of Roy Garnish wearing city clothes as usual, and carrying a brief-case.

At the Yard they had waited in Superintendent Crowe's room for the agreed five minutes before Pollard made a carefully rehearsed call. After a short delay he was put through to Roy Garnish.

' Sorry to trouble you again, sir,' he could hear himself saying, with a touch of excitement in his voice, ' but there's been an unexpected development in the case. It involves the outer door of your garage at the west wing. I see that you say in your statement to Inspector Dart that this door was locked when you left for Polharbour last Saturday. I take it that you are positive about this?'

The ensuing silence had been almost – but not quite – too brief to register. Then Roy Garnish's rather rough voice with its cockney undertones had come across with an emphatic affirmative.

'What's more,' he added, 'I'm prepared to go into the box on it. Shut and locked it myself. With all those kids around we make a point of it in term-time. What's the big idea? Or isn't one allowed to ask?'

'From information received, sir, it's virtually certain that a man entered your garage immediately after the time when we believe the murder to have taken place.'

'——!' Roy Garnish had commented. 'Couldn't have. There are only two keys. I keep one on my ring, and the other's up here in the flat. If the lock had been tampered with I'd've noticed when we got back.'

'The information we have had is reliable enough to make us feel that it must be followed up immediately,' Pollard had persisted. 'It's a matter of possible prints. Presumably, as it's an integral garage there's a door from it leading into the house?'

'Obviously.'

'Did you lock this door too, when you went out last Saturday?'

'Not that I remember. What on earth are you driving at?'

'Anyone who could get into the garage, could get into the house then, and in theory could have hidden there over the week-end. One of the puzzling things about this case is the way in which the murderer managed to vanish into thin air. Did either you or Mrs Garnish go up into the roof space during the week-end, sir?'

Again there had been a fractional pause.

'Christ! What a thought!' Garnish had ejaculated. 'Pretty far-fetched, though. Whoever your informant is, I think the whole thing's ruddy nonsense from start to finish.'

Pollard remembered the feel of a glass paperweight he was fingering as he steered the conversation in the direction of its climax.

'Well, sir,' he had said, 'to come to the point we've decided that the garage and the house must be fingerprinted and examined for other clues as soon as possible. I propose to take down experts today. We can eliminate your prints and Mrs Garnish's at once, as we already have them. You won't, I'm sure, have any objection to our entering the house in your absence: I take it that Mr Ainsworth has a key in case of an emergency. I fully realize how busy you are, but we do want Mrs Garnish to come down. If the murderer made use of the house – and particularly if he hid there – there'll almost certainly be missing stores and other traces of him. It's the lady of the house who can get on to that sort of thing in a brace of shakes.'

This time there had been an agonizing pause which seemed like an hour. It was ended by Roy Garnish cursing Affacombe and everything connected with the place in lurid detail.

' How the bloody hell do you expect me to ask my wife to go chasing down there again, and sleep in the house alone after what's happened?' he demanded belligerently. ' I suppose the only thing is for me to bring her, though how I'm going to get away...'

So, apparently, the bait had been taken. There had been a brief word with the Old Man who'd wished him luck, and then a dash to the waiting car.

The drive down had been a time of reaction. He had repeatedly wondered if Roy Garnish could possibly have failed to suspect a trap? Or had the success of the impersonations made him confident that the police hadn't got on to them, and that it was better to take a hypothetical risk than to make difficulties about the fingerprinting which might arouse suspicion. Probably it was the suggestion that Pamela should come alone that had tipped the scales. Anyway, it didn't look as though X's prints were in the Yard's archives, because there must be some of them about the house.

After a drive which seemed interminable they had arrived at

Highcastle. A report was waiting for them at the police station. The Garnishes had left London and were *en route* for the West under discreet observation. At any rate they hadn't tried to run for it – yet. Reinforced by Inspector Dart and Sergeant Metcalfe the Yard party had gone on to Affacombe after a hasty meal.

At the sound of a car Toye and Dart were instantly alert. Then Toye, who was watching through the rear window, gave an exclamation of disgust.

' Bleedin' little Morris!'

The small car, decorously driven, came to a halt outside the front door of the school. Dart exploded with indignation.

' If it isn't that Strode dame again! You can't move an inch without she turns up. Mark my word – '

' Shut up!' said Pollard violently. ' There's another car coming.'

Within a couple of seconds the Garnishes' Mercedes had swung in at the gate and swept up the drive. It braked violently outside the West Wing.

Feeling astonishingly cool Pollard got out of the police car, followed by Toye, and went forward. As he did so, Roy Garnish heaved himself out of the Mercedes.

' Well, we're here,' he said ungraciously, ' and bloody inconvenient it's been, too, coming chasing down at a moment's notice for what we know perfectly well's a mare's nest. Nobody could have got into the garage without busting up the lock, as I told you.'

' Good afternoon, sir,' Pollard said politely. ' Good afternoon, Mrs Garnish,' he added, as Pamela emerged from the passenger door, courteously held open by Toye.

She acknowledged his greeting briefly, and stood looking bored as her husband extracted his keys.

' As you see, I have brought our experts down,' Pollard went on, indicating the two cars. ' If we can have access to the garage from the outside they can start the printing there, without disturbing you by bringing all their equipment through this way.'

Without replying Roy Garnish unlocked the front door and strode into the house, making no attempt to stand aside for his wife. Great beefy lout, thought Pollard, with an upsurge of distaste, as he watched Pamela turn into the sitting-room, and fling down her coat and other belongings.

'You'd better come this way,' Roy Garnish called over his shoulder, 'and let in your chaps by the garage door if you want to. Here, what's all this in aid of?' he demanded, wheeling round at the sight of Toye and Dart behind Pollard. There was an unmistakable movement of his hand towards his hip pocket, checked by a swift gesture from Pollard enjoining silence.

'We can't take the slightest risk, sir, especially with Mrs Garnish in the house. It's unlikely that anyone's still in hiding here, but we must make sure.'

At this moment Pamela came out of the sitting-room and stopped dead with a startled exclamation.

'A routine search of the extensive premises,' Roy said ironically. 'For God's sake make some tea for everybody. It might speed things up.'

Without replying she went past them into the kitchen. There came the sound of a tap running. Overhead there were muffled footsteps as Toye and Dart searched, the squeak of a seldom-opened trap door being pushed up. A few minutes later the two men came down.

'No one up there, Mr Pollard,' Dart reported.

Roy Garnish gave a snort of contempt and led the way to the door into the garage.

'I'll go in first, sir, just in case. I take it the door is unlocked.'

'As far as I remember. God, what damn nonsense all this is!'

Pollard stepped forward, unemotionally conscious that the man behind him carried a gun. He opened the door on darkness.

'Switch on your right,' Roy Garnish said.

A few moments later the outer door swung up. Detective-

202

Constables Boyce and Strickland were standing stolidly against a wintry background.

Pollard gave business-like instructions as they unpacked their apparatus.

' You can muscle in, too, Toye,' he said. ' I expect you'd like to be getting back to Highcastle, Inspector, unless you'd care to wait for that cuppa Mr Garnish kindly suggested.'

' Make yourself at home, by all means,' remarked Roy.

They turned at the sound of Pamela's step in the passage.

' Tea in the kitchen if anyone wants it,' she announced, and disappeared again.

' Leave you to it, chaps,' Pollard said, following Roy into the house, Dart and Metcalfe bringing up the rear. He saw Pamela carrying a tray of tea things into the sitting-room. Roy went to join her, leaving the door ajar. Background noise of voices and of objects moved about came through from the garage. In the kitchen a vigorous triangular conversation was kept up, accompanied by the clinking of crockery. Once there was a short burst of laughter. After an interval Pollard slipped out and went back to the garage.

He found an atmosphere of tense excitement as Toye finished unscrewing the metal plates of the mortice lock and gently eased them off the door leading into the house. Underneath was a sunken chromium knob controlling a burglar-proof bolt.

' This may have the print to end all prints,' Pollard said in a low voice as Strickland advanced with his powder. With a subdued exclamation he stood aside for Boyce and his camera.

Re-entering the house Pollard nodded as he passed the kitchen, and knocked at the sitting-room door. The short November afternoon was closing in, and the lights had been switched on.

' Well?' Roy Garnish enquired sarcastically. He had lit a cigar, and sprawled at ease in a haze of blue smoke.

' A number of prints have come up, sir, but of course we shan't be able to classify them until the photographs have been developed and blown up. If Mrs Garnish has finished her tea, perhaps we could start a general look round now?'

'I really don't think this is going to be the slightest use,' Pamela said fretfully in her high metallic voice as she stubbed out a cigarette. 'Last week-end was such a mess-up that I can't possibly remember what tins and stuff were in the cupboards.'

She rose unwillingly and went out of the room, followed by Pollard.

'You'll be surprised at what you can remember,' he told her. 'Oh, I see my chaps are starting on the kitchen. Could we take the upstairs rooms first and work downwards? I particularly want you to check things like blankets and any clothes of your husband's.'

'You'd better come yourself, Roy,' she called back from the top of the stairs. 'I haven't a clue about the stuff you keep down here.'

The door of the main bedroom of the house faced the head of the staircase. Pamela pushed it open and flicked down the light switch. It gave a click, but nothing happened.

'Damn!' she exclaimed. 'The blasted bulb's gone.'

As she spoke there was a faint click from the other side of the room, and a flood of light. For a measureless length of time she stood frozen, confronted by a stocky, bull-shouldered figure with a red face and ginger hair, incongruous in striped trousers and morning coat.

Then she began to scream, a high continuous scream.

The heavy footsteps crossing the hall below became an animal stampede on the stairs. Roy Garnish burst into the room. For a split second he seemed transfixed by sheer primitive terror. Then he whipped out his revolver.

'Rat on your own brother would you, you dirty swine?' he bellowed. 'I'll send you where I sent the nurse.'

The bullet struck the elegant Adam ceiling as Pollard wrenched the arm upwards, and Toye and the others closed in. Pamela's screams suddenly ceased. She stood frozen between Strickland and Boyce.

Pollard turned to Roy Garnish, now safely handcuffed.

'It's unwise to jump to conclusions,' he said. 'Allow me to introduce Detective-Sergeant Blair. Make-up by Scotland Yard. Roy Garnish, I charge you with the murder of Joan Emily Roach.'

Pollard found Olivia Strode alone in the Ainsworths' drawing-room. She explained that John was away, and offered to fetch Faith.

'It's not necessary,' he said. 'Frankly, I'd rather you told her what I'm sure you know I've come to say. Roy Garnish has just been charged with the murder of Sister Roach, and his wife as an accessory together with a second person at present unknown. He admitted to the crime in front of half a dozen witnesses. I'm just taking them both into Highcastle.'

Olivia steadied herself with a hand on the mantelpiece.

'I thought it would be the most colossal relief,' she said slowly, 'but now it's happened it seems quite horrible.'

'In my experience it always feels that way in the end. Incidentally the case would probably have remained unsolved without your evidence, you know.'

She stared at him in astonishment.

'Do you think that one day you could possibly unravel it all? At the moment everything is just incomprehensible.'

'I'll do that, Mrs Strode,' he promised her.

Chapter Eighteen

The news that the Garnishes had been charged with the murder of Sister Roach reverberated round Affacombe like a sonic boom. At first it met sheer incredulity. A variety of reactions followed.

'Us be well rids o' the lot o' they,' was the main theme of comment in the Priory Arms, bracketing killers and victim. It was felt that the nurse had got what was due to her for trying to come between Fred and Ethel. As to the Garnish money, it could only have come through beggaring hundreds through crooked dealing, as well as by highway robbery, as the papers were saying now. The topic of the demolition of the North Lodge was resurrected, and a surprising number of people said they had thought it a proper queer business at the time, and now anybody could see for themselves.

In other circles reactions were more complex. There was genuine shock and horror, but also a certain unconscious satisfaction born of resentment of the Garnishes. Such absolutely impossible people with that fantastic amount of money, and actually having the nerve to say they didn't want to get involved with local society instead of coming cap in hand trying to get into it. But those experiencing these feelings would have been appalled to know of their existence, and their conscious minds were charitably concerned with the future of the Priory School.

John Ainsworth, once reassured by his lawyer about the terms of his lease, was one of the very few to feel genuine distress, at least on behalf of the Garnishes. Old Roy had turned out a wrong 'un, of course, and you couldn't stand for bank raids and what-have-you in a civilized country. But he'd been pretty well as smart as the train robbers, come to that. And when Roach cornered him, well, he fought his way out. Blackmail was a filthy stinking business. Faith Ainsworth was unable to rationalize the situation as successfully as her husband. She ached with confused compassion for all concerned, and the school gained from the sympathy she aroused in parents.

After the initial impact of the news Olivia Strode was overwhelmed with relief. It felt like waking up from the grimmest kind of nightmare, she thought, turning eagerly to her normal preoccupations. Rather to her surprise, however, she found it difficult to give them an undivided mind. In spite of David's cheerful reassurances she was still uneasy in case action were taken by the authorities over the false registration of Julian's birth. Also the puzzling circumstances surrounding the murder intrigued her. She often wondered if Pollard would remember his undertaking to elucidate them.

' That, my darling,' David Strode had remarked on hearing the news over the telephone from Julian, ' is that. There'll be some tiresomenesses, I expect. Giving evidence, perhaps. But you and I can at last give our minds to essentials. Listen, sweetheart...'

There followed a lengthy and recklessly expensive conversation, mainly unintelligible to anyone overhearing it.

The two Garnishes were duly committed for trial at the Highcastle Assizes. After a lull during which local interest began to show signs of flagging, it was revived by reports in the Press of the arrest of one Peter Baker in connection with the mail van robbery at Bristowe on September 19th. Accused was the half-brother of Roy Garnish, at present awaiting trial on a charge of

murdering Sister Joan Roach, a school nurse. It was understood that further charges of a different character were likely to
be preferred against him.

Olivia read the paragraph over and over again, illumination
slowly dawning in her mind.

A few days later she had an unexpected telephone call from
Pollard, who was in Highcastle, offering to pay her a short
visit that afternoon. She accepted with pleasure, but, as she put
the receiver down, suddenly wondered if she really wanted to
see him after all. If they did prosecute Barbara, it would be on
his information. She decided that she was being emotional and
silly.

'I remember that attractive map,' Pollard said, standing in
front of the fire and examining it closely. 'In fact, I've thought
of this room more than once. It was here that you gave me the
pointer to Garnish, you know.'

'What *was* it?' asked Olivia. 'I've racked my brains. Do sit
down.'

They settled in a couple of armchairs, and he accepted a
cigarette.

'It was Dettol,' he told her, and smiled at her bewildered
expression.

'Dettol?'

'Yes. When I asked you about your arrival at the Priory on
the night of the murder, you described it so vividly that you
transported yourself back there: right into the smell of baked
beans, wet clothes and Dettol. Let me explain a bit more fully.'

Olivia listened absorbed to Pollard's narrative of charred
bandages, Streak's bruise and the subsequent deductions leading
finally to the tracking down of Roy Garnish's half-brother, Peter
Baker.

'But the Garnishes' alibi in Polharbour?' she asked. 'Did you
bust it wide open, as my son would say?'

'I don't know about wide open, but it transpired that no one saw or spoke to the alleged Roy Garnish who was in a position to identify him beyond any doubt.'

'Wait a minute,' said Olivia. 'This is incredibly complicated, but from what has appeared in the papers, wasn't Sister Roach blackmailing the wrong person for the wrong thing? I mean, Pamela for a non-existent – or incidental – lover, instead of Roy for using the impersonation set-up as a cover for crimes like the Bristowe mail van robbery?'

'Congratulations, Mrs Strode. You'd better join us in the C.I.D. Yes, she'd jumped to the same wrong conclusion as the boys. It was a very daring and cleverly worked-out scheme. Take the Bristowe business. Peter Baker did the job – with suitable assistance, of course, while Roy went about his usual work in London. Late that night, Baker, who'd made a clean getaway, was dropped off near the second Affacombe turning, and doubled back through the North Gate into the West Wing garage where he laid low until Pamela arrived the next day. Then he stepped into Roy's identity, Roy having gone to ground elsewhere. On the Monday, Baker, disguised as Roy, returned to London with Pamela, and the two men unobtrusively became themselves again.'

'But surely it was terribly risky for Baker to have been in the West Wing? There was some arrangement with the Ainsworths about having the place kept clean.'

'I don't know if you've ever noticed it,' Pollard said, 'but that garage has no windows. If it could be made impossible for anyone to open the connecting door from the house side, it would be a very safe hideout indeed. It didn't take my chaps long to find a concealed burglar-proof bolt, so there was no risk at all of a cleaning woman or even one of the Ainsworths coming through. They took a risk over letting Pamela drive down alone on the 20th, of course, and pulled it off. No one seems to have noticed that she arrived without Roy.'

Olivia considered.

'I don't think it really was much of a risk – not at this end, anyway. You see, nobody knew anything about their comings and goings. If I'd seen her driving up the village alone, I should just have thought that they'd arrived together earlier. Then on other occasions like October 28th, I suppose Baker came to establish Roy's identity here, so that there couldn't be any question of his being involved in whatever he was really doing elsewhere?'

'Yes, that's it. There is a remarkable physical resemblance between the two brothers, and it was a well-established impersonation, all ready to step into when they decided that Roach had to be eliminated. She'd tumbled to it, and become much too dangerous to them to be allowed to go on living.'

'But surely,' Olivia covered her face with her hands and thought furiously, 'the murder was unnecessary? I mean, the letter they must have had from Sister Roach showed that she had got the wrong idea about the purpose of the impersonation? Why not let her go on having it? Roy and Pamela could have gone to the Leap, and he could have said that Pamela had confessed everything to him, and unless Sister Roach signed a confession of attempted blackmail he'd go to the police. A bit risky, perhaps, for people like themselves, but nothing like as risky as committing murder.'

'Think about the letter,' suggested Pollard.

She exclaimed aloud.

'Of course! How stupid of me! It would have been anonymous, like the one Mrs Winship had, and they wouldn't have known who they were up against.'

'Exactly. They might have found themselves confronted by someone not at all easy to silence and intimidate. One of the masters from the school, perhaps. Or even John Ainsworth. Or even yourself.'

'Me?' she gasped.

'Yes, you, Mrs Strode. I shouldn't be surprised if they speculated about you. After all, you'd had several contacts with them: more than anyone else locally, except the Ainsworths. In fact, after I saw you here last time, I decided that you'd been a bit too much in evidence if there really was something fishy about the Garnishes. Hence that phone call of mine about any more invitations to the West Wing.'

'Good heavens,' she said, unpleasantly chilled at the thought of having been at risk. 'But I still don't understand,' she persisted, 'why Roy Garnish, when he found it was only Sister Roach at the Leap, didn't fall back on the story of knowing all about Pamela's lover.'

'I don't suppose we shall ever know why he decided to take the greater risk all the same. My theory is that he was badly rattled by the Streak incident, and that Roach showed signs of being difficult. In confidence, she was quite an experienced blackmailer.'

Olivia stared into the fire.

'What I find so staggering,' she went on after a pause, 'is the part sheer chance seems to have played in all this. Things like the time Barbara Winship happened to start out that afternoon, and Streak electing to come and paw at you and get picked up. It makes me wonder if there's any cause and effect in history after all.'

Pollard laughed.

'In the long run I'm quite certain there is. But pure chance does play a bigger part in life than a lot of people realize. I've come across it again and again in my cases.'

'By the way, you haven't told me yet how Roy Garnish came to admit to the murder. It seems astonishing: not a bit in character, somehow.'

'His wife was confronted with an impersonation of his impersonator, and it broke her. A gamble, but it came off. He reacted by trying to shoot his way out.'

Olivia listened absorbed, looking at Pollard with undisguised admiration.

'Was this brilliant and imaginative idea yours?' she asked him.

'Well, yes, it was. But don't credit me with running Baker to earth too. That was a master stroke by one of my colleagues. I only contributed a fingerprint from the bolt I told you about.'

'I shall watch your future career with the greatest interest,' she told him, smiling. Then suddenly her anxiety about Barbara's future returned.

'Is something still worrying you?' he asked, puzzled by the change in her expression.

'There is, actually, although perhaps I oughtn't to ask you about it. It's so bound up with my son's engagement, though. Will Mrs Winship be prosecuted for registering Julian as her own child? It would be so terribly painful.'

'As you know,' he said sympathetically, 'I can't say anything officially. In any case it doesn't rest with me. But my personal opinion is that the Registrar-General may very well decide to let the matter rest.'

'Thank you,' she said. 'That's most comforting. I – why, there they are! They've been up Sinneldon as it's such a lovely afternoon. David had a couple of days' holiday due to him.'

David and Julian came into the room, glowing from a moor walk in the crisp December air and each other's company. Julian assured Pollard that the top of Sinneldon was the finest viewpoint in the entire West Country.

'You can see the whole coast right down to Thirl Point,' she said, 'and all Crownmoor and the rest of the county spread out like a map.'

'Everything's lined up for tonight,' David told his mother. 'Tar barrel, brushwood, paraffiny rags – the lot. St Lucca's Revel,' he explained to Pollard. 'We have a comic beano here every fifteenth of December, after dark. It dates from the Lord knows when.'

'Certainly from Saxon times,' said Olivia. 'David's disgracefully flippant about my interest in the past. It's a fascinating survival of an old pagan ritual. Would you care to stay and watch, Inspector?'

'Would that I could,' Pollard replied, 'but unfortunately I've got to be back in London tonight.' He glanced at his watch. 'In fact, I must dash off at once, I'm afraid.'

They went outside to see him off, and stood watching his car

212

reach the turning, halt and vanish.

'Decent chap,' remarked David dismissively as they turned back into the cottage. 'Is there any tea going, Mamma?'

The sunset was dusty pink and gold, the frosty air motionless and sharp with wood smoke. In accordance with ancient custom St Lucca's Lights sprang up in every window overlooking the street. Families from the outlying farms began to arrive in the village, which echoed with the shouts of Sergeant Murch and his constable as they struggled to control the traffic and organize parking. A packed coach came in from Leeford and was greeted with cheers and catcalls. Its passengers flooded out and melted into the crowded street.

From her bedroom window Olivia Strode watched the people streaming down to the field by the Sinnel where the festivities began. Everyone carried a light: a torch, or a hurricane lamp with a candle inside, or a nightlight in a glass jam jar. Timeless, she thought. Women with scarves over their heads in the immemorial way. Excited children and barking dogs running along. Old men gamely hobbling on their sticks. Pairs of lovers borne by the tide, oblivious to everything but themselves.

Voices below announced that the Winships and Julian had arrived. She roused herself, and went downstairs to welcome them.

As they all came out of Poldens a few minutes later it struck her that the Revel atmosphere was even more hilarious than usual. The perfect evening, perhaps? Or was there an unspoken feeling that a shadow had lifted from the village? David hooked her firmly on to one of his arms and Julian on to the other. A head taller than most of their neighbours in the crowd, he started a ridiculous running commentary which was received with roars of laughter. Glancing back Olivia caught a glimpse of Hugh Winship stalwart in a duffel coat, protectively shepherding Barbara through the throng.

Once they reached the field it became easier to move, and

213

they manoeuvred for a good riverside stance. She realized that they had become separated from the Winships.

'Hopeless to find anyone in this crush,' David said unconcernedly. 'We'll join up all right at the Parish Hall.'

She saw he had not noticed that she had tactfully detached herself, and moved a short distance away along the river bank. Alone, she gave herself up to enjoyment of the scene. Over head there was an unbelievable splendour of stars. Across the water reared the huge dark mass of Sinneldon, a tiny cluster of moving lights indicating the barrel party, about to go into action under the restored leadership of Fred Earwaker.

An expectant hush descended, in which the running of the Sinnel became loud and dominant. Olivia stared down into the water, its blackness flecked by dancing golden pinpoints, reflections of the traditional lanterns. Timeless too, and unrelentingly purposeful, she thought, listening to the unseen movement at her feet. She felt a stab of compassion for Sister Roach falling like a plummet into that cold impersonal embrace. The dark into the dark. Could you help being dark in spirit if you had never lived in the light?

Her attention was suddenly riveted by a triumphant yell as tongues of flame leapt into the sky from the crest of Sinneldon, and a ball of fire streaked down the slope with gathering momentum and plunged into the river with a great hissing splash.

The watchers held their breath, gripped by a superstitious anxiety to which few of them would have admitted. Then a column of flame shot up from the Sinnel amid a roar of cheers.

'Oh my!' rang out a hearty feminine voice. 'Did 'ee iver see 'un flare up better'n that? Us'll 'ave pop'lation splosion yur in Affacombe, sure 'nuff. Why, Miss Wrey, luv, 'twill be orange blossom for 'ee Jan'ry, an' orange juice for a liddle 'un come October!'

The crowd shouted with laughter, and applauded as David Strode hoisted Julian high.

X